# DEVOTED

EVELYN FLOOD

**Devoted**

**Evelyn Flood**

First published by Evelyn Flood in 2023

ASIN B0BJC3G2PF
Formatting by Diana TC @ Triumph Book Covers
Cover by Penn Cassidy @ PC Designs

# TRIGGER WARNING


This book includes references to previous neglect, severe illness and use of medication.

# ABOUT THIS BOOK

This book is an **omegaverse**. That means that the characters have some of the characteristics often seen in wolves, but they **do not shift.**

*To my little sister, who has just as much sass as Jessalyn Rogers, but in a much smaller package.*

# 1

# SIENNA

Sharp pain radiates through my foot as I stumble over a jagged rock. The forest is full of them, tiny little circles of hell hidden under leaves and twigs for me to step on like some fucked up game.

Slumping against the huge trunk of an oak tree, I stare around me desperately.

I'm pretty sure I've already passed through this way. The forest is deceptively peaceful, the trilling sounds of birds trickling through the thick thatches of branches above my head. Rays of the fading afternoon sunlight cast shadows across the moss-covered floors, and I shiver as I move away from the tree and onwards.

I've been walking for hours. There's no sign of any shelter.

And the sun is fading from the brief glimpses of sky I can see above me.

I'm trying really hard not to melt into a giant puddle of panic, swallowing down the urge to curl up into a ball on the floor and rock back and forth until I wake up from this nightmare.

If I lay down, I won't be getting back up.

The pain is increasing. It's everywhere, raging down my veins, in every beat of my heart in my chest, burning the very edge of my fingertips. I choke back a sob, and keep going.

I have to keep going, or there is a very real risk I'll die here, in this forest where every tree looks the same as the one next to it.

Although if my limited knowledge turns out to be true, I'm not long for this world anyway.

My vision blurs, and I pause yet again to try and drum up just a little more energy.

It takes me a second to notice the quiet.

The birds have stopped chirping.

The cracking sound of leaves up ahead gives me just enough warning to drop down and crawl into a thick gathering of leaves. Twigs scratch at my face as I pull in the edges of my dress, making sure none of it can be seen.

Just in time. I hold my breath as several pairs of large, laced black boots stomp into the clearing I was just standing in. I count three pairs before a deep voice breaks into the silence.

"He's fucking played us."

"Shut up," another hisses. "We're supposed to be silent."

The first voice scoffs. "I don't believe she's in here. We would've spotted her by now."

My heart jumps in my chest, my whole body locking up.

"It's this fucking forest," the third voice grouses. "Everything looks the fucking same."

"Makes it easy to spot our little prey," the second voice suggests. "She's got bright fucking pink hair. How hard can it be?"

I shove my fist against my mouth to try and hold in my absolute panic. They're looking for me. What the hell? Why?

A grunt. "Better be worth it. I heard omegas have magic pussy. I might even take her for a run myself, since she's had us walking through this fucking place all day."

"Don't be stupid." There's a thump, and a curse. "She's worth a lot of fucking money to someone. We have a job to do, so move it."

The boots start to move away, crunching into the ground in fading steps. Nausea burns the back of my throat and I swallow it down, staying exactly where I am. I don't trust them not to come back.

*She's worth a lot of fucking money.*

*Magic pussy.*

The bile churning in my stomach makes a rapid exit, and I turn my head to the side, trying to keep the noise down as I choke up the scant remains of what's in my stomach. It's not much.

I can't remember the last time I ate a proper meal.

My eyes close, and I wrap my arms around my knees as I huddle under the bush. Every time I think I can't possibly hurt any more, something else hits me over and over again. I'm nothing but a handful of fractured pieces stitched together by sheer fucking will at this point.

My closed fist rubs frantically against my chest. How could they?

I'm their Soul Bonded. Their fated gods damned fucking *mate*.

And even despite everything that's happened in the last few weeks, this is one twist I didn't see coming.

But then I guess I never really knew them at all.

The light is fading rapidly now. Digging my hands into the dirt, I scrape away until I reach a damper, wetter section. Gingerly, I claw at it with my hands, gathering clumps and rubbing it into my hair.

Having pink hair in a green forest will be a fucking beacon if any of them spot me.

I'd get rid of this dress, too, except it's the only item of clothing I have. The beading is broken now, the pale blush color streaked with mud and filth from the forest floor. I *really* don't have a good track record with dresses.

Adding to the dirt, I rub as much as I can into the soft material until it's stiff and dark and not anything near its original palest pink.

It's the best I can do.

It's close to dusk by the time I gather the courage to leave my little bush, gingerly crawling out and listening for any sign of the three males coming back. I move away and head in the opposite direction, but my steps gradually falter, my breathing choppy and harsh as I list from one tree to the other until the thick trunks are the only thing keeping me upright. Pain pulses dully inside my head, and I'd fucking kill for some water.

Just the tiniest sip.

A desperate noise leaves my mouth when I finally spot an opening in the trees, a worn path forming in the ground ahead of me. At this stage, I don't even care where it goes, relief making my head spin as I stagger through the gap and spot a low, timber building ahead of me. Warm lights flicker in the window, a hint of gray smoke curling from a small chimney on the roof.

My body is screaming, but I force myself to pause, to think.

They could be anyone. They could be part of the group I overheard earlier.

Instead of heading directly for the door and the promise of water like I desperately want to do, I take slow, measured steps as I look around me. There's no sign of life out here, nobody to spot me slipping around the back of the building.

There's some sort of barn ahead and I try the door, letting out a breath when it opens smoothly under my hands. I don't bother looking for a light, my eyes landing straight on a crate of drinks.

It takes precious, shaking minutes to pry the lid open, and I send a silent apology to the owner as I snap open a can of soda. It's not the water I need, but it'll do, the fizz grating on my aching throat as I chug it down before I force myself to take a breath and look around.

It's some sort of storage area, the stacks of boxes giving me echoes of my shitty little excuse for a nest.

My hand clenches around the can, and I shove those memories down.

I'll never see that room again.

Edging past the stacks, I find a small corner to curl up in, grabbing a large, empty burlap sack from a stash to the side to pull over me.

I just need a little rest. A few hours to close my eyes, and hopefully stave off the pain radiating against my insides.

A few hours to forget the agony in my chest for the family I left behind.

And for the pack who sent me here.

## 2

# TRISTAN

SEVEN HOURS EARLIER

My eyes stay glued to the gates until well after Mal has pulled out in the escalade, taking Sienna with him.

My Soul Bonded chose to travel alone to our Mating Ceremony rather than sit in an enclosed space with us for the journey. With me.

I don't blame her for it. No, all the blame for this shitshow is settled well and truly around my shoulders, dragging me down like an anchor.

A throat clears behind me and I blink, turning away from the gates. Logan stands there, his eyes averted. "We're ready to go."

I nod wordlessly, taking in the way he angles himself away from me. My pack can't bring themselves to look me in the eye, our pack bond full of shame and worry that bleeds through into my chest.

I haven't slept for two days. Exhaustion weighs down my bones, every step heavy as I move towards my car, opening it up as Jax passes me, his shoulder jamming into mine without apology.

After today, we can start to heal. Every angle, every secret will be out in the open, the scale of our deception laid out for Sienna like some sort of twisted offering.

But she'll be *safe*. Safe from Erikkson and his twisted plans. Safe from Alicia and her scheming.

Everything else will settle in time. I'll spend the rest of my life making this up to her.

Jax chooses to get in the back rather than sit next to me, Logan following his lead. I stand by my door, my fingers gripping the handle with whitened knuckles as Gray slides in next to him, his mouth pressed into a firm line.

We might be dressed for a Mating, but this feels more like a funeral.

My jaw sets before I yank the door open, getting in without saying anything. I'm not about to waste precious minutes trying to hash out the dynamics of our pack when the person we really need is alone and waiting for us to get there.

Before I can start the engine, a noise jerks my head up. There's a car pulling in through our gates, an escalade similar to the one that just pulled out.

"Did she come back?" Logan asks in confusion, pushing his head forward between the seats to take a look. Shaking my head, I watch in growing disbelief as a door opens wide, a stiletto-heeled foot appearing.

"What the fuck is that bitch doing here?" Jax growls furiously behind me. Alicia steps out and walks over to us, her steps smooth and measured, not an ounce of fear in her face.

There should be. This bitch dragged our Soul Bonded into a shed and locked her in when she was in heat. Sprayed her with chemicals to try and put us off the scent.

And today, she's going down.

"We need a fucking security system," snaps Gray. "This is ridiculous."

"Quiet," I bark. "Let me deal with this."

"Like you've dealt so well with everything fucking else,"

mutters Jax, but he doesn't say anything when Alicia taps on my window.

I can almost taste the fury of my pack on my tongue when I roll it down. Putting my hands back on the steering wheel, I grip it tightly, imagining it's her neck. "What do you want?"

She fucking *laughs*. A trilling, chirpy glee that burrows into my eardrums and ratchets the anger in the car up by a good few degrees.

"Oh, Tristan," she coos. "So masterful."

Fuck this.

My hand shoots through the window, grabbing her throat as she chokes. Her face darkens as I flex my fingers, squeezing until her eyes bulge.

"Listen to me," I breathe, pulling her towards me and leaning closer. "I want nothing more than to keep squeezing, Alicia. Nothing would bring me greater pleasure than to finally wipe that demented, fucking smirk off your face once and for all. But we have somewhere important to be. Far more important than whatever the fuck you're here for. So get back in your car, turn the fuck around, and leave us alone."

When my fingers open, she pulls herself back with a gasp, massaging the skin at her throat. Her swollen, pouty lips tremble as she eyes me with the first hint of self-preservation I've seen.

"I know what you think of me, you know." Her words are softer than I've ever heard, so quiet I have to lean my head further out of the window to hear them. "But you'll change your mind in time, Tristan. It'll all be fine once she's out of the picture."

My eyes flash to hers, taking in the manic gleam. "Alicia—,"

My words cut off as she pulls something from behind her and throws it through the window. It lands with a clatter, rolling under my seat, and I cough as a dark green fog fills the car. A second clatter follows, Jax, Logan and Gray shouting from the back seat as the fog swallows them up.

"Tristan," Jax chokes. "*Sienna.*"

Desperate, my fingers grapple for the doors, but I locked them when we got in. My head starts to spin, something in the mist fogging up my mind.

Alicia's face swims in my view as I try to push my head out of the car window to take a breath. "What…,"

"Don't worry," she taps my nose. "I'll say your goodbyes for you."

Fuck.

*Fuck.*

*Sienna.*

# 3
# JAX

A metallic taste coats my tongue, fills my mouth with iron as my eyelids crack open.

Where the fuck am I?

A blinding pain fills my head, making me groan as I struggle to sit up. There's something in my way, and I blink slowly as the light filters in and I realize where I am.

A weight leans against my left side, and I look down to see Logan slumped against me, his head hanging down.

"Logan." My voice feels thick, slurring, the words not forming properly in my mouth. Wetting my lips, I try again for something a little louder than the rasp I managed the first time around. "Logan."

He doesn't respond, and I turn my head blearily, eyes blinking until Gray swims into sight. His head is leaning against the window.

Clarity filters in slowly, too slowly.

The Mating Ceremony.

*Sienna.*

"Fuuuck." Lifting my hand is a struggle, but I manage to whack it against the back of the chair in front of me. "Tristan."

Silence, and my head clears a little more, leaving plenty of space for panic.

What the fuck was that about?

Leaning forward, I squint at the clock on Tristan's dashboard. The numbers solidify, and my hand jumps to the door handle, jiggling it frantically. "Tristan! For fucks sake, wake up!"

We're not just late, we've missed the entire fucking ceremony. Fucking *shit*.

Our Soul Bonded will never fucking forgive us, and fuck knows how the Council will take it.

Undoing my belt, I lean forward and stretch my fingers past Tristan's still figure to slap the lock, and the doors open with a click.

It takes precious seconds to stumble out of the car, to get my legs steady underneath me, before I'm able to open Tristan's door. He's slumped over into the seat next to him, his belt undone and his hand dangling down into the stairwell.

Not bothering to be gentle, I shove and lift until his body flops completely into the seat and I can slide into his place. We don't have the time to wait around for them to wake up.

Fingers shaking, I switch the ignition on. The tires squeal with the smell of burning rubber as I swerve out of the gates, turning right and slamming my foot down on the ignition to get us to the Hub as fast as I can.

The sinking feeling in my stomach warns me that we might already be too late.

I put all the windows down as we fly down the highway, hoping the fresh air will help the rest of them wake up faster. I'm rewarded when I hear a groan behind me. "Jax?"

"We missed the ceremony." Twisting my neck quickly before facing the road again, I take Gray in, pale-faced and swallowing as he blinks drowsily. "We what?"

My hand smashes into the wheel in frustration. "We missed the Mating Ceremony! Sienna's there, on her own, and I think Alicia has something planned."

His eyes flicker over to Logan, and he swallows. "Shit," he slurs. "Where's Tristan?"

"Here." Leaning over, I smack him in the arm, hard. "Tris, wake *up*."

But he's still and silent, and it's not until we reach the outskirts of town, a few minutes from the Hub, that he stirs. "What happened?"

"Alicia," I hiss. God, I hate that bitch with a fucking passion. I can't wait for her to get her comeuppance. It's so close, I can almost taste it.

Tristan jerks upright, his body sliding to the side until he pulls himself up, slapping at his cheeks with a curse. "Sienna."

"I know," I say grimly.

I just hope we get there in time.

4

# TRISTAN

M y chest is pounding as we stumble up the steps, a chaotic mess of staggering limbs as we all pelt for the courtyard.

The bottom drops out of my stomach as we follow the growing noise, retracing the steps we took at our first disastrous fucking Bonding Ceremony.

It sounds like—

"Screaming," Logan mutters, his face leeching of color. "That's screaming."

I find a burst of energy, pelting past the others to burst through the double doors, my eyes scanning frantically for Sienna. Heads turn to me in the chaos ahead of us, the shouting and yelling bouncing off the pillars and hitting me like a brick.

The noise cuts abruptly, and I race forward, down the petal-strewn carpet to the group congregated in the middle of the room.

"Sienna," I gasp, my head swinging to my father. "Where is she?"

Because she's not in this room. There's no trace of pink to be seen anywhere.

My dad's face is more grim than I've ever seen it. He opens his mouth, but I'm blindsided by pain in my right cheek.

I go down with a crash, taking out a flower display that

crashes to the floor. Gasping, I shake my head and look up, my eyes blind in the afternoon sunlight until a shadow looms over me.

"I will *kill* you."

John Michaels, Sienna's father, looks down at me, his whole body vibrating. He looks as though he's aged a decade since I last saw him, furious and shaking at our Bonding Ceremony.

"Get the fuck up," he spits. "You spineless excuse for an alpha. Get up!"

I stagger to my feet, holding my hands out. "Wait. *Please* – where is Sienna?"

His face purples. "You know exactly where she fucking is!"

Nobody intercedes when he launches himself at me, his fist landing straight in my face. My head snaps back, a spike of pain erupting.

"Shit." Bending over, I pinch the top, trying to stifle the blood I can feel dripping from my nose. "Enough," I growl, shoving Sienna's father back. We have too much to sort out for this to happen now. Later, I'll put my hands behind my back and let him take all the hits he wants.

Jax steps forward, finally deciding to intercede. "Where is our Soul Bonded?" he demands. "Why isn't she here?"

My dad pushes between us, holding his hand out as he looks back at me grimly. "We got your letter."

My head spins. "What letter?" I demand. "I didn't send a letter!"

My dad frowns. "The letter," he says slowly, "announcing your Denial of Sienna Michaels."

Staring back at him, I blink as the jigsaw pieces start to move together in my mind.

Alicia. The stunt she pulled with the car.

*Sienna.*

Shaking my head, I turn again, scanning the faces around us. My mother doesn't meet my eye, her face solemn as she stares at the ground.

"I didn't write that letter," I say slowly, turning back to my dad. "We absolutely do not Deny Sienna. Where is she?"

My dad pales, holding his hand out. "She... she's gone, Tristan."

Gone.

*Gonegonegonegone.*

The word burns into my brain. "That's not possible," I croak. "She can't be."

The heaviness that's been sitting in my core for the last few days expands, filling my body until I'm pretty sure I could look down and see stone.

She's not gone.

They're punishing us for being late.

"Tristan," my dad says grimly. His hands land on my shoulders, squeezing. "Son. Sienna has been sent over the wall."

My knees hit the floor, my dad coming down with me as he talks frantically. There's noise around us, people demanding, asking questions. My hands grip the carpet beneath my knees, crushing flower petals into the material.

But all I can see is my Soul Bonded's face as she stood in the hallway and asked me if we would be here.

We didn't show up. And now she's gone.

Denied.

Sent over the wall, alone and defenseless, where Erikkson's cronies are waiting for her.

Jax's face swims in front of me as he lands next to my dad. His desperate words sound muffled as he grabs my shoulders, shaking me.

"Tristan!" His words break through the stone wall. "Snap out of it!"

The noise breaks through in a rush, filling my head with crying and screaming. My hands push against the floor as I pull myself upright.

"That's enough!" I roar, and the courtyard silences immediately. Sienna's father comes for me again, but my dad pushes him back. "John, wait. There's been a misunderstanding."

"Allowing my daughter anywhere near your son was a misunderstanding," John Michaels snaps. His wife, Sienna's mother, comes up next to him, devastation on her face, and puts her hand on his arm. His shoulders shake as he turns to her, pulling her to him.

I have to pull myself together. I can't afford to fall apart now.

I take a few steps, my eyes scanning the crowd. They land on someone, lounging in a chair and picking at her nails.

Stalking forward and pushing people out of my way, I grab Alicia's arm, ignoring her squeal, and drag her back to the crowd of Councilors and parents gathered around. People gasp as I throw her down, and I pull my phone from my pocket.

"Tell them," I demand. "Tell them what you fucking did, Alicia. Tell them everything."

She whimpers, and my dad turns to me. "Tristan."

I'm shaking, and I feel my pack step up behind me. On this one thing, at least, we're completely united. Alicia Erikkson will not fuck with us again. And there's no way we're leaving here to find our Soul Bonded without making sure everybody here knows it.

I lean forward with a snarl. "You won't tell them? Then I will."

Hitting the button on my phone, I hold it out, turning to volume up to max. The room goes silent as the recording plays out.

*"Such a lovely shade of blue eyes. Quite unmistakable, really. And to think, she nearly fell into the road. Why, if I hadn't grabbed her arm, who knows what would have happened?"*

*"Threatening children now, Alicia?"*

*"It's more of a promise, really. Quite simple. You keep your word, and Elise Michaels remains unharmed."*

*"You think holding the safety of Elise Michaels over our heads will make us dance to your tune? Your father is already extorting us with what I strongly suspect is false evidence—,"*

*"It's not false! My father has you tied up, Tristan!"*

When the recording ends, Sienna's father steps forward. He looks pale. "What the hell is going on here?"

I take a deep breath. This is it.

"Two days before the start of the Bonding Trials, Counselor Erikkson came to my office with two folders, which he claimed included evidence that would destroy our family if it were to be made public."

"What kind of evidence?" my father asks. My throat aches as I turn to him. Fuck, but I hope he's the man I think he is. I didn't want it to come out like this.

"Firstly, that you were extorting Council funds and engaging in corruption, being paid to make certain decisions that would benefit criminal groups across Navarre."

Gasps ring out across the room, and my dad pales. "Oh, Tristan."

*Tell me I haven't done all of this, to try and protect you, for nothing.*

"It's not true." He shakes his head. "Tristan, if you had come to me with this – I could have explained. Milo is fully aware of what's been going on."

The Justice Councilor nods, his usual sour face replaced with intense concentration. "Tristan. Are you telling us Erikkson blackmailed you?"

The relief to finally know threatens to buckle my knees. "Yes, he did."

"Tell them the rest," Alicia snaps. We all turn to her, disheveled on the floor . She cackles when she looks up at me. "Tell them the truth about your *alpha pack*, Tristan Cohen."

My lips tighten, and I turn to where Gray and Logan stand next to me. Both of them are pale, but they nod at me.

It's time. The secrets we've been keeping have torn us apart.

For better or worse, we need to start stitching ourselves back together.

"You want me to do it?" I offer, but they shake their heads.

Grayson holds out his hand to Logan. "Shall we?"

Jax comes to stand next to me as their hands curl together.

Gray clears his throat, and eyes move to him, dropping down to take in their joined hands. Turning away, I watch the faces in the crowd, looking for their reaction as Gray starts to speak.

"I've been in love with this man for three years." His voice shakes. "I was too afraid to admit it, too afraid that people would turn their backs on our pack and we'd all suffer for our choices."

He turns to Sienna's parents. Her dad is frowning, but her mom is watching them both closely, a contemplative look in her eyes. "They blackmailed you with this."

It's not a question, but Gray nods anyway. "They did. And Tristan made the decision to do as they asked whilst we tried to find a way to expose the Erikksons for what they are." His lips tighten. "Blackmailers. Liars. And traffickers."

Sienna's parents freeze. "Traffickers?" her dad asks slowly. "What do you mean?"

"I found evidence in Councilor Erikkson's office that show he's working with people in Herrith to traffick Denied omegas." Everyone turns to me. "There was a list of names. Mine was at the top. If Erikkson could force us to Deny Sienna, she would be sent over the wall and the traffickers would be waiting."

Sienna's mother looks petrified. "But… she's *gone*. More than an hour ago."

"Tristan," my dad demands. "Why the hell didn't you approach the Council?"

I shake my head, looking down. "I thought… I could fix it all, dad," I admit. "Thought I could protect Gray and Logan, protect you… and protect Sienna. But I failed."

Looking up, I hold his eye. "The Denied status doesn't apply. The letter was forged. It needs to be retracted immediately."

Justice Milo interrupts. "There's certainly a lot to discuss." I don't miss his side-eye at Gray and Lo, the way his lip curls in distaste, and my fists clench at my sides. "I too would question why you did not approach us with this, Tristan."

"Because you're Erikkson's little Council buddy," Jax interrupts. "Everyone knows it, Justice."

Milo's eyes widen a little, and he draws himself up. "I am not so blind to my faults that I do not recognise them. But I will not accept accusations of corruption. The law is the law, and I will follow it."

He glances around. "Where is Erikkson, so he can respond to these claims?"

I stay where I am. "He's gone. He was gone before we came in."

Alicia's head jerks up as she looks around. "Daddy?"

Jax leans forward, his tone cutting. "Looks like daddy isn't around to get you out of this one, princess. He left you behind to face the music."

Alicia keeps looking around frantically. "He's not – he would never leave me."

"Well, he did." I raise my voice over the muttering. "Alicia prevented us from coming today by throwing a gas canister into my car, knocking us out to give her time to get here and offer a forged letter of Denial. I have never signed a letter of Denial, and I never will."

I turn back to Alicia, my eyes flicking to Sienna's parents. "During Sienna's heat, Alicia locked her in a shed in our grounds and threw chemicals over her to disguise her scent. If we hadn't found her, I don't know what would have happened."

Gasps ring out, and Ollena Hayward steps forward, her face thunder. "Is this true?" she demands. Alicia huffs, looking away.

"She threatened your daughters," I say softly to Sienna's parents. "Both of them."

I don't look at Alicia. I'm not giving her a single second more of my time, even as she wails, scrabbling and crawling to my feet. She tugs at my trousers desperately.

"Tristan," she cries. "You know I only did that for us. All of it, for us."

I keep my eyes up, refusing to give her even a single second

19

more of my attention. "I do not want you, Alicia. I do not care about you, except to wish you as much pain and suffering as you have heaped on our Soul Bonded."

Her cries are drowned out by a scream, and everyone turns to Sienna's mother. She sways in her mate's arms, and the look on her face, the terror, makes me step forward.

"I swear to you," I begin, but she holds up a shaking hand. "Soul Bonded. You are... Soul Bonded, to my daughter? *All* of you?"

When I nod, the courtyard erupts. Sienna's father turns gray as he runs a shaking hand over his face. "Oh, Sienna."

"We'll find her—," I begin, but her mother interrupts me.

"You find her *now*," she demands. "You have to leave immediately. If you don't, it will kill her. She cannot *survive* being separated from you!"

The bottom drops out from my stomach.

Health Elio comes to stand next to them, his face grave as I try and comprehend her words.

"What?" Jax demands next to me. "What do you mean?"

Tears start to roll down Sienna's mothers cheeks. "Soul Bonded cannot be separated. It causes physical pain for the omega, and it grows the longer they're apart."

"Not just that," Elio says softly. "We believe that the distance can be physical, or emotional. Whilst we don't have many Soul Bonded to study, Sienna's visit to the Healer's Center raised my suspicions. Although she denied it at the time, you have just confirmed them, Tristan. Aside from the physical dangers you have mentioned, her body will begin to fail. And she was already significantly weakened by the emotional stress caused during the Bonding Trials."

My mouth dries as the implications of his words hit me directly in the chest. Every action, every word I've spoken to Sienna, every cold shoulder, hits me like a dagger, and I stagger into Jax.

"Soul Bonds need care," Helena Michaelson whispers, her lips pale. "And as soon as I saw her, I suspected something wasn't right. She's already fading, thanks to you and your pack."

We've been killing her. Killing her, with our coldness, with our failure.

Every decision I've made has been slowly killing the girl who's supposed to be our soulmate.

I cannot fall apart. My hands are shaking as I look Sienna's mother, her father, in the face.

"I will find her. I will find her, and I will bring her home."

And I will never, ever forgive myself.

# 5

# GRAYSON

Logan's hand feels firm in mine, the eyes on us filled with disgust.

"Ignore them," he mutters. "It doesn't matter, Gray."

He's right. It doesn't matter. Now that I'm standing here, his hand in mine and our secret out, I couldn't care less about the assholes who want to judge someone for wanting the same freedoms they take for granted every damn day.

All I care about right now is Sienna, and how the fuck we get her back from over the wall.

Tristan strides over to us, his jaw clenched as Jax throws questions at him.

"We're leaving," he says shortly. "Right now."

As we move out, David catches up to us, grabbing Tristan by the arm. "Wait."

"We can't," Tristan spins, pushing his dad back. "We're leaving, dad. Sienna will *die* without us. We can't fuck around here any longer."

Wait. *What?*

Logan looks as confused as I feel, but David nods. "We have a lot to talk about when you're back. I'll see what I can do here – Erikkson is missing, and we need to look at replacing him before

Milo will support another vote on Sienna's Denied status. I'll try and send word if things change."

Tristan shakes his head. "I don't care about that. We need to be wherever she is."

"She has a family here," David says softly. "So do you, Tristan. All of you. So stay safe, and bring her home."

I grab Tristan's shoulder as we head out of the Hub at nearly a run. "Tristan - wait. What the fuck was he talking about?"

"You didn't hear?" Jax asks, his tone furious as he stares at Tristan. "Soul Bonded omegas can't survive without access to their mates. Sienna is dying. Unless we find her as soon as fucking possible, she will *die*. Thanks to us and our shitty decision-making."

I stagger back. "No - that's not true."

*That can't be fucking true.*

My eyes swing between Tristan and Jax. When Tristan nods, confirming it, I lose my balance, and Jax drags me upright. "Fall apart in the car," he snaps. "We're going to get her. Right, Tristan?"

Tristan stops short, turning to us. His face is pale. "We'll leave immediately. A quick run to the house for supplies. We don't know how long it will take to find her."

That's if the traffickers don't get to her first.

*What the fuck have we done?*

6

# SIENNA

A gony.
Wave upon wave of unyielding, searing torment rips through my body, gripping my muscles mercilessly as I cry out.

*Need to be quiet – they'll find me –*

"Shhh." Cool, damp cloth across my brow.

"Tristan," I sob. "Tristan, it hurts."

Not Tristan. Tristan left me alone.

"Jax," I wheeze. "Please."

But he left me, too. Gray, Logan. All of them left me alone.

Anguish tightens its grip, my back bowing as hands press me back down.

"Come on, now," a voice demands softly. "You can do this."

My head shakes wildly. I can't do this.

"Mama." The sob slips from my lips. "Mama, please."

*Help me. It hurts so much.*

Warm fingers curve around mine, gripping me tightly. "Hold on," the voice demands. "The fever will break."

It won't. I'm dying. I can feel it.

I can see them all, standing there with cold eyes.

"Why did you leave me?" I beg. "Why didn't you come?"

Tristan takes a step forward. "You need to wake up," he orders, his eyes sweeping over me. "You can do it."

"I can't," I whisper. "Something is broken inside me, Tristan."

His hands land on my shoulders, shaking me gently.

"I'm not Tristan," he murmurs. "You need to wake up." "

# 7

## SIENNA

My eyes fly open on a gasp, Tristan's face still swimming in my mind as I turn my head blindly. The room around me is dark, and my hands shoots out in a panic as I scramble back. Something crashes to the ground and I flinch as the door opens, a broad figure filling the space.

My whine rings out as I press myself against the cool wall.

Low light fills the small space, and I squint at the male in front of me.

"Hey," he says, leaning against the door. "You're awake."

I take him in as my eyes begin to adjust. He's tall, broad-shouldered with chestnut curls tight against his scalp. Deep brown eyes watch me carefully, and he eases back a step.

"How are you feeling?" he asks gently. "You've been in pretty bad shape."

I glance down at the bed I woke up in, taking in the blankets, the chair to the side. I'm still wearing my Mating Ceremony gown, if you can even call it that. It's ripped to hell and there is zero sign that it was ever the pale blush color that Logan handed to me.

I take a deep breath. Can't think about him now.

I've got bigger issues.

"Where am I?" I ask directly. He's not giving me kidnapping omega vibes, and I don't feel like he's about to wrangle me into a cage and sell me off... but I don't trust my instincts anymore.

He straightens and takes a small step into the room. "You're above my bar. I found you in my storage shed, burning up and half-dead, so I brought you in here."

He folds his arms, cocking a brow at me. "Feel free to explain why you were hiding in my shed at any time."

Swallowing, I press my hand against my cheek. It burns against my hand, my temperature still high.

Even now, the familiar pain pulses dully in my stomach, a twisting, taunting fist that'll never let me forget what happened.

"I don't remember." The lie drops from my lips, and I glance down. He seems nice enough. I don't want to lie to him. But I'm also not about to set myself up.

When I glance back up, he nods. "Fair enough. There's a jug of water on your nightstand." He nods to the tall, filled glass, a smaller glass placed carefully beside it. "Some painkillers too."

When my eyes move back to him, he holds up his hands. "You don't want to tell me where you're from, that's fine. You're clearly running from something, and you need rest. So get some sleep, and come find me when you're feeling up to it."

It's a generous offer. I'm not likely to find better, not out here in the middle of nowhere. I mull his words over before I give a slow nod.

"I'm Emmett," he offers, before he closes the door. He doesn't ask for my name, and I'm grateful, just in case word is getting around.

Although if anyone's looking for me, the hair will probably do it.

Gingerly, I settle my aching bones back into the mattress, but not before I glug down two full glasses of water, ignoring the painkillers. I lie back, leaving the overhead light on and trying not to freak out.

This is probably a good thing. It's better than wandering around the forest, waiting to be scooped up by traffickers.

As the adrenaline leaves my body in a rush, I swallow down the ache at the back of my throat. I wonder where my parents are. If they're still fighting the Council. If Jessalyn is with them, her snark in full force as she tries to persuade them to turn over their decision.

I wonder if my pack ever showed up, or if they're just getting on with their lives. My stomach flips.

Did they ever care about me at all? Even the tiniest bit?

Turning onto my side, I squeeze my eyes shut.

None of it matters now. I can't afford to dwell on it. I have to look forward, put a plan together.

It won't be long until my body fails me completely. I can feel it in my energy levels, in my shaking hands as I gripped the glass in both hands to drink my water.

I don't know how long, exactly. And truthfully, I can't bring myself to care.

8

# SIENNA

I'm curled up in the little bed, staring blankly at the wall when the door opens. Quiet footsteps pad across the room, making the hair on the back of my neck stand on end in warning.

Bracing myself for a fight, I flinch when Emmett's whisper floats across the room.

"There are men outside looking for you."

My whole body locks up, and I bite back a whimper. "Did you… did you tell them I'm here?"

When I turn over, Emmett has crossed to the window, peering through the small crack in the cream curtains. "No. But they're asking around. How much trouble are you in, exactly?"

He doesn't sound hugely concerned. More like he's preparing himself.

I swallow. "I'm not entirely sure. Are there three of them?"

He nods, turning his face towards me with a serious look. "They're not messing around. Who are they?"

I draw up my knees to my chest, hugging them. "Not… nice people. They seem to want me quite badly."

"Because you're an omega." My head shoots up as I recoil, and he rolls his eyes. "A girl like you, this close to the wall? I've heard enough about what happens in Navarre to put the pieces together."

My fingers pick at the covers. "You gonna tell them?"

Emmett sighs. "Do I look like that kind of asshole?"

My locked up muscles relax a little, but the tension doesn't leave me completely. "Are they trying to get inside?"

Emmett shakes his head. "I don't think they suspect you're here. More like they're covering as much ground as possible. They told me they were looking for a girl with pink hair. Acting all concerned for your welfare. Figured I should come and check just in case, but I told them I hadn't seen anyone like that."

"Thank you," I whisper. "I'm sorry to be a trouble."

Emmett nods. "Seems like the people around you are the trouble. Not your fault. You might want to lie low for a while, though."

I peek at him. "Here?"

He shrugs awkwardly. "Room's empty. So's the bar most of the time since we're pretty far out, though I've got a few regulars that come in. All of them are good people. So if you're looking for a place to hide out, omega, I'd say this might be your best bet."

My heart flips over. "I'm Sienna."

He clicks his tongue. "Nice to meet you. I'll leave you in peace, just wanted to let you know what was happening and not to go near the window."

Nodding, I wrap my arms around myself as Emmett closes the door softly behind him before I lay back down, my eyes focused on the window.

I'm tempted to look. Just a little. Just in case.

Maybe it's *them*.

Maybe they've come back for me.

My feet land on the bare wooden boards, my toes scrunching as I wobble to my feet.

I won't open the curtains. I'll just... take a really quick peek through the crack, like Emmett did. My feet aren't particularly steady as I weave my way across the room until I'm standing in front of the crack. Leaning forward, I look through the gap cautiously. The setting sun highlights the yard in front of the building I'm holed up in, and I can see the storage shed straight ahead of it.

My eyes move straight to the three men standing in a loose circle, talking animatedly, and I shove my disappointment down. Of course it's not them.

*Fucking pathetic, Sienna.*

The trio in front of me I recognise from the black boots and khakis. All three look big, menacing, with shaved heads and hands that flex on the handle of the guns they're carrying.

If they get hold of me, I won't be getting away.

I stumble backwards, putting enough distance between me and the window to help me breathe as I crawl back into the bed, tugging the covers over myself until I'm cocooned and my chest doesn't feel as tight.

Fucking hell. What an absolute shitshow. I'm separated from my family, abandoned by my pack, stuck in the forest with a strangely good-looking beta bar owner and a pack of neanderthal meatheads who want to *try out* an omega prowling around outside.

Maybe I'll write a book one day. You know. If I survive.

The minutes tick by, and I stay where I am until Emmett taps on the door.

"They're gone. Some food here for you," he calls through the wood. "Figured you might be hungry. Bathroom is across the hall."

I unwrap myself enough to call back to him. "Thanks, Emmett."

"Welcome." He whistles lightly as he moves away from my door, his footsteps creaking.

Curious, I dig myself free of my blanket prison and pull myself upright. My head swims with dizziness, and I hold on to the little table next to my bed until it recedes enough for me to walk.

Emmett's offering is surprisingly homely. A thick bowl of steaming stew, filled with meat and vegetables and with a large hunk of bread next to it. It actually makes my stomach rumble.

When I lean down to pick up the tray, my head lists, my hands shaking and making the tray tip to the side. Biting my lip, I put it down and tug it forward instead until I can close the door.

I've got very little appetite, but I do manage a few mouthfuls, forcing myself to drink all of the liquid and eat some of the vegetables in the bowl.

My bladder makes itself known in a sudden demand, so I shuffle back to the door, opening it gingerly and peeking out. There's a door directly opposite my room and I scuttle over, finding a small but very clean shower, sink and lavatory.

I take a few minutes to clean up, as much good as it can do with this fucking pink monstrosity still on. I swear to god, if this is a repeat of what happened during the Trials and I end up wearing this dress until it's crawling off me, then I'm going to lose my shit. I avoid glancing in the mirror as I scrub at my hands, my arms, my face.

I don't need to see what I look like. I'm sure I'm on par with one of the walking dead at this point.

I drag myself back to bed, wincing at the filth on my dress as I climb back in, my eyelids already drooping. I feel exhausted just from that small burst of activity, but at least I'm fed, and sort of clean.

9

# LOGAN

Hoisting my bag back onto my shoulder, I hold out a hand
for Gray. He pulls himself up, not letting go as he threads
our fingers together absent-mindedly, his eyes already scanning
the forest.

"Nothing," he mutters. "Where's she gone?"

Ahead of us, Tristan's shoulders tense, but he carries on
walking. None of us want to consider why we can't find any
goddamned trace of our Bonded in these fucking woods. If
someone was waiting for her at the gate, she might not have even
set foot in here.

"She's here somewhere," Jax says determinedly. "I can feel it.
Can't you?"

We all shake our heads, but I trust him, so we follow without
complaint when he veers off down a path. Tristan shouts after
him. "We've been down there before!"

"Bite me," Jax snaps back. "I'm following my fucking instincts,
and it's telling me to go this way."

I quietly pull on Gray's hand until we're following after Jax.
We move into single file down the worn path, our boots crunching
over the jagged rocks and twigs in our way.

Tristan stomps after us, muttering something under his breath.

"What do we do when we find her?" I ask out loud. It's the elephant in the corner, has been for the hours we've spent traipsing through the woods, looking for any hint of Sienna passing through.

"Pray," Jax shoots over his shoulder. "Pray to gods that she actually forgives us for abandoning her at our Mating Ceremony."

"And for everything else," Gray says quietly.

I nod in agreement. Where the fuck do we even begin making the last few weeks up to her? Fuck. If it wasn't for us being Soul Bonded, she'd be gone, and we'd never see her again.

My chest squeezes at the thought. Soul Bonded or not, Sienna belongs with us.

We just have to show her. All she's seen are the worst parts of us.

My heart thumps. I don't have anything to give her, really. A few pieces of art. But if she forgives us, I'll spend the rest of our lives making sure she understands exactly how much she's wanted.

Tristan huffs behind us. "We're just going around in circles!" he shouts down to Jax. Jax throws up his middle finger in response, carrying on.

We just have to *find* her.

1 0

# SIENNA

I don't know what makes me jerk awake, my breath see-sawing out of me as I push away yet another dream where I'm taunted by the possibility of what our pack could have been.

I pick up the slight change in the room, the smallest creak of a floorboard before a figure flies at me, covering my face with a hand.

I let out a muffled scream before the voice hissing in my ear registers.

"Sienna! Come on. It's me. We have to go, now."

My eyes widen as a familiar face spins into view, corkscrew bronzed curls hanging on either side of my face.

*Jess?*

For a small, euphoric moment, my heart cracks in sheer happiness. She's here. How the fuck is she here?

"Jess," I whisper hoarsely when her hand releases. "What the hell—,"

"We don't have time," she hisses back. "We have to go, before he wakes up!"

I blink. "Who?"

We're interrupted by the tread of footsteps. Jess jumps up as the light gets switched on, and I flinch as Emmett charges in, a raised gun in his hand. "Get the hell away from her!"

I'm not sure what he expected, but it's clear he has no idea that he was facing down a small but *extremely* angry female. He stops, blinking as he looks between us..

My best friend doesn't blink. The second Emmett's gun lowers, she whips out a handgun of her own and points it at him casually. Gasping, I scramble out of bed. "Jess!"

"Jesus fuck," Emmett grumbles. Lowering the gun, he lifts his hands in the air. "There's *two* of you?"

Jess doesn't waver, her hands steady as she holds the gun pointed straight at his chest. "We're leaving," she says calmly. "And you are not going to stop us."

"Damn straight I'm not," Emmett mutters. "Sienna, you've got some interesting friends."

I see the moment Emmett's deliberately casual tone registers with Jess. She frowns, her eyes sliding to me. "Is he keeping you here against your will?"

Gingerly, I move between her and Emmett, pressing the barrel down with a single finger. "Pretty sure he saved my life, actually. Could you put the gun down now, please? I'd kind of like to give you a hug, and I can't do that while you're holding live ammo."

Jess drops the gun suddenly, and it clatters to the floor as she jumps on me. Her arms wrap around me tightly, and I can't stop the tears from streaming.

"Jess," I gasp, her face buried in my neck. "What are you doing here?"

She mumbles into my skin. "Told you I wasn't leaving you."

"But the wall!"

She huffs. "Oh, please. It wasn't hard to find a gap that I could get through. They're not exactly spending bucketloads on maintenance."

"I can't believe you're here," I whisper. My eyes dart over Jess's shoulder to where Emmett is standing, his arms crossed and eyebrows raised questioningly. Flushing, I pull back from Jess.

"Jess," I say slowly. "This is Emmett. He owns the bar downstairs."

Emmett looks bemused as Jess gets a proper look at him. "Pleasure. Do you always introduce yourself with a loaded gun?"

I watch in slight shock as Jessalyn Rogers blushes. I don't think I've *ever* seen Jess blush.

It only lasts for a split second before she tosses her hair back. "Sorry about the lock on your door. You have terrible security."

Emmett half-grins as he eyes her. "Never needed it before I met you two, but thanks for the heads up."

He looks at me. "She staying, too?"

"I...," I glance at Jess helplessly. She nods abruptly. "Damn straight I am. We can leave if it's an issue."

Emmett purses his lips. "Well, I don't think I could set you loose on the locals. I'll get some more blankets."

I blink as they nod at each other, forming some sort of silent agreement,, before Emmett ducks out and Jess turns back to me. She swallows as she steps back, taking me in in my dirty dress. "Oh, Si."

My lip wobbles. "Jess."

She points her finger. "You've got thirty minutes before you can fall apart on me. Is there a shower in this place?"

She wrinkles her nose when I nod. "Good. You're going to have a long soak in the shower, and then we can talk."

Bending down, Jess grabs a large backpack from the floor and starts unzipping it, digging around until she produces a bottle of shampoo. "Go on. I've got spare clothes in here you can put on. Turn around and I'll do your dress."

My shoulders shake as she gently undoes the buttons lining the back of my dress, before she nudges me forward. "Shower. I'll see if the new member of our trio has any coffee downstairs."

Holding up my dress and clutching the shampoo, I head obediently towards the door before I turn around.

"Jess?"

She turns, pushing her hair back. "Yeah?"

I manage a wobbly smile. "I wish you hadn't come, but I'm really glad you're here."

Jess sniffs, but I catch the gleam in her eyes. "Like fuck was I letting them send you over the wall on your own. Good job Monty taught me how to use a gun."

I choke. Monty, Jess's butler, must be close to a hundred. "He did?"

"Yep. I knew it'd come in handy one day." She points, giving me a stern look. "Shower. Clean. Then crying."

Nodding, I take her at her word, spending a good twenty minutes washing all of the forest filth, the sweat from my fever off my skin. The bruising on my arm is still a garish green, and I turn away from it. I try not to notice the bones poking out, the protruding feel of my ribs beneath my fingers as I wash.

God, it feels good to be clean. As I climb out, Jess sticks her head around the door and tosses me some clothes. "Coffee's on, bitch. Time for tears and retribution."

I snort out a laugh as I pull on the pajamas. They're ridiculously loose on me, and I catch Jess's look of concern when I look up from pulling the drawstring as tight as they'll go.

Another mattress has been dragged into the bedroom when I enter, a neat pile of blankets and a pillow at one end. Jess is stripping the bed briskly, swapping out the dirty sheets for fresh white ones. Emmett stands in the middle of the room, wild-eyed with a tray of coffee in his hands.

"I'm sorry we're invading your space," I say awkwardly. He shrugs, the tips of his ears tinging pink. "It's pretty boring up here. Nice to have some company for a change."

I don't miss the way his eyes follow Jess, but he glances away when she springs upright, puffing hair away from her face. "Done."

Emmett puts the tray down on the table, grabbing the empty jug. "I'll leave you two to it. Help yourself to anything you need from the kitchen, but just watch out for anyone hanging around."

"Thanks," Jess says begrudgingly. "Sorry for threatening to shoot you."

He gives her a cool look. "Threaten all you want. You wouldn't have gotten very far if you'd tried."

She huffs, her cheeks darkening again as she looks away. "Guess we'll never know."

"Nope." Emmett pops the 'p' as he passes me, giving me a smile. "You need anything, Sienna? More painkillers?"

Jess's shoulders tense, but I wave him off. "You made sure I was pretty well stocked. Thanks, Emmett."

After he leaves, Jess collapses down on her mattress. I perch on the bed.

"I can't believe you came after me," I say softly. "Jess."

"Like I said, I wasn't going to leave you on your own." Her eyes slide away. "Your parents... they weren't doing so well. I left them a note with Monty."

"How'd he take it?" Monty is very protective of Jess. All her staff are.

She shrugs. "Badly. But he couldn't stop me."

My hand traces patterns on the light blue cotton of my pajama pants. "Did you... did you see them?" I hate that my voice breaks at the end.

Jess shakes her head, her lips set in a line. "I left right after the Justice officers took you. Didn't want to waste any time, but I lost your trail anyway. I only found you because you left some footprints by the forest."

I sit up. "I did?"

She gives me a look. "I wiped them. Talk, Si. I want to know everything."

We curl up with our coffee as I spill the beans on everything that's happened in the last few weeks. Jess curses, shouts and swears at appropriate times.

"I'm going to shave her head," she snarls. "Bet she looks like a plucked turkey without all that hair. That fucking bitch!"

When I finish, my breathing a little heavier than when I started, Jess stares at me, her mouth opening and closing. "I... I don't even know where to begin."

I shrug weakly. "I know. The worst thing... I was so certain they'd show up, Jess. After everything, Tristan still lied to my face. I should've known better."

"But they're your Soul Bonded," Jess says softly. "Oh, Sienna."

She picks up my wrist, circling it with her fingers. "I feel like your bones could break under my fingers. What's up with that, Si? It's like you've dropped half your body weight."

My mouth dries, and I shift uncomfortably. "Jess...,"

She picks up on my tone. "What? What is it?"

"The Soul Bond," I croak. "It... I need to be close to them, Jess. It hurts to be away from them."

Jess frowns. "Like, your heart hurts? Heartbroken hurt?"

"No – well, yes, but... actual pain. Everywhere. I spoke to Health Elio when I was at the Healers Center. He thinks that Soul Bonded omegas have to have maintained contact to stay healthy."

"So if you don't...," Jess says slowly, watching my face. "What happens? You get sick?"

I nod. "And worse. Maybe." My whisper drops like a stone between us.

Jess swallows, flipping her hand over and lacing our fingers together. "We can fix this."

She sounds so certain that tears fill my eyes. "I hope so, Jess. It feels like I'm fading away."

"I won't let that happen," she says fiercely. "I won't, Si."

I laugh croakily. "I believe you." Leaning my head against her shoulder, I let the tears fall. One, then another, then another. My breath shudders as I let it all out.

"That's it," Jess whispers. Shifting, she works herself back until my head is in her lap, her hands playing with my hair. "Let it all out, Si. I've got you."

I cry until I have no tears left, my eyes gritty and dry.

I cry until my swollen eyes start to close, Jess stroking my hair in silence as we curl up together, abandoning the bed for tonight.

"I'm glad you're here, Jess," I whisper as I drift off. It's maybe the most selfish thing I could feel. But I'm so glad that I'm not on my own.

"I wouldn't be anywhere else."

# 11

## SIENNA

**M**y eyes feel full of grit when I crack them open again, yet another broken night of tossing and turning. Vague memories of Jess talking to me surface, shaking my shoulders, wiping my face.

It doesn't feel like either of us got much sleep.

Gingerly, I push myself upright. The mattress behind me is empty, blankets tossed aside haphazardly and no sign of my best friend.

After taking a few minutes to make myself presentable, I take a deep breath and make my way along the hall from my room. We're at the end of the long hallway, and I pass several doors until I reach a narrow set of dark wooden stairs. Voices float up to me from downstairs, and my feet pad down the steps as I follow the low buzz.

Jessalyn is leaning on a long, dark bar that runs the length of the low-ceilinged room. I glance around, taking in the worn but well cared for wooden tables, the dartboard, the bare cream walls.

"Sienna!" Jess says brightly. She uncrosses her arms, leaning back from where she and Emmett had been having what looked like a fairly intense discussion. "How are you feeling?"

I shift on my feet. "I feel okay."

To her credit, Jess doesn't call me out on my absolute horseshit, even as her eye twitches.

"Good. Well, I was talking to Emmett about what I could do to... I don't know, earn our keep?"

She directs her words to him, and he nods. "I could always use another hand around here."

"Ah... do you get busy?" I glance askance at the small space, thinking of the remote forests around us. What made him decide to set up a bar in the middle of nowhere?

His lips twitch. "Not really. A handful of regulars and that's it.. You'll get to meet them."

"But in the meantime," Jess adds, "Emmett is going to take me down to the store to grab a few things."

I blink, looking between them. They both avoid the other's eye. "Ah. Okay?"

"Good." Jess pats Emmett's arm. "Come on, hot stuff. Show me your truck. I need to see if you're compensating for anything."

I hear him choke as he leaves, and a grin pulls up the corners of my lips. Jess hangs back, her expression turning serious. "Stay upstairs," she says quietly. "The gun is under the bed. I'll call out when we get back."

Swallowing, I nod. "You sure you need to go to the store?" I ask weakly. Jess nods. "It's important, but we'll be quick."

When she leaves, I do as she said and head back upstairs. My feet drag a little as I lift them, and it's a relief to curl back up into my covers and close my eyes.

The small amount of rest I've been able to get is interrupted as I wake with a choke. Air catches in my throat as I struggle to take a breath, eventually breaking into a cough that sends something spattering against the hand pressed over my mouth.

Rolling over, I push myself up and open my fist.

Dark, red, viscous liquid sits like a pool in my palm. My fingers close over it quickly, and I stumble to the bathroom, frantically running the water and scrubbing until there's no trace of blood. My skin turns red under the scalding rush of water, but I keep going until the pain is worse than the panic clawing up my insides.

I hit the water off abruptly, my hands landing on the side of the sink as I take deep breaths. I catch a glimpse of my face in the mirror, red staining my lips, and rub at it until it disappears.

"Si?" Jess hollers from down the hall, and I push myself upright. Quickly, I wash my hands again and snatch one of the neatly stacked, worn towels from the rail as her footsteps sound from outside the door.

"We okay?" she asks, popping her head around. Her hair bounces as she cocks it in question.

"Fine," I say hastily, putting the towel back and following her into the bedroom. "How was the shopping?"

Jess wrinkles her nose. "I don't think I'd call it shopping. Not when the clothes look like they went out of fashion a century ago. But..." she drops a full bag onto the bed, "I did get what I wanted."

I watch over her shoulder as she unpacks what looks like dozens of small boxes and tubes. "What's that?"

Jess tosses the empty bag aside and starts laying them out. "Vitamins. I spoke to the chemist – nothing about Soul Bonded, obviously, but about general health – and he gave me a list. They had most of it in stock, and we can pick the rest up in a few days."

She turns to me, hands on her hips. "You're not eating properly," she says softly. "And if we're going to fight this, Si, we need to make sure you're in the best possible condition."

I swallow back the metallic taste in my mouth. "These are all for me?"

"Yep." Jess pulls another tub out, holding it out to me and turning back to her haul. I turn the plastic over in my hands.

"I'm going to split them into a batch for each day, and you're taking them."

"Jess." My voice is quiet, and she pauses for a second before her shoulders tighten, her back to me as she carries on. "I'm not sure—,"

Her eyes are bright, too bright, when she turns around.

"I can't sit here and do nothing, Si," she says fiercely. "You expect me to just watch you fade away in front of me – and what? Twiddle my thumbs and make sad faces? Not. Happening."

She points to the bed. "Sit your ass down and take your vitamins."

I sit on the bed, and I take every one of the endless vitamins Jess shakes at me threateningly.

Every little helps, right?

When we're done, and my stock for the next week is packed into the little tabs of my new vitamin box, Jess stands up and dusts her hands.

"Just one more thing," she says firmly, throwing another packet at me. I catch it, peering down at the text. My heart thumps painfully. "Hair dye?"

"Those men are looking for someone with pink hair," Jess points out. "We change your hair color, it's one less thing to make it stand out."

She's right. I know she's right. But it still hurts.

"Great," I force a smile and a nod. "Let's do it."

Jess rolls her eyes at me. "Liar. It'll wash out. I bought plenty to keep us topped up."

My breath leaves me in a whoosh. "Oh, thank god."

I'm messing with my newly-dyed brown hair when Jess clears her throat.

"I told Emmett we'd come down and do some work," she admits. "Well, I will, anyway. You need to rest, Si."

"I can work," I protest. I need something – anything – to get my mind off recent events. Jess eyes me dubiously, but she doesn't protest when I follow her down the stairs, her pace slowing to keep up with mine.

"We're heeere!" she sings out. "Two wenches, at your service."

Emmett's head pops up from behind the bar. His curls look a

little rumpled and his eyes widen as he takes us in. "Right. Nice hair. You still want to do a shift?"

Jess strikes a pose, her hand on her hip. "Of course. Your regulars will love us."

Emmett stands, wiping off his hands on a cloth with a frown. "And if those men come back?"

Jess smiles sweetly. "I'll shoot them." She turns and yanks up her top, showing off the sleek handgun tucked into her waistband.

Emmett and I both stare at her, open-mouthed. "What?" She shrugs. "You think I'm stupid enough to let us wander around here without protection?"

*My best friend is a badass. A slightly petrifying, tiny, wild-haired badass.*

I'm feeling mildly smug about it as I shrug at Emmett. "What do you need us to do?" I ask.

With a sigh, he gestures at the bar. "Have you ever done this before?"

"No," I consider the idea. "It can't be that hard, though, right?"

---

*"Motherfucker."*

I grin smugly at Jess as she swears at the pieces of glass on the floor. She actually stamps her foot at me, and I snicker as she grabs the dustpan Emmett put close to us 'in case of any more accidents'.

Jess has had quite a few *accidents*.

Meanwhile, I've progressed from pouring beers to operating the till, and I'm practically preening. Jess snarls at me as she stands from scooping up the glass.

"I hate you right now," she grumbles. "Why the hell is this so difficult?"

I don't point out that she's only dropping glasses when Emmett is standing next to her, *helping* her.

I don't want to ruin the small amount of fun I'm actually having watching them interact. It's like a wildcat and a bear, creeping round and sniffing each other.

I'm so entertained that I fail to notice the door opening, and I jump a mile when a voice booms out behind me. "Who the hell are you?"

Yelping, I watch in dismay as the shelf I just smacked into wobbles. A glass teeters ominously, falling as I jump to catch it.

Shit. I was doing so well, too.

Emmett groans, covering his eyes as he steps around Jessalyn. His huge hands cover my shoulders as he steers me away from the danger zone and onto a bar stool. "I'll clean this up."

I push my hair back to get a look at the newcomer.

Or... newcomers.

Three males are standing on the other side of the bar, mouths slightly open as they take in Jess and I and the chaos we're causing. One of them, an older male with bushy white hair and a bristly, trimmed mustache, lifts a hand to his chin and scratches carelessly. "Got yourself one of them packs, Emmett?" he asks, a hint of mischief in his pale green eyes.

Emmett stands abruptly, nearly hitting Jess and sending them both scrabbling away from each other. "Mind your business, Jack," Emmett says grumpily. "They're guests. *Temporary* guests."

Jess's shoulders stiffen, but she throws them back and offers the men a bright smile as she not-so-gently muscles Emmett out of the way. "Hey there! I'm Jessalyn. This is Sienna. We're just... traveling through."

The male next to Jack, a little younger though still well into his fifties, offers Jessalyn a smile. "Well, hello there, Jessalyn. I'm Rick." He jabs a thumb at the bulky male next to him. "And this is Otto."

Otto nods, but doesn't say anything. His brown eyes linger on me, taking in the sharp angles of my face, the bruising poking out of my sleeve. His mouth thins, and he looks away from me.

"Leave 'em alone," he says gruffly. "Three beers please."

"Coming right up!" Jess says eagerly. I catch Emmett's eyes flicking up and what looks like some sort of prayer as Jess grabs another glass.

## 12

# GRAYSON

I shake hands with the burly beta, and he holds out a set of keys.

"Thanks." Turning back, I head over to Logan, Jax and Tristan and jangle the set. "At least now we can move faster."

Two fucking days. Two days of finding our way out of that gods-forsaken forest and into a small community. We've made discreet enquiries, and there's no sign of Sienna passing through here.

"Good," Logan straightens, hoisting his backpack across his shoulders. "I think we should head to the other place."

Jax is rubbing his chest, his eyes scanning the empty road ahead of us. "You feel it?"

If he means the solid weight of regret dragging down my chest, it's not something I can ignore. Looking at Tristan, I see him staring down at the floor, his lips pursed. He's been close to silent since we left Navarre, the dark circles under his eyes evidence of the hours he spends sitting upright, keeping watch during the night while the rest of us have been restlessly stirring.

He's going to break, but I'm not sure the rest of our pack cares anymore.

Crossing over, I jangle the keys in front of his face, and he nods, reaching out for them.

"Not a chance," I snap. "You want to kill us? You need to sleep, Tris. At this rate we'll be carting your ass around, and that's the last thing we need right now. *Fix it.*"

He gives me a short nod. "You're right."

"I – I am?" Somehow I expected more of a fight. "I mean, I know I am, I'm just surprised you're agreeing with me."

He falls into step beside me as we make our way to the truck, a familiar brush against my side.

"I've been going over everything in my head, the last two days. Where I went wrong."

"I think we all went wrong," I say softly. "I'm not saying I agreed with all of your decisions, Tris. But I understand them."

His face twists. "I don't think Sienna will feel the same, and I don't blame her" he admits. "I can't breathe, Gray. Every time I close my eyes, I see her face. At the ceremony, at the house, the hospital. And then I imagine how she looked when Alicia handed over that fucking letter and I—,"

He stops, his breathing ragged. "I need to make sure she's okay," he says quietly. "Work through this Soul Bonded mess. And then… I don't know, yet. But… I'm thinking of leaving, Gray."

I stop abruptly, and he pauses next to me, his eyes flicking to Jax and Logan. Staring at him, I search for the right words.

"You what?"

Not the most eloquent, but I'm not sure what the fuck I'm supposed to say to that. Tristan half-smiles, and it's the saddest fucking thing I've ever seen.

"I think you can make it work," he murmurs, "with Sienna. But I don't deserve her forgiveness, Gray. I lied to her over and over again and forced you all to do the same, and that's not how you treat your Soul Bonded. She won't forgive me, and I'm not going to try and force her into it."

He looks down. "I've done enough of that already."

My heart twists in my chest. Tristan is our pack leader. The beating heart of our pack.

Except... that's not quite true. Not anymore.

I swallow. "I don't want you to go."

He looks ahead, his eyes sad as he takes in Jax and Logan talking. "I'm not going anywhere yet. Not until I know she's safe. I'm guessing three Soul Bonded will be enough, but if not, I'll be close enough to keep her healthy."

Frowning, I follow his eyes. "So, what? You're just condemning yourself to a life on the outside? Come on, Tris. Where the hell has your fight gone?"

He shakes his head. "It was my fight that got us into this fucking mess, Gray. I was so adamant I could keep everything going, and look how it fucking turned out. I'm not saying I'm definitely leaving, and not until I know she's healthy enough for me to be able to do that. But if she can't cope with having me around... it's something we have to consider."

Everyone piles into the truck, and I set the navigator to take us west. It looks like we might've missed a path somewhere, and apparently there's a small community up there where our Soul Bonded could have ended up.

We have to drive around a mountain to reach the new place, and we drive slowly through the trees. There's a few log cabins scattered around, but no sign of Sienna. I keep driving, looking for somewhere we might be able to leave the truck to head out and search.

Logan leans forward between the seats. "How about there?"

It looks like a bar, although what the hell a bar is doing in an area this deserted, I don't know. I pull into the yard, parking a short distance away from the entrance.

We all get out, and I walk up to the entrance. It swings open before we reach it, and the beta male in the doorway stares at us. Not the most friendly welcome.

"Can I help you?" he calls.

"Yeah. We're looking for a girl that might have come through here. She's pretty distinctive, long pink hair. Have you seen her?"

He frowns. "We don't get many visitors up here. Sorry."

The faint sliver of hope in my chest dims again. "Right. Sorry to disturb you."

We trudge back to the truck, the male watching us with his arms crossed. Sighing, I climb in. "Come on. We'll drive back down, maybe stop off at those log cabins."

## 13

# TRISTAN

As we drive away, something twists inside my chest. "Wait."

Gray looks over at me with a frown. "Why?"

"Just – stop the truck."

I'm opening my door before Gray can brake completely, ignoring his curses as I jump out. For once, I'm trusting my instincts, and it's telling me that we've just driven in the wrong fucking direction.

Our Soul Bonded is in that building. I'm certain of it.

The others catch up to me as I stride forward, all of us falling into the familiar line as I lead us back to the small bar. The beta appears back at the door as we approach. His thinly-veiled civil demeanor falls away as he takes in our faces, replaced by a scowl.

"I told you," he says casually, leaning against the doorway. His nonchalant pose doesn't fool me. I can see the tension lining his shoulders, the set of his jaw.

The tugging at my chest is becoming more insistent, a driving force that pushes me forward until we stand toe to toe.

"I know she's in there," I say firmly. "And I will go through you if I have to. But you will not stop me from getting to my mate. Move."

When he doesn't budge, a growl ripples out of Jax as he comes to stand beside me, both of us united. "Do as he says, little beta. We're not fucking around here."

The male shifts on his feet, spreading his legs a little wider. He's not moving.

"She's ill," I say quietly, watching his face. He tries to stop it, but I catch the flicker of awareness in his eyes, and my gut clenches.

*Sienna.*

"We can help her. We're the only ones that can."

A hand curls over his shoulder, and he jerks his head back. When he turns back to us, there's something else on his face.

*Amusement.*

My confusion lasts as long as it takes for him to shift to the side, and a tiny ball of absolute fury comes darting out, crashing into Jax.

"Jesus wept." He drops to his knees, cupping his balls. "She got me!"

"I will fucking kill you," the omega snarls. Not our omega, but I recognize her, relief and shock sinking in and lightening my muscles as she turns to face me, even as I see the anger on her face.

If Jessalyn is here, then that means—

"Sienna," I say urgently. "Where is she, Jessalyn?"

Jessalyn stares at me, her bronze curls just as wild as they were the day I saw her at our Bonding Ceremony as she moves towards me, her finger jabbing with every word.

"You," she hisses. "You son of a goddamned bitch. What the fuck are you doing here?"

I catch her fist in my hand as it flies towards me, and for the first time, true menace enters the beta's face as he takes a step forward. "Get your fucking hands off her, *now*."

Dropping it, I hold up my hands, as much an apology as it is to ward Jessalyn off. She vibrates with fury as she looks around at us. Gray and Logan have closed in behind us, Jax staggering to his feet with a groan.

"Oh, shut up," she snaps, rolling her eyes. "A little punch in the babymakers is nothing compared to what you've put Sienna through, you little weasel. Take it like a damned alpha."

"Enough." I'm done being patient. "Where is Sienna, Jessalyn?"

She scoffs. "Like I'd tell you. What – you didn't finish the job? Here to stick the knife in a little more, really twist it? She gets the fucking message, asshole. Now crawl back into your little hole and stay away from here."

Crossing my arms, I resist the urge to bare my teeth. "We're not going anywhere. You tell Sienna that. We're here to explain."

"I don't want your apologies."

Every one of us freezes at the quiet, steady voice that sounds from behind Jessalyn. I catch the worry on the omega's face as she spins around, and my stomach drops as I catch her hurriedly whispered words.

"…should be resting…,"

Jessalyn's shoulders slump as she moves to the side. The beta adjusts himself casually so he's stood between us, a furrow in his brow as he moves aside for Sienna to move past.

The first glimpse of my Soul Bonded pushes the air from my lungs, threatens to take me to my knees.

She meets my eyes, her own sunken with deep, dark purple circles in the thinness of her face.

It's been two days.

*Two days.*

And she looks…

"Sienna." The choked word falls from my lips, but as I step forward, she holds up a wavering hand.

"Do not," she says quietly, "come near me, Tristan."

"Shortcake," Jax breathes, and I see the flash of pain across her face as her eyes flicker to him. "Don't call me that."

Her eyes continue moving, and I hear Logan swallow next to me. I can't take my eyes from her, our broken Soul Bonded, but I can feel their absolute devastation in my chest, a beating, pulsing wound in my heart.

I'm looking at the consequences of my bad decisions, and I know with sudden certainty that my words to Gray were true.

I can never atone for this. Never.

But she has to live. And right now, I'm certain that our Soul Bonded is walking a very thin line. My fists clench, my nails digging into my palms so hard I can feel the warm trickle of blood spreading in my palm.

"You deserve an explanation." My throat is dry, the pain in my chest blinding, but I know, I know, that it's nothing to what she's feeling. I can see it in the way she holds herself, heartbreakingly careful, as though one touch would shatter her completely.

As if we haven't done that already.

14

# SIENNA

I can't breathe.

They're here, all of them, staring at me with sad, broken faces. Pretty lies in perfect faces, even if they all look like shit.

*Good. Join the fucking crew.*

I'm not buying what they're selling.

I made that mistake too many times. And I don't have the time to fuck around waiting for their pretend apologies and half-truths.

Tristan opens his mouth, and I flick my eyes back to him. "You deserve an explanation."

"You fucking think?" Jess snarls, but Emmett taps her arm, and she crosses them with a dark glare at Tristan.

"I deserve a lot more than that." I take a careful, measured step forward, keeping my body as straight as I can, battling the urge to hunch over at the blinding pain in my stomach that's tugging me towards them.

*Betrayed by my own fucking body.*

"I deserved a pack who would have given me everything," I say to them all. Gray looks grim as his eyes scan down, taking in the changes in my body underneath the oversized shirt I borrowed from Jess.

"Short- Sienna. *Please*." Jax shakes his head in despair, dark hair flying everywhere and his violet eyes dark. "I can see you fucking fading away. It's only been two *days*."

"It hasn't only been two days." My words land like a whip. "Because you never showed up at all."

Jax drops his head. Logan steps forward. "Sienna—,"

"And *you*," I say coldly, taking in his soulful, kicked-puppy eyes. "All I asked for was the truth. And after everything, you still lied to me."

"Sienna," Tristan leans forward. "You're sick. I know you don't want us close, and I do not blame you. But we can help you."

"I don't want your help. I've seen what it looks like."

"But—,"

"I choose this." My words cut Tristan off. "I would choose this over and over, and over again over your so-called *help*."

Tristan pales, but I'm not finished.

"I would have given you everything," I whisper. "But I have nothing left to give. You can live with your mistakes, Tristan. Because I won't be. Go home. There is *nothing* for you here."

They're silent as I turn my back on them, Jess and Emmett spreading out to put a barrier between us as I shuffle towards the stairs.

"I told you before," Tristan calls out. I pause, my hand shaking on the handrail. "Hate me if you want to, Sienna. But we're not leaving."

I don't acknowledge his words, dragging myself up to the small haven of our room as Jess follows me. She doesn't say anything, uncharacteristically silent as she tugs the blankets over me.

When I meet her eyes, she looks away. "Si—,"

"No." My resolve is firmer than the shaking in my voice. "No, Jess."

Her shoulders slump, but she doesn't say anything else as I roll over and close my eyes.

I meant every word. I have nothing left for the Cohen pack. I'll see myself through the Soul Bond.

And even if I can't... I'd choose short-term agony over a life filled with nothing but pain.

15

JAX

All four of us are struck dumb as we watch our Soul Bonded walk away from us.

*Shortcake.*

She's so much thinner than she was even a few days ago. The sharp, pointed edges of her elbows poke out of her shirtsleeves as she shuffles away. Jessalyn swings her head between us and Sienna, clearly torn between laying into us and going after her.

"Leave," she says finally. "Please."

Tristan shakes his head. "We can't do that, Jessalyn. We won't. We're not leaving her again."

The harpy frowns. "She doesn't want you."

"Maybe not," Tristan admits. "We understand that. But we're not going to sit back and watch her wither away, Jessalyn. We're Soul Bonded. She needs us close. Her mother told us that before she left."

Jess pauses, and I see a flicker of indecision on her face. "Helena did?"

He nods. "We're not here to hurt her, Jess. I swear it."

Jess glances behind her, takes a step away. "She doesn't want you. If it wasn't for the Soul Bond—,"

"We know. But we are Soul Bonded. That has to mean something."

I see the moment Jess stiffens. "Pity it didn't mean anything to you sooner. The only reason we're here, the only reason my best friend is looking more like a corpse every day is because of you and your pack."

Tristan doesn't look down, holding her gaze. "I know. And we'll spend the rest of our lives making it up to her."

Jess looks at the beta, indecision in her eyes. He looks over us before sighing and crossing his arms. "More guests."

"They're not stepping foot in here," Jess snaps. "Let them camp outside."

With that, she stomps off, following Sienna's steps. We're left in an awkward silence, the beta studying us intently, a small frown on his face.

"So you're the reason she looks like that?" he asks. The affable look he wore around the omegas slides away, and he bares his teeth. "I'm not having abusers under my roof."

I flinch at his stark words. But they're fucking true.

"We have to stay close," Tristan responds carefully. "We'll respect her wishes for distance as much as we can, but we're not going anywhere."

The beta nods slowly. "There's a storage shed behind this building. You can use that, but you're not coming inside."

"Agreed." Tristan sounds weary as he turns, nudging us all away.

Gray and Logan are quiet as we unload our packs, their eyes sliding to the windows around the building. Awareness prickles the back of my neck. We're being watched.

"I need a minute," Logan says abruptly. I watch as he stalks away from us into the trees. Gray hesitates, but he follows him, leaving Tristan and I in uncomfortable silence.

"Fancy words, considering you're leaving." The drawl in my voice hides the pain I don't want him to see. How the fuck can he even consider walking out on us?

EVELYN FLOOD

Tristan sighs. "I'm not going anywhere right now, Jax. Not until Sienna is healed and healthy. Then it's her decision. But she doesn't want me around. The rest of you... I think you can make it work, in time."

"So you're just fucking off?" I demand. "That's it, thanks for the memories, see you fuckers later?"

He shakes his head as we move towards the building Emmett pointed out. "What do I do, Jax?" he asks. "I won't force her to accept a Soul Bond with me. I don't know if I *can* leave, if three Bonds are enough to keep her healthy."

"You're being a fucking martyr," I point out. "No wonder she doesn't want us. You can't be assed to even fight for her, Tris."

He snarls, throwing his pack down. "You think I don't *want* to?" he demands. "Think I don't want to walk in there right fucking now, fall on my fucking knees and beg her for forgiveness? I would do anything to make this right, Jax. *Anything.*"

"There it is." I shove him. "So pull your head out of your ass, and fight for our Soul Bonded, Tristan. For all of us. That's what I'm going to do."

He stays silent, grabbing his pack and stalking into the storage room. Following him, I glance around at the stacks of crates and mess lying everywhere.

This feels a little bit like karma biting us in the ass.

Sinking down onto a crate, I wince as I shuffle to get comfortable. God, the wildcat can pack a punch. Straight into my balls.

I'd take a dozen if Sienna would just talk to us.

16

# LOGAN

The trunk splinters under my knuckles as I hit it.

Harder.

Again.

Sienna's face is burned into my mind. What the fuck have we done?

Arms wrap around me, pulling me back, and I shove Gray off. He stumbles to the side before he comes back. "Logan."

"No," I snap. "This is on us, Gray. All of us, not just Tristan. Fucking Christ. Did you see her?"

Gray swallows. "Yeah."

"We did that." I jab a finger into his chest and then mine. "Us. We could have made the whole thing so much better for her, Gray. We were too wrapped up in our own fucking stupid problems, and now she—,"

My knees hit the floor of the forest, the pain rocketing through my chest a sledgehammer as I try to catch my breath. Gray drops down next to me, his hands reaching out and cupping my face.

"We'll fix this," he vows. He presses our foreheads together, our breathing ragged and disjointed. "Nothing is going to happen to Sienna, Logan. I swear it."

"You can't," I whisper. "We did this to her. It's already done."

And we can't take it back. Every single bad decision we've made has brought us here, to our judgment. And Sienna is paying the price for our mistakes.

"She lost everything because of us." Shifting away from him, I stare out into the forest. "Her family, her home. We're supposed to *be* her home, Gray. And all we've given her is pain."

He moves until he's next to me, our arms brushing together.

"I don't even know where to begin," I admit. My voice shakes as I voice it. "How do we even start to fix this?"

Gray's jaw is tight as he lifts my hand, gripping it tightly between both of his. "We keep trying. We don't give up. We didn't fight for her before, Lo, and now we have to give it everything."

*We don't give up.*

"Whatever it takes," I whisper, and he nods. "Whatever it takes."

17

# SIENNA

**M**y ceiling has a crack that's shaped like a dick.

I can't stop staring at it. Have been for hours, unable to get to sleep. My stomach is burning, the pain running around my right side and into my back.

Jess stirs next to me. I'm in the bed and she refused to share, saying I needed rest, but she's been up and checking on me every hour without fail.

My eyes flick to hers as her tousled head appears, and her lips thin. "Does it hurt?"

Hesitating, I nod. Jess chews on her lip before she follows my eyes up to the ceiling. "Is that a dick?"

I can't stop the snort that comes out. "Right? It really, really looks like one."

"Kind of crooked, though." Jess tips her head to the side. "I haven't seen one in so long I'd nearly forgotten what it looked like."

My laugh sounds rusty in the darkness. "Remember when you made Jonny Vega show you the goods?"

She sniffs. "We were eight. It was not an accurate impression."

"I was so grossed out," I cackle. "And he swung it round like a helicopter."

Jess starts to shake next to me. "He was so proud!"

My laughter trails off, and Jess's hand finds mine in the dark. "Are you thinking about them?"

I press my lips together. "Not if I can help it."

I'm trying really, really fucking hard not to think of the Cohen pack at all. It helps that we're not under the same roof. I think I'd go mad if I could pick up their scents.

But I'm still aware of them, very fucking aware that they're so close and not here.

Jess stands, shifting and moving to the window. She pulls the curtain back, staring out into the yard. "Huh."

I jerk my head to her. "What? Is there someone out there?"

When she chews on the inside of her cheek, I heave myself out of bed to join her. Our faces press together as we stare through the crack.

"That is... pitiful," Jess mutters.

Jax is sitting in the middle of the yard, his hands hanging over his bent knees as he stares at the door below us. We watch him silently for a minute, but he doesn't move.

"What is he *doing*?" Jess pulls a face. "This is kinda giving me creepy stalker vibes."

I drop my hand, letting the curtain fall closed and pushing Jax's puppy eyes out of view. "It doesn't matter. I'm going back to bed."

Jess lingers as I crawl back in, pouring me some water and forcing me to drink it before I lay down. She settles back down on the mattress, but I can tell by her breathing that she's not going back to sleep.

But we both pretend.

18

# TRISTAN

The early morning sun feels like a taunt as I exit the shed where I've spent a night tossing and turning. Images of Sienna taunt me, memories from the last few weeks playing in a loop through my mind.

*Look at all the ways you've fucked up.*

And every dream ended with the same, nightmarish image.

But that's not going to happen.

Pausing, I watch Jax as he stares at the door where we first saw Sienna yesterday. It looks like he hasn't moved all night.

"Jax." I approach him slowly. "Did you get any sleep?"

He shakes his head at me. "Couldn't."

I get it.

The door starts to open, and Jax and I both bolt upright, Jax scrambling to his feet and then deflating as Emmett exits. He eyes us as he makes his way over.

"You stay out here all night?" he asks Jax. Jax shrugs. "Couldn't sleep."

Emmett purses his lips. "I'll put some coffee out."

I nod at him. "Thanks. Is Sienna up?"

He raises an eyebrow. "Oh, no. I'm not gonna be your go-between here. Jessalyn would have my balls, and I'm quite attached to them."

Jax grunts. "I think she keeps them as trophies."

Emmett grimaces, but I notice the gleam in his eye as he talks about Sienna's friend. "What exactly is your plan here?" he asks, crossing his arms. "You just gonna linger around my yard and hope she talks to you?"

Blowing out a breath, I stretch out the kink in my neck before I face him. "We haven't got the best track record of being dependable. So for now, that's exactly what we're doing. We're not going anywhere. The only thing that matters to us right now is Sienna, and if that means we're camping out in your storage shed for the next year, that's exactly what we're gonna do."

Emmett rolls his eyes. "Is everyone as dramatic as all of you in Navarre?" he asks with exasperation. "Because I'm picking up a real vibe, here."

"Who's dramatic?" A voice rings out.

I watch Emmett flush a deep claret, clearing his throat as he turns to face Jessalyn. "Mornin', Jess."

"Morning, Emmett," she says sweetly as she approaches, before she turns to us. "Morning, asswipes."

She nods at Jax. "Creepy stalker asswipe."

To Jax's credit, he doesn't blink, offering her a lazy smile. "Wildcat. How's our girl this morning?"

Her lips tighten. "Fine."

She can't lie for shit.

If we're going to get anywhere near our Soul Bonded, we need Jessalyn on board.

I shift on my feet. "Jessalyn. We really, really need to talk to Sienna."

She waves her finger at me, her lip curling. "Don't even think about it. I'm not out here for you, you son of a bitch."

Then she blanks me completely, turning to Emmett. "We need to do another run."

I'm lost, but Emmett nods. "'Course."

"A run for what?" Jax asks curiously, and she shoots him a glare. "Bullets. How fast can you run, Jax?"

"With you behind me? Like a fucking racehorse."

We don't have time for this.

"Please, Jessalyn," I push. "We'll wait as long as we need to, but Sienna is running out of time."

The stare she gives me is almost glacial. "I know that. What the hell do you think we're doing here?"

Turning back to Emmett, she jerks her head towards the truck parked to the side of the building. "Come on. I don't want to leave her alone for long."

"Wait," I interrupt. "We can go. If it's something for Sienna, we'll go."

Maybe it's an opportunity, But I don't want to barge into her space when she hasn't asked for us. This, we can *do*.

I can see Jess wavering. "Let us do this. That way, you can stay with her. We'll make sure we get whatever you need."

She sniffs. "Fine."

I reach out for the piece of paper in her hand. My heart flips over as I scan the detailed list. "She needs all of this?" I ask, looking up. Jess nods as Jax cranes in to scan the list over my shoulder, a low curse escaping his mouth.

"Is it helping?" Jax asks, and I can see the answer in her eyes, in the slump of her shoulders as she turns away.

"Don't leave anything off," she shoots over her shoulder as she walks back to the building.

Emmett scans us. "The town is that way," he says, pointing to a track leading away from us. "Around a thirty-minute drive."

My hands clench on the list as I nod. "Tell Gray and Lo we're going," I say shortly to Jax. "It's better if they stay here. I don't want her to think we've all left."

He leaves without argument, and I head over to our truck, digging my keys out of my pocket.

At least this way I'm doing something.

## 19

# SIENNA

I'm hacking my guts up over the toilet when frantic hands land on my shoulders. "Sienna!"

I can't stop retching, the dark, bloody bile spattering against the white basin.

When it finally stops, Jess presses a damp towel into my hands, feeling my forehead. "What the hell?" she demands. "How long has that been happening?"

With a groan, I wipe my face. "I thought you were going into town?"

The silence is deafening, and she's chewing her lip when I look up. I give her a flat stare. "Jess."

She throws her hands up. "They need to make themselves useful. They're just lingering. And they look like little kicked puppies."

When I glare at her, she shrugs. "They're still assholes. At least this way, they're useful assholes. Anyway, stop deflecting. How long have you been coughing up blood?"

I struggle to my feet, and her hand slips under my elbow. "This is the second time," I admit.

But this time was so much worse. It feels like I'm drowning, my breath choking in my lungs.

Fear grabs at my throat, threatening to steal the last little piece of air I have left. My balance tilts, and I go down with a thud, Jess crying out as I land heavily on the tiled floor of the bathroom. "Sienna!"

"I'm alright," I gasp. "I'm fine, Jess."

Except I'm not fine, and we both know it. I'm about as far from fine as I can be.

Jess lets out a broken sob as she lands next to me. "Sienna. *Please*."

She grabs my face, forcing me to look at her. "You're dying," she says fiercely. "You're dying on me, Sienna. And there is nothing I can do to stop it."

I try to look away, but she won't let me. "Jess—,"

"You're leaving me." Her voice breaks, and my eyes snap to her. She's shaking. "You're leaving me, and I don't have anyone else, Si. It's me and you, and if you don't get better, it's just going to be me. I'll be *all alone*."

"Jess." I'm crying too, both of us sobbing on the floor of this tiny bathroom. "It's not—,"

"Please," she begs. "I know you don't want them. I get it. But you will die if something doesn't change, Si. And I can't watch that."

"Oh god, Jess." Her arms wrap around me, and I hold onto her as tightly as I can manage. "I'm sorry," I gasp. "Jess, I'm so sorry."

"Stop it," she snaps. "This isn't your fault, Si. You've been given a shit hand of cards, and now you have to play. But you have an ace out there, even if it's a shit one. Play your damn ace. Let them *help* you. When you're better, we can give them the finger and drive off somewhere where we can drink margaritas and flirt with ridiculously tanned, handsome alphas."

My throat threatens to close up again, the idea of them coming anywhere near me. "I can't be with them. I can't, Jess. It will break me."

"You're already broken," Jess says quietly. "But maybe they can be the glue, too. Just think about it. You don't have to be *with* them to have them close, Si. You don't owe them a glass of water if they were on fire, but they owe you fucking everything."

She dashes her hand across her eyes. "Dammit," she mutters half-heartedly. "Mascara everywhere."

"Don't let Emmett see," I tease as she gets up and helps me upright. "I think he might have a soft spot for you, Jessalyn Rogers."

"Hah," she tosses her hair back. "Obviously. Man's got excellent taste."

But the twin spots of color that flare on her cheeks stay where they are as we shuffle slowly back to my room, Jess hovering as I lower myself back into the bed. She perches next to me, pushing my hair back from my face.

"Think about it," she urges. "Please, Si."

Letting them back in. Letting them close. Even if it's nothing more than that, just the idea hurts almost as badly as the pain in my body. But I nod.

"I won't leave you alone, Jessalyn Rogers," I squeeze her hand, and she gives me a wobbly smile. "There's always Monty," she says with a shrug. "I think he's got at least another twenty years."

We both jolt at the knock on the door. Emmett stands awkwardly in the doorframe, his eyes lingering on Jessalyn's stained cheeks. Moving his eyes back to mine, he offers up a bowl.

"You hungry?" he asks gently. "You haven't been eating much."

I'm about to refuse, the idea of food making nausea rise up my throat. But I glance at Jessalyn, at the way her hands tighten against the blankets, her knuckles whitening.

"Sure," I say quietly. "I could eat. Thanks, Emmett."

He nods, bringing in the bowl and placing it on my nightstand. He very obviously doesn't look at my best friend as he rubs the back of his neck.

"Ah – Jess? You want to eat with me? Or I can bring some up?"

His adorable awkwardness makes me smile. Jess purses her lips, her eyes darting to me. "I should—,"

"You should go and eat," I nudge her gently. "Go on. I'm feeling pretty tired. I'll have this and crash out."

"Okay." Jess looks uncharacteristically fragile as she stands up. "I'll just be a few minutes, and I'll come back to check on you."

"Okay," I whisper. Emmett holds the door open for her, his frame protectively curving over Jess as she walks through, her hands clutching her elbows. He glances back at me. "Sure you're okay? Do you need anything?"

I shake my head, my throat tight. "Look after her?"

He gives me a nod. "Of course. Call if you need us."

After they've gone, I stare at the bowl on the side. I do need to eat. But the first spoonful tastes like iron in my mouth, and I push it aside, abandoning it in favor of picking through the thoughts crowding my head.

Just the idea of letting them back in, opening that crack a tiny bit, makes me shake. The Soul Bond makes me crave them, but it feels jagged, twisted in a way that doesn't feel right.

But Jess is right. They owe me. And if I curl up here and let myself waste away, the only person I'm punishing is myself.

And they deserve to feel a little of the pain they've put me through.

My lips firm. And I shove off the covers.

I hope they choke on it.

20

# LOGAN

Groaning, I cross out the last idea on my shitty list. "We suck at this."

We're trying to come up with ideas, suggestions for things we can do to prove to our Soul Bonded that we're sorry.

And we're really, really shit at it.

"Because we're trying to plan it," Gray points out. "We can't plan this, Lo. I mean, we can, and some of those ideas were fine. But she needs us to prove ourselves. That's not something we can do with a giant sign."

I frown. I quite liked that idea.

I want her to know that we're proud to be her Soul Bonded. That we've always been proud, despite the fucking chaos of the Trials. Is that so bad?

"I just... I need to know she's okay, Gray." There's something building in my chest, something that's pulling me straight to the door where our Soul Bonded refuses to see us. It's been growing for a while, but now it feels like a pressure around my chest, a need.

Is this how she felt? Worse?

Swallowing, I reach up to rub my chest when Gray's head

shoots up. He scrambles to his feet as I turn around, shading my eyes against the sun.

Sienna is leaning heavily against the doorway, her own hand up to her eyes as she scans the yard. I jump up, Gray and I staying where we are as we wait.

*Please. Please speak to us.*

When she takes a single, unsteady step, it's enough. I'm across the yard in a second, Gray just behind me as I pause a few paces away from her. "Hey."

I drink her in, the pain in my chest growing with every second. I take in the weight she's lost, the way her clothes hang loose around her frame, how her shoulders curl in, her collarbones prominent in the glimpse I get before she tugs up her shirt.

And her hair. Her beautiful, pink hair, covered in a brown dye. There's nothing wrong with brown hair, but it looks *off* on her. Everything that made her Sienna, vibrant and beautiful, is hidden beneath a cloak of agony. I can see the fucking pain in her face, and it kills me.

"Sienna," I murmur. My hands shoot out, but she recoils and I pull them back in. Gray steps up next to me.

She lifts her eyes to mine, and even they look cloudy, the bright, azure blue almost gray.

"What do you need?" Gray's words are soft, equally aware as I am that our Soul Bonded looks breakable. Heartbreakingly breakable, and all because of us.

She glances behind us, her spine straight and her body tense. "You get thirty minutes to tell me everything," she says finally. Even her voice sounds broken, rasping and thin. "And I mean everything. No more lies. Not a single, unspoken truth. Tell Tristan. Come back in an hour."

"Of course," I breathe. "Everything, Sienna. That's all we—,"

She slams the door in my face.

Gray grabs my arm as I stumble back. "This is good, right?" he asks, a stunned tone to his voice.

"Yeah," I answer finally, my eyes still stuck on the door, "this is good."

Maybe.

I just hope Tris and Jax get back here in time.

We pace the yard, both of us lost in our own thoughts until Tristan and Jax pull up. I'm first to Tristan's door, yanking it open when his hand is still up.

"Sienna will see us," I say abruptly. "She'll be out in a minute."

Jax comes around the truck, a large bag in his hands. "She will?"

I nod as Tristan gets out.

"She wants to know everything, Tristan," I say quietly. "This is it. No more lies."

He doesn't hesitate to meet my eyes. "Everything. Everything on the table."

And then we'll see if our Soul Bonded can forgive us.

## 21

# TRISTAN

My hands tap against my side as we wait silently in front of the door. It's a few minutes past the hour Sienna told us, but we'll wait for as long as it takes.

Running my hand through my hair to try and tidy it, I glance across to the others. Logan is completely still, Gray leaning into him where they stand together.

It's funny. We've been a pack for six years, and I never noticed how seamlessly they fit together until now. Like two puzzle pieces.

Jax is shifting restlessly, humming a tuneless sound as he bounces up and down on his feet. I can see his nerves in the way he keeps shaking his hands out, stretching. As if he's about to go on stage.

Even though I'm expecting it, I still jolt when the door opens, slowly. Our Soul Bonded stands with her lips pressed together, thin lines bracketing from her eyes highlighting the pain she can't hide from us.

Pain we fucking caused.

"Sienna," I murmur. When she stands aside, I walk past her, taking in the long, low-ceilinged room, the dark wooden bar, A few tables are dotted round, and I follow Sienna's lead as she sinks heavily into a seat and I take the one at her left side. Gray takes the other, Logan and Jax settling opposite us until we're all sat in silence.

Sienna sighs. "You're wasting your thirty minutes."

She's leaning as far away from me as she possibly can, and it stings. I want nothing more than to pull her closer, to lift her onto my lap the way I did in our garden, when the letter from the Council came and she looked to me for reassurance.

But a lot has happened since then. So I swallow it down, place my hands on the table.

Then I tell her everything.

Our excitement over the invite to the Bonding Trials. Erikkson, coming to my office and presenting me with the evidence that could destroy my family from both sides. The first argument with Gray and Logan, when we found out they were lying.

Sienna drinks it all in, not giving anything away as she frowns down at the table. "So... you never wanted Alicia."

"Never," I swear fervently. "She's a psychopath, Sienna. I didn't realize how much, not until your heat happened."

Sienna doesn't say anything else, not until I pause. She looks up, finally, her eyes traveling across us all as we hold our breath.

"The Mating Ceremony," she presses her finger into a wooden whirl on the table. "You didn't come."

My heart breaks at the soft, sad tone of her voice. Jax leans forward.

"We were coming, shortcake," he promises. "We would never have left you there alone. Not in a million years. We were all in."

Her eyes lift. "So what happened?"

"Alicia," Jax hisses. "She gassed us."

Sienna jerks. "She what?"

"She pulled in through the gates, and we thought you might have turned around." My throat is dry as I watch her. "We were in the car, Sienna. A minute or two behind you at most. But she pulled in, and came up to my window. I told her to fuck off."

She looks unimpressed. "And then?"

"She had some sort of gas canister. She threw them in and it knocked us out. We didn't wake up for over an hour, and by the time we did, it was too late. We rushed to the Hub, but the ceremony was over, and you were gone."

I swallow. "Alicia faked that letter. You're our Soul Bonded fated mate, Sienna. You are the one we want."

Jax nods. "You're all we ever wanted, shortcake."

"And I'm sorry." My voice drops. "I'm so damn sorry for everything. If I could take back every stupid decision I've made in the last three weeks, I'd do it in a heartbeat."

"We all had a role to play." Gray sits forward, his eyes focused on Sienna. "That day – in your nest – I didn't want to leave you, Si. It tore at my chest walking away from you, but I panicked."

Sienna looks at Logan. "And you," she says softly. "What pretty words do you have?"

Hesitating, he nods. "I don't have any, except that I'm sorry. You deserve action, and that's what I'm going to do."

"See, you say that, but it's still just words." Sienna jumps as I reach for her hand, grabbing it before she can pull away.

This might be the only chance I ever get, and I'm not leaving her without saying my piece.

"You're right," I duck down so she can see my face. "But I swear on my life, Sienna."

"I spent years waiting for a mate. And you… you are everything. Everything I ever wanted, and so much more than I ever realized. And I swear to you, I will spend the rest of our lives making sure that you never feel the same way that you did during those Trials. I'm not asking for more than you can give. I know we have a lot of shit to work through."

She tries to pull away, but I hold onto her hand.

"I told you that you could hate me if you wanted to." Her eyes jerk to mine. "I meant it. I'll spend the rest of our lives working to change your mind. But you will live, Sienna. That's the one thing I will not apologize for. I will do whatever it takes to make you well again. And you can hate me for it, but hate me when you're healthy and whole. I'll even leave, if that's what you need, and if it works with the bond."

She flinches.

"I do hate you," she whispers, and it fucking guts me. "And I don't need your fucking permission to do it, Tristan."

She yanks her hand out of mine, my fingers closing around empty air as she pushes her chair back. Panic laces up my throat as she struggles to her feet.

"Sienna—,"

"Tonight," she snaps back at me. "One of you per night. No touching. Jess seems to think that having you close would do it. And that's as much as I'm willing to give."

My fists clench around the promise in her words. She'll let us help.

"Yes," I swear. "Whatever you want."

She gives me a death glare as she turns around. "Not you. Jax can be the first."

I glance at him, and he's damn near bursting out of his seat. "I-uh-," he says, clearing his throat when Sienna turns to him. "I'll be there, shortcake."

"Fine." Sienna walks slowly over to a doorway, dark wooden stairs leading out of sight. "And you're all idiots, by the way."

She turns back to me, and the pain in her eyes... fuck.

"If you had just been honest with me," she says plainly. "None of this would have happened, Tristan. *None* of it. I would have kept your secrets."

She glances at Gray and Logan, and away. "I would have fought for you," she says bleakly. "I *did* fight for you. But not one of you did the same for me."

She leaves us to simmer in a pool of our own shame, drowning under the weight of our decisions.

## 2 2

# SIENNA

I manage to make it to the top of the stairs before I bend over, my hands gripping my knees for support.

Now I know.

And I'm not sure what – or who – I'm most pissed at.

Jessalyn pops her head out of our bedroom door and rushes down the hall. "Si? What happened?"

"They told me everything," I say numbly. Straightening with her help, we walk back to the bedroom, and I huddle up in my covers as I talk her through everything they told me.

Her eyes are round as saucers. "They knew? About those men, and they didn't say anything?"

"Yep." Keeping my eyes on the door, I laugh weakly. "Remind me again why I thought having Soul Bonded would make this the easiest thing in the world?"

Fucking hell. My Soul Bonded are a bunch of morons. I don't even know where to start on unpicking the clusterfuck they've just talked me through.

"I understand why Tristan made the decision he did," I muse. "They didn't know me. Any other omega would have withdrawn at the Bonding Ceremony."

"But they're your Soul Bonded," Jess snaps. "And they just carried on!"

I swallow. "Guess I wasn't enough to make them rethink."

"Oh, fuck off with that," Jess stands up, her hands flying up as she paces up and down the small space next to her makeshift bed. "All the way off. They do not fucking deserve you, Sienna. They deserve to live the rest of their lives on their own, staring out of windows with sad little faces and chewing over the mess they fucking made."

She whirls, pointing her finger at me. "Tell me you're not softening."

"What? No!" My fingers twist around.

"I'm so angry, Jess," I admit. "I don't even know where to start with them."

She collapses next to me in a huff. "Vengeance," she muses, "is a dish best served to alphas who have royally fucked up."

I snort. "I don't think I'm in the best condition to plan out any sort of revenge right now."

She leans over and squeezes my hand. "But you spoke to them? About... about helping?"

Nodding, I swallow back my misgivings at what I've just agreed to. "Jax is coming tonight. I can't... I can't see Tristan yet. Not like that."

Jess's curls bounce as she nods her head. "Si... thank you." Her voice wobbles at the end, and I lift up my arm and wrap it around your shoulders.

"This isn't for them," I promise. "This is for me and you, Jess. I'm going to get better."

"Damn fucking straight."

## 23
## JAX

I'm rocking back and forth on a stool in the bar, waiting for Sienna to call me up.

As I tilt the legs back again, Emmett slaps his hand down on the bar in front of me. "Will you quit that?" He asks exasperatedly. "I don't need any more broken furniture."

The legs slam down on all fours, and I give him a salute. "Sorry, man."

I start to tap out a rhythm on the wooden bar with my fingers, and he moves down the other end with a shake of his head. A wireless is playing music quietly in the background, the bar empty apart from me and a few older guys huddled in the corner, giving me the stink eye.

I focus on the music, listening to the rise and fall of the bass underneath the main melody. It's catchy. Not a band I've heard before, but that's not a surprise. The wall stops most things from crossing over, and the wireless in Navarre plays its own stuff. Mainly from Haven's End and a handful of other bands. Our own gloriously fucked up little fishbowl.

"Hey," I call down to Emmett. "You got a guitar here?"

He glances down where he's pouring a beer. "Maybe," he calls back. "You play?"

The bones of an idea are shaping in my head. "Yeah. Mind if I borrow it?"

He walks closer to me, wiping his hands with a cloth. "I'll dig it out. You're staying upstairs tonight, right?"

When I nod, Emmett's face settles into something more serious. "You take care of that omega," he murmurs, his eyes steady on mine. "I'll be listening. Any hint that she needs help and I'll be there. You get me?"

His tone gets my back up, and I have to bite back my snappy response. I owe him. We all do. He took in our Soul Bonded – and her batshit best friend – without batting an eye. Hell, he's putting the rest of us up in his damn storage shed.

And if the fact that he's a good-looking son of a bitch winds me up, I'm not about to fucking admit it.

"What's your story?" I ask carefully. He's living in the middle of nowhere, out on the edges of a fucking forest, running a tiny little bar that's clearly shitting money.

His face tightens, and he turns away. "None of your damn business."

Studying him, I lean back in my seat and clear my throat. "Fair enough. I'll look after her."

Hell, it's all I've wanted to do since the moment I found her in that crowd before our first Bonding Ceremony. Even if she despises us for it, Sienna knowing the full truth feels like a truck's been lifted off my shoulders.

A full night with my Bonded. Alone. My knee jiggles. I just want to talk to her. To breathe in the same damn air as her, and try to work out a way for us to move forward. Learn what she needs from me.

I might've been a shit Soul Bonded so far, but I'm planning on an A in my next assessment.

I hear Sienna coming before I see her, slow, shuffling steps that twist my heart inside my chest. She still takes the breath from my lungs when she appears. Still beautiful, even when she looks like one strong breeze is gonna blow her over.

Not on my watch.

Slipping off my stool, I approach her where she's standing in the doorway. Her eyes meet mine and it fucking hurts to see them so flat, the sparkle that she still had in Navarre despite all the shit we threw at her well and truly extinguished.

"Shortcake," I murmur. I keep my distance even though it fucking kills me as she turns without a word, and I have to watch her struggle up the steps. My hands reach out and then back to my sides.

Not yet.

I follow her down a clean but worn hallway, the dark wooden floorboards creaking under my feet as she leads me to a small bedroom. There's a tiny single bed pushed up against the wall with mounds of covers, and a mattress on the floor.

"Don't worry," she mutters when she sees my look. "It feels like luxury compared to the attic."

*Aand* she scores a direct hit to my chest.

Swallowing at the reminder of just how much we have to fucking atone for, I hang back. The cream curtains hanging across the tiny window flutter in the breeze, showing glimpses of the setting sun. It's not late, but my Soul Bonded looks too exhausted to care as she crawls beneath the covers, tugging them around her in a way that tells me she's feeling uncomfortable.

"Where do you want me, Bonded?" I ask softly, and her head snaps up.

"Don't call me that," she rasps, pointing to the other end of the bed. "You can sit by there."

I'm not sure how this Soul Bonded connection works, or how exactly my presence is supposed to help, so I follow her instructions. It's a tight squeeze with both of us and the bed creaks dangerously as I climb on. Sienna pulls her legs up, curling them beneath the blankets to give me space as I prop myself up with my back to the wall.

Leaning my head back, I listen to the harsh sound of her breathing, the slight rattle in her lungs. Every drawn breath sounds painful, and my whole body twitches with the need to crawl up the damn bed and drag her into me.

*Baby steps.*

We sit in broken silence as the sun sets fully and the room grows dark. Sienna reaches out and switches on a small lamp next to the bed.

"You sleep with the light on?"

"I do now." Her voice is quiet, and the shame of our fucking actions hits me like a wrecking ball. It keeps doing that, coming and going in never ending fucking punches.

She sleeps with a light on because of us.

"You're not going to get a great night's sleep, just to warn you," she mutters.

I shake out the cramp in my arm. "Baby, I don't plan on doing any sleeping tonight. All I'm interested in is watching you."

If her breathing carries on like this, I'll be counting every inhale.

"Will you *stop*?" She sits up, covers falling away and highlighting the frailty of her body in the dim light. "You know the first ceremony? I didn't withdraw after Tristan because of *you*."

My head jerks to her. "Sienna—,"

"We'd already met," she snaps, "and I was so certain that even if the others didn't want me, you did. So when Ollena asked me to withdraw, I didn't. And then you did exactly the same as the rest of them, and it hurt *so much*, Jax."

I shift on the bed, leaning down towards her. "Sienna."

"Why'd you do it?" she asks, and I stop short, my hand out in mid-air. "Why'd you go along with it?"

"I...," I search for the right words. I've practiced them in my head over and over, knowing this moment might come, hoping that it would, but now that we're here and she's looking at me with shattered eyes, it's not enough.

It will never be enough.

"I was... cocky," I admit. "I didn't want to, but I figured we'd find a way out of it pretty quickly. I didn't know it was going to be you, shortcake. I thought we'd turn up and there would be some random omega standing there, and she'd withdraw and we could work something out and I could go off and find you. I knew that whoever it was, I didn't want them. Not when I'd already met you."

Her eyes are wet, and I reach out, catching a tear on my finger. "And then I saw you at the Bonding Ceremony. You were everything I ever wanted," I tell her softly. "And when it hit me that we were going to do that to you, when I watched Tristan go ahead of me and I saw your face… I will never forget it. Not for as long as I live will I forget how you looked at me."

She looked then like she's looking at me now. As if something precious has shattered.

"I made a choice," I tell her hoarsely. "Trying to do what was best, for my pack, for you… and it was a shitty one. I'm so sorry, shortcake."

And Sienna is paying the price.

"Sorry isn't enough, Jax," she says. She turns her face away from me, slowly laying back down. "You had so many chances," she whispers. "And you never took a single one."

I can see her body shaking, and I can't fucking take it. Sienna jolts when I half crawl, half drag myself into the small space next to her. My frame swallows up most of the bed. "What are you doing?"

"You're shaking." Staying on top of the covers, I turn on my side and wrap my arm over her, bundled up in her blankets. She feels like all covers and no Sienna, there's so little of her.

Her body vibrates even through the layers. "Stop it."

"You need this," I draw her against me until her body settles. "We did this, Sienna. Let me help put it right. And then you can beat my ass when you're back up and running."

She lets out a half sob. "I'm going to."

I prop my head up on my hands, ready for a night of watching over her. "I'm counting on it, shortcake."

## 24

## SIENNA

W hen I wake, the curtains can't stop the sunshine from filling the room, muted and golden. I blink my eyes open lazily.

I slept. All night.

Jax's arm is a warm weight around me, and I can feel fingers stroking through my hair, gently running lines down my scalp.

My eyes nearly drift closed again. The sharp pain that I've been battling for the last few days feels slightly more muted today than yesterday, although it's still there, churning at my insides. Maybe Jess was on to something.

I should push Jax away, stop him from taking advantage when he thinks I'm asleep, but I'm enjoying the contact too much to deprive myself of it just yet. Something must give me away though, because Jax's fingers falter, before they withdraw completely.

"Shortcake," he murmurs. "How'd you sleep?"

"Better." Shifting away from him, I sit up. "Thanks. You can go now."

The words hurt, but I need to be clear on exactly what this is. They owe me this, and I don't owe them a damn single thing, except maybe a pinch of the same pain that I've felt these last few weeks.

I can feel Jax's flinch, but he shifts anyway. "Of course. Do you need anything before I leave? Or today? Is there anything I can do?"

Shaking my head, I turn away from those violet eyes, his mussed hair and his kicked-pup expression.

"I think this helped," I admit. I don't want to admit just how much better I feel after a single night. Soul Bonds are really, *really* weird. "Can Logan come tonight?"

"I'll tell him." His hand ghosts over my hair, the softest touch before he moves over to slide his boots on. "I'm here if you need me, shortcake. I'm not going anywhere."

I nod, but that's as much as I'm willing to give, and I don't look up until I hear his footsteps moving away down the hall.

## 25

# TRISTAN

I'm sitting in Jax's place outside when he wanders through the door. Emmett gave us descriptions of the goons who looked for Sienna when she left Navarre. I'm not leaving this place unattended unless we're with her.

He looks tired, but his expression is lighter than I've seen it in days as he comes to a stop in front of me.

I shade my eyes, glancing up. "How'd it go?"

To my surprise, he takes a seat on the ground next to me, bringing up his knees and leaning his arms on them. "She slept all night."

"Good." That's good. If the deep circles under her eyes are any indication, she hasn't been getting much sleep. Looking over at him, I catch the expression on his face before he can wipe it away. "What?"

Jax spreads his hands out helplessly. "Her room is empty, Tristan. She doesn't have anything. And she can't sleep without a light on. Now, I mean."

His voice is dark, and a lump appears in my throat. "Because of us, you mean."

"We've got a hell of a lot of making up to do, Tris." Jax sighs. "I don't know if a lifetime is going to be enough."

"As long as it takes," I answer firmly. "Nothing else matters, Jax. Not anymore."

I'm leaving all of our other shit behind us in Navarre. The only thing that matters to me right now is Sienna, and bringing our pack together the way it should have been from the start, if I hadn't let panic cloud my mind.

"I agree." Dusting off his hands, he gets to his feet. "I've got something I need to do. What are you doing today? Sienna asked for Logan tonight."

I push down the disappointment. I'll be grateful if she asks for me at all. "I don't know. I'll find something, though."

I need to keep my hands occupied.

Gray crosses over with Jax, the two of them exchanging a few words before he comes over to me. "I need some stuff," he says, crossing his arms. "Logan too, but he won't want to leave Sienna if he's going to her tonight. Want to go into town?"

"I'm not sure they'll have everything you need, but yes." Calling it a town is a stretch, but Jax's words have given me my own ideas.

It's our job to provide for our omega. Fuck knows we did a shitty job of it before, even if it was unintentional, thanks to Alicia's games in the attic. But I'm not letting her go one more day without anything to call her own.

I get to my feet. "Let's go."

My fingers drum on the steering wheel as we drive down the track. The wireless is patchy out here, bursts of static making my ears ring.

Reaching out and turning it off, I glance at Gray. He's staring out of the window, his copper hair blowing around at the top with the window down. A familiar face, one I grew up with, formed a pack with.

But I've realized I don't really know the person he's become. The secrets that have spilled out have held up a mirror to my role as pack leader, and it's not a reflection I'm comfortable with.

"Gray? How are things with you and Lo?" He spins his head

to me, surprise etched into his expression. "You've never asked before."

"I wasn't a very good pack leader before."

Understatement.

Gray hums. "You weren't that bad. Just busy."

Too busy for my pack. Too useless to help my Soul Bonded.

"Well, I'm not busy now. Is everything okay?"

I catch a smile I don't think I've ever seen before on his face. Gray is… stoic, I guess. Always has been. Quick to anger, but maybe Logan has helped to iron out his rough edges.

"We're good, Tris. Better than we've been for years, now everything is out in the open."

"And you're okay with that?" I press. Hindsight is a *thing*. I remember Gray's panic being much more than Logans, his hesitancy at the idea of bringing their private life into the open.

His smile fades. "I… I didn't want Logan to suffer for my choices. I was the one who pushed it in that parking lot when Erikkson took the photos." He swallows. "But Sienna suffered instead. And I only made that worse. I would have swapped with them both if I could've, Tris."

"But you do want Sienna?"

Gray laughs sadly. "She's my Soul Bonded. Of course I want her. It was hard at first. It felt like… like I was betraying Lo, to want another person like that. I was harsher on her than I should've been. Took me a while to pull my head out of my ass."

I take a turn. "You want her just because she's our Soul Bonded?"

"No. That's what drew me in, but… it's her, Tris. She makes me feel *complete*. Logan too. She belongs with us." He sighs. "If we can persuade her."

Pulling into the little square, I switch the engine off. "I don't know what's gonna happen, Gray. But all we can do is try. I'm glad you and Logan have sorted things out – I'm sorry if you felt you needed to hide that from us. We're a pack, Gray. Family. And we stick together."

He raises his eyebrow. "You been practicing your motivational speeches in the mirror again? That one was pretty good."

"Shut up." I actually grin for the first time in a long time. "Come on."

The little bell tinkles above us as we enter the store. It's surprisingly large for such a small strip, but I guess they serve the surrounding areas too. Gray and I split up as he heads towards the section where they keep the tools, and I turn towards the toiletries, picking up a basket on the way.

It becomes apparent very, very quickly that I am out of my depth, even with the relatively small selection they have.

Everything is scented. *Everything.*

Putting the basket down, I start to scope out the products on offer, sniffing at different lotions and random shit until my head hurts. It all goes into the basket until it's close to full and my head is aching from the different smells shoved up my nose. Nothing smells anywhere near as good as the soft sweet raspberry scent of my Soul Bonded, but hopefully there'll be something in there she enjoys.

Leaving the aisle with a grateful inhale of scent-free air, I tackle the next one, grabbing another basket. Gray finds me wild-eyed and clutching something called a – a throw pillow?

"Tris," he says carefully, approaching me slowly. "Ah... what are you doing?"

I show him the pretty pattern on the green pillow. "You think Sienna would like this? Jax said she didn't have anything in her room. I thought—,"

I can feel the heat creeping up at the back of my neck. I'm no good at this stuff, not really. Logan did the bulk of the work in making Sienna's room presentable at the house, and I don't think he ever went shopping for this kind of stuff.

"I'll get a trolley," Gray says, glancing around. "I think we might need it."

He's right. We work our way through the store until the trolley is overflowing, grabbing a second one. Anything that looks like something Sienna might like goes in. I spend ages looking at different types of lights, picking out several sets of stringed warm white lights. I also slip something else into the trolley.

Gray comes back with his arms stocked up. "Candles," he says testily. "Why the hell are there so many different types?"

He spills them into the trolley, and we both stand there. "You think that's everything?" he asks.

I start pushing one of the trolleys towards the grocery section, and he does the same. "We can't keep relying on Emmett to feed us, and I want to get some things for Sienna. She's not eating enough."

Maybe some treats will tempt her. We were always taught that omegas like sweet things. I remember that much of my training at least.

It takes an age to ring everything up, and the cashier, a thin-faced young beta male with a messy ponytail eyes us suspiciously. "You with that group?" he asks. "The ones looking for the girl?"

Gray and I both stiffen. "What group?"

The kid shrugs, tossing things into bags haphazardly. "I dunno. I heard it from my manager. They came in a few days ago looking for a girl with pink hair."

"Huh." Gray studies the bags, faking waning interest. "Never seen a girl with pink hair before."

"They haven't been back?" I ask, and he shakes his head. "Don't think so. Thought you might've been with them."

"Nah," I say casually. "Just traveling with my wife and brother."

Gray chokes as I nod to the kid and we load the bags into the trolley as quickly as we can. I spare a brief moment of thanks that the debate the Council had last year about changing Navarre currency didn't go through, and we still use the same money. We'd be fucked if we couldn't access our accounts.

"Shut up," I mutter as we leave. "They don't have packs here, remember?"

"You think they're gonna come back?" Gray shifts closer as he asks the question, his mouth pressing together.

"I don't know." But if they do, Emmett's bar isn't exactly the safest place. We might have to move on and hide Sienna in a more built-up area, but I can't see our Soul Bonded agreeing to travel anywhere with us at the moment.

We spend the drive back in contemplative silence. I'm trying to work out a plan to get this stuff into Sienna's room, and when I pull in and see Jess in the yard when we get back, I dive out.

"Jessalyn!"

Her lips curl as she turns. "Did someone call me?" she asks nobody, putting her hands on her lips and twisting around. "Nope. Just an annoying little alpha with a god complex."

I take a breath. Good job she's on Sienna's side.

"Jess, I need your help."

She squints at me. "I know," she says slowly, "that there's no way in hell you're stupid enough to think that I would help you, Crispin."

I fight the urge to bare my teeth. She knows my damn name. "Not for me. For Sienna."

It's plain as day that there is nothing this girl won't do for Sienna. Her hostile demeanor changes slightly as her eyes flick towards the bar. "What?"

As I explain, her face changes from cold anger to reluctant interest. "Well," she declares finally. "It's not an apology, but... not bad, Cristine."

My relief is instant. "So you'll help us?"

She rolls her eyes. "Her, Crispy. Like hell am I doing any of this for you."

"I know. Thank you, Jess."

She flicks me a middle finger before she turns around. "Emmett will get you when it's safe," she calls. "Don't touch any of my shit, Cristina."

"That's not even close," I drawl back. "Can I call you Julia?"

"Try it," she calls back cheerfully. "If you dare."

I do not dare. So I stay by the truck, waiting for Emmett to come out. Gray grabs the bags for him and Logan. "You want a hand?"

I shake my head. I want to do this myself.

It's a good thirty minutes before Emmett comes ambling out. His head tilts and he whistles when he catches sight of the bags. "I'm not sure all of that will fit," he deadpans. "Jess has taken over my living room for a movie night, so you've probably got two hours, max."

Perfect. Refusing his help, I carry the bags up, Emmett directing me to their room before withdrawing back to the bar downstairs. Setting the first batch of bags down, I look around.

The room is soaked in Sienna's scent, though there's a bitter aftertaste to its usual sweetness that catches at the back of my throat. It smells like sickness.

My stomach clenches as I get to work, unpacking the bags and heading out to the truck until the room is awash with various bits of stuff.

Omegas can be territorial about their bedding, so I lay the blankets and pillows out towards the bottom of the bed so she can choose her favorites. The lights get untangled and I wind them around the wooden frame, making sure the plug is easily accessible. We bought some wicker baskets, and I make use of a nearly bare bookshelf on the other side of the room to stack up her lotions, spreading out the candles and adding a few other pieces.

When I'm done, I feel a satisfaction I haven't felt in a long, long time as I gaze around.

It's not much – not in light of what I could have given her, if we were home, in Navarre. But we're not there, thanks to me, and this is the best I can do.

I wish I could see her reaction, but it'll be something entirely different if I'm here when she gets back. So I gather up all of the trash into the bags, taking it with me and closing the door softly as I head back outside. Emmett calls me as I pass the bar.

"Coming in tonight?"

When I turn to look at him, he shrugs. "Sienna hasn't been coming down much. Doesn't make much sense, you sittin' out there when you could be in here."

Slowly, I shake my head. "We'll wait," I say with a half-smile. "Omegas can be territorial. I'd rather have an invitation."

Emmett looks around before he beckons me closer. When I approach, he leans forward. There's a panicked look in his eye.

"I don't know much about omegas," he says quietly. "But I might need to learn. Think you can help me?"

My eyebrows fly up as I read between the lines. "Truthfully, I'm the absolute worst person to ask, given the circumstances. But I can probably give you something."

He exhales. "Anything that stops me feeling like I'm doing everything wrong would be great."

Leaning against the bar, I can't help but grin. "Jessalyn tying you up in knots?"

He shrugs, but the tips of his ears turn red. "She's something."

"She is," I agree. I've no idea if an omega and beta relationship could even work, but something tells me that if Jessalyn is set on Emmett, they'll work it out.

2 6

# SIENNA

I blink as I notice the credits rolling on the screen. "Wow. It finished already?"

Jessalyn shoots me a wry look. "It was a two-hour film, Si."

Grimacing, I stretch, trying to work out the painful knots in my back from hunching my body into weird positions to try and make this damn pain feel better. "Sorry. My head wasn't really in it."

It's currently stuck on the four alphas lingering downstairs. It doesn't help that I can pick up traces of Jax's misty scent coming from the hall, thanks to his sleepover last night. My gut clenches. Logan will be here soon.

"It's helping, though, right?" Jess scooches closer to me, her voice soft. "Having them here?"

I half-shrug, half-nod. It might be helping my body, but I'm not sure it's helping my heart. It definitely doesn't help that they're giving me all the soft words and promises I needed from them to start with.

My lips firm. Too little, too fucking late.

"I need to get Logan," I mutter, but Jess jumps up. "I'll get him," she offers, edging towards the door. "Why don't you go and get yourself sorted?"

She's acting a bit weird, but I let it slide as I head down the hall. After doing my business and brushing my teeth, I shuffle across into my room.

And then back out.

Back in. *Aaaaand…* there's a whole lot of stuff here that wasn't here earlier. My heart swoops inside my chest as my head spins around, taking in the soft warmth of the fairy lights wound carefully around my bed frame. There's a whole heap of blankets and pillows laid out carefully at the end of my bed, and on my nightstand is a basket filled with… snacks?

I step forward to get a better look, when my eyes catch on something plugged into the wall. Frowning, I lean down awkwardly and pull it out, holding it up to get a better look.

*A nightlight.*

Sinking onto the bed with the light in my hands, I blink at the wall opposite. Baskets that weren't there earlier have been carefully laid out, full of different toiletries. Candles are dotted around too.

There's a note propped against the snack basket, and my hands shake as I reach out for it.

*Bonded,*

*This isn't an apology. This is what you should have had all along.*

*It's not enough, I know.*

*Tell me if you need anything else – please.*

*T*

My eyes burn, tears coming thick and fast and landing on the paper in large drops that I brush away, as though his words actually fucking *mean* anything when he's broken my damn heart into pieces.

There's a creak, and my head shoots up, my eyes landing on Logan where he stands in the doorway. His face drops when he sees mine, and he rushes forward.

I flinch when he lands on his knees in front of me, the things he's carrying clattering to the floor.

"Sienna." His voice is low, anxious. "What's wrong? Are you in pain?"

I dash my tears away angrily with the back of my hand, avoiding his chestnut eyes. But he ducks down, and his hand comes up, nudging my chin. "Tell me."

It's a demand, but his voice is soft enough to ease the snap I can feel in the back of my throat.

"Why did you lie to me?" I ask him instead, searching his face. He holds my eyes, enough for me to see the flecks of gold in his irises.

"Because I'm an idiot," he whispers. "A stupid idiot who didn't realize what I was doing."

"No." I slash my hand through the air in irritation, narrowly avoiding his face. "I don't want to hear bullshit, Logan. I want the *truth*."

He takes a deep breath. "Let's get you comfortable."

I scramble back on the bed, my hand snatching at a pretty, soft green blanket that I can't resist and wrapping it around me as Logan clambers on. He sits closer than Jax did, our shoulders brushing together as we both lean our backs against the wall. His legs dangle over the edge of the bed as he shifts, his fresh, lemony scent soaking into my nose.

Logan clears his throat. "I... I wanted to tell everyone. About me and Gray. A long time ago."

I stay silent, waiting for him to find the words

"He struggled with it," Logan says sadly. "And every time it came up, it was never the right time. We had to wait for *progress*, for Tristan to ascend to the Council and change things."

"But then... Erikkson gave Tristan the folder."

He nods grimly. "It was out of our hands then, but I still didn't care, Sienna. I was a little worried about how an omega might affect our relationship, if it would be an issue... but all of that went out of the window when I met you."

Swallowing, I bang my head softly against the wall. "But I wasn't enough for you to tell me the truth."

"You were more than enough," he says forcefully. "Always, Sienna. We made shitty decisions, but not one of them was because we thought you were lacking in any way."

Logan grabs my hand, hanging onto it when I try to turn away. "Listen to me. You, Sienna Michaels, are perfect."

"Stop it," I say quietly. "I don't want—,"

"Yes, you do." I jerk my head to look at him. He's completely serious, his fingers tight around mine.

"You deserve all of the pretty words, Sienna. All of the compliments we should have given you from day one. And you can ask me anything, and I'll do it, but I will not stop saying the things that I should have been saying from the second I saw you at our Bonding Ceremony."

My lip quivers, and I turn away from him. My jaw clenches.

*What do they want me to say?*

"Did you know," he says softly, "that my studio at home is filled with paintings of you?"

My head snaps around, and he half-smiles, the dimple in his cheek deepening. "I painted you every day. Painted the future I wanted us to have. And I'm working for that, sweetheart. I know you're angry, and I'm not asking for your forgiveness. I have to earn it."

Lifting my hand to his mouth, he twists it, his lips barely brushing the skin on the inside of my wrist. "I'm going to earn it," he whispers. "I swear to you."

I can't take any more tonight, so I turn away from him, curling up wordlessly on the bed and closing my eyes. I keep the green blanket with me, and I flinch as Logan leans over, his hands gently tucking the sheets around me until I'm cocooned.

When I feel him climb off the bed, my eyes fly open in sudden, irrational panic, my heart thumping.

He spins around, holding up the pad he dropped on the floor earlier in a silent apology. The tension in my shoulders doesn't loosen until he's back on the bed.

"Sleep, Sienna," he whispers. "Heal. Everything else can wait."

His hand traces gentle circles on my leg over the bedding as I drift off.

27

# GRAY

I'm leaning over the branch in my lap, working away furiously when Logan finds me the next morning.

"Hey," I say, looking up at him. "How is she?"

Lo pushes his hair back from his face as he settles in next to me. The lines on his face highlight his sleepless night. "She's devastated, Gray. We did that."

*No. I did that.*

Much more so than Logan.

Swallowing, I keep going, the knife in my hand whittling away. I only stop when Logan's hand closes over mine.

"Talk to me," he urges, pulling the knife away and dropping it to the floor. His hands come up to cup my face. "Tell me what's going on in that head of yours."`

Sighing, I wrap my hands around his, keeping them where they are, soaking in the warmth of his palms. "I just... I don't see how she can forgive me, Lo."

It keeps playing on my mind. Every harsh word, every snap, every fucking bad decision I've made. Lo is a far, far better alpha than I am, because I don't think I could ever forgive myself for the shit I pulled on him over the last four years.

And my Soul Bonded? My fucking fated *mate*? I wouldn't blame her if she never let me near her again.

Logan shakes his head. "That's the thing, Gray. I'm not asking her for forgiveness. I'm just going to love her. The way she needs to be loved. And of course, I hope she forgives me. But I'll wait as long as it takes. Will you?"

"Of course I will."

It's the least I can do. Logan leans in, brushing a kiss across my lips. "Then show her that. She doesn't know you, Gray. All she knows is the harsh alpha face you put on. I know the *real* you. I *love* the real you. And she will, too. But you have to show her."

I close my eyes, breathing him in. "I love you too, you know."

"I know." His words are affectionate. "Even when your head is up your ass."

He looks down at my little project. "I haven't seen you whittle for years."

"I thought I might've forgotten how," I admit, holding it up to the light. "I can't exactly design her a building, but I thought she might like these."

It helps to keep my hands busy while I drive myself insane thinking of all the ways I've fucked up. I keep seeing Sienna's face, over and over again. The Bonding Ceremony. That tortuous, blissful moment in the shitty excuse for a nest we gave her, before I took what little trust she had in me and snapped it under my shoe.

If regret was money, I'd be a fucking billionaire by now.

"You should talk to Emmett," Logan says, tilting his head. "Get some feedback on your ideas for the beta housing in Navarre."

My jaw clenches. "None of that matters now."

The only thing that matters to me now is my pack. Sienna. Logan. Jax and Tristan.

I'll never lose sight of that again.

I spend the rest of my day in the forest, messing around with pieces of wood and grabbing a sandwich from Logan before I head into the bar. I sniff cautiously at my shirt as I walk up to Emmett.

He grimaces when he sees me, and I look down. "It's bad, right?"

There's no shower out there, just an outhouse with a tiny sink. My heart sinks when he nods. I don't want Sienna to smell me before she can see me, but I don't have much of a choice.

"It's… pretty bad. You'll have to use the shower tomorrow. You'll drive my customers away."

I glance around the empty bar. "Yeah."

He motions towards the stairs. "Go on up. Her door's on the right."

With a nod, I make my way slowly up the small wooden staircase. Creaking noises announce my imminent arrival, and Jessalyn pokes her head out of a doorway.

"Asshole number three!" she calls. "My *least* favorite one."

She doesn't miss my flinch, her eyes narrowing as they take me in. "Is Sienna here?"

"Yeah," she says dubiously. "But – dude. Seriously?"

"There's no shower," I say defensively. "I can wash up in the bathroom."

"There's no shower?" A small voice interrupts my stare-off with the she-devil, and I twist to face Sienna. Scanning her, I try not to let the relief show on my face that she looks a little healthier than the last time I saw her.

She shifts on bare feet, and I belatedly realize that I'm staring her down like I'm about to take a bite out of her.

Switching my gaze hastily to my feet, I shuffle uncomfortably. "I – ah – we were just—,"

"I was just giving Grayson here a little lesson on personal hygiene," Jessalyn announces.

I swear my cheeks light on fire in embarrassment, my shoulders stiffening as I stare at the floor. "You know, maybe one of the others would be better. I can go and get Jax—,"

"Wait," Sienna says tightly as I turn around. My foot freezes mid-step as she disappears inside the room, rustling around before she reappears with a towel in her hands. She presses it into my hands.

"Go and shower. We'll get you something to wear."

"You don't have to—,"

"I know," she says abruptly. "Go."

Slowly, I make my way into the bathroom and push the door closed.

Then I bang my head against it. Once. Twice.

The third time, it swings back and smacks me in the forehead. I stumble back with a curse as a hand appears through the door, waving a clean pair of sweatpants.

"Courtesy of Logan. Are you done with your pity party? 'Cause I can hear your head smacking into the door down the hall."

I snatch the sweatpants with a snarl. That girl is the spawn of fucking Satan. I can hear her cackling as she walks back to whatever lair she's got set up now she's not sleeping in with Sienna.

The hot water feels like heaven as it pounds against my back, but I don't waste time. I'm in and out, slipping the sweats up past my hips and pulling the door open.

Sienna's door is open, and I pause. She's sat on her bed, her hands clasped together and her eyes focused solely on my torso. Cautiously, I keep rubbing the towel through my hair and run it over my chest to catch the last of the droplets.

She looks away, her jaw tight.

"Sienna…" I don't *have* any pretty words. I'm a damn architect, good with my hands but not so much the social side. I'm fucking petrified that if I open my mouth, more stupid shit will pour out that'll drive an even bigger wedge between us.

When I don't say anything, my Soul Bonded presses her lips together. "You can sit at the end of the bed."

"Okay." Placing my boots down, I shuffle my way onto the bed, careful to avoid her legs. The final rays of the evening sun are fading, filling the room with golden light that bathes Sienna's skin.

I snatch glances at her as we sit in silence, breathing in the soft, slightly bitter scent of raspberries. She's curled up, her head on the pillow and eyes open as she stares at the opposite wall.

My concern grows as I watch her, giving up any pretense and openly staring. She looks pale, even paler than she has before, and I can see sweat beading on her upper lip.

Something is wrong.

When she twitches, I reach out for her. "What—,"

Her body convulses violently, an agonized retch ripping from her throat.

"Sienna!" I can't move fucking fast enough as she jerks, her head twisting over the bed. As I land next to her, my hands pushing back her hair, I'm spattered with something viscous, and I stare down in horror.

Blood.

"Fuck, Sienna, *baby*." My hands shake against her skin, my heart fucking ripping apart in my chest as she groans weakly.

My fault. This is what we've done to her.

She doesn't protest as I lift her, carrying her out of the room and into the bathroom. Her head lolls against my shoulder as I carefully prop her up on the bathroom counter, taking her weight as I reach my left hand around to flick on the faucet. Grabbing a washcloth from the counter, I dampen it, nudging her back and gently holding the back of her neck so I can wipe her face. Her eyes are dazed, a touch more awareness filtering in as I rinse the cloth and work it over her neck, her collarbone.

When she meets my gaze, her own wary and shuttered, I take a deep breath.

"It's not working, is it?" I say quietly. "You need more than we've been giving you. Maybe proximity helped a little, at first, but it's more than that."

Instead of answering, she buries her face in my shoulder. I can feel her shaking, damp tears soaking my skin. My hands reach up, slowly, so fucking carefully, as I cup the back of her head.

She feels like the finest, most delicate china under my hands, so fucking fragile as I run my hands over her dyed hair, over and over again.

My words start falling out, rambling as I hold her to me.

"I'm sorry," I whisper desperately. "I'm so sorry for everything, Sienna. I can't take it back. I can never take it back, I know, but I'll never stop making it up to you. I'm sorry you've got me as a Soul Bonded. I knew it the second I saw you. You were so hopeful, so happy to see us. It was like you had this – this *light* inside you, and I knew I'd crush it, the same way I break everything else."

Swallowing, I glance down, but her forehead is pressed into me, gentle huffs warming my skin as she breathes in.

"That's what I do." It hurts, saying it out loud. "I break things. I broke Logan over and over again, and I knew when we were in the nest, that I'd break you too."

She stirs. "You didn't break me." Her voice is a little stronger now. "You didn't break me, Gray."

She pulls back, huge blue eyes looking up at me. There's a crease between her brows, her face still pale but a little better than it was a few minutes ago. "It feels like there are so many different versions of you," she mutters. "You're giving me emotional whiplash, Gray. Angry, nasty, protective, sad, caring... who do you *want* to be, Gray Cohen?"

I hold her eyes. "Yours."

I catch the faintest flare in her eyes before it disappears. "And Logan?"

Swallowing, I nod. "I need him to breathe, Sienna. Lo is my oxygen, the air in my lungs. But you...I think I might need you to live."

"What does that make me?"

"Everything."

Her smile is so fucking sad. "You have no idea how much I want to believe you, Gray. But I can't take another run of this."

"Never again," I swear. "And I'm not asking you to believe me, sweetheart. I just... give me the chance to be a better man. A better Bonded."

My hand is still entangled in her hair, and I move it away from her face. "For now, just let me help you. Please."

She wets her lips, indecisive but not kicking me out of the bathroom, so I'll take that as a small win. "How? I don't want—,"

"Not that," I interrupt. "Just sleep. Skin contact."

She chews on her lip as she considers it. "I think... I think you're right. What we were doing helped, but it's not enough. Skin contact... I can do that. Don't read into it, though."

"Okay." My hands feel clumsy as fuck, huge on her body as I carefully lift her, not thinking about the angle until she's pressed against me, her legs hitched around my hips and my hands gripping her thighs.

Fuck, but she feels perfect in my arms. Too light, but I'm going to fix that.

"Have you been able to eat?" I ask her as I walk us back across the hall to her room. Sienna shrugs. "I guess so. Not a lot, but enough."

Definitely not enough. I can feel the sharpness of her bones pressing into my skin as I lay her down on the bed.

"I need to change." She sits up, slowly, and I run a hand over my hair.

"Sure. I'll just – I'll give you some space."

I quickly wash myself off in the bathroom, my ear cocked for every small movement from her room as I grab the small figures I left with my jeans earlier. When she calls my name, her voice small and hesitant, I'm inside in a second.

Several of the blankets have been removed, giving a little more room for me to slide in next to her, Sienna cocooned between my body and the wall, a fingertip's worth of distance separating us.

*Skin contact.*

When she shifts, an irritated huff escaping her throat as she turns to face the wall, I roll with her. Sienna makes a startled sound as I wrap my arm around her waist, pulling her in until she's tucked against me, our bodies pressed together and my knees up, our feet tangled.

My Bonded sucks in a breath. "Gray."

"Skin contact," I remind her. Nudging with my hand, I get her to tilt up her head so my arm can slide underneath, my head pressed into the sweet scented crook between her head and shoulder as my other arm moves slowly under her camisole, my hand spreading out to cover the soft skin over her abdomen.

"This okay?" I whisper into her neck. "Too much?"

She shakes her head. "Skin contact, right?"

Her words are a little higher pitched.

"Mmhmm." I stroke my fingers over her skin, softly back and forth until she relaxes, her body becoming soft and pliant around mine. The last of the evening light disappears, the fairy lights around the bed illuminating her in soft warmth.

Soft fingers grip my arm. "You're not leaving?"

I swallow, remembering her face when I walked away from her in the nest. "No. I'm not going anywhere. Not unless you want me to."

She doesn't respond, her breathing deepening into sleep as I hold her close.

2 8

# SIENNA

I rouse slowly, my eyes blinking sleepily at the bright light that makes it through the curtains. It takes me a minute of laying there, staring at the ceiling to work out why I feel so weird.

The pounding inside my head, the jagged pain in my stomach... it's still there, but it's barely noticeable, a background irritation.

Wow. Maybe Gray has magic hands.

Talking of... I suck back a ridiculous feeling of disappointment when I twist my head and don't see him.

Of course he didn't stay. He probably just meant the night.

My eyes skitter over my nightstand, before they jump back. A tiny, wooden bear has been put there, and my hand reaches out for it as my eyes widen. It's perfectly crafted, one paw lifted in the air as though it's about to come to life.

Fascinated despite myself, I turn it over in my hands before I reach for the note.

*I haven't left. I made a promise.*
*Making you breakfast. You need to eat.*
*The bear is for you.*
*Gray*
*PS. You look beautiful when you sleep.*

Well. Slightly flustered, I press the back of my hands to my cheeks.

It's just a note. Doesn't mean anything.

But despite myself, I still fold it carefully, opening the drawer and placing it next to Tristan's.

I'm still examining the bear when footsteps sound outside, and I hear a brief curse before the door pushes open. Gray carries in a tray, his hair in disarray as he tries to balance a glass of juice.

"This always looks better in the movies," he mutters. "Good morning."

"Morning." Shyly, I grab my green blanket, tucking it round me as Gray places the tray down in front of me. "Did you make this?"

His ears go red. "I tried, but I'm not the best cook. Emmett helped, though, so it should be edible."

The French toast even has strawberries sliced across it, and I pause as Gray settles next to me. He leans in, grabbing a knife and fork and slicing up the toast before he holds it up.

I stare at him. "You're kidding, right?"

He wants to *feed* me?

He shrugs. "I need to see you eat, Bonded. If you eat it, then I'll give you the rest of your present."

My hands clutch on the bear. "There's more?"

He hums as he waves the fork. "Find out."

Grumpily, I lean forward and take the food from the fork, my lips sliding off the tines and making Gray swallow as I pull back. "Good. More."

"Can you make airplane noises too?" I ask haughtily. "I'm not sure I feel enough like a three year old."

"Trust me," he mutters, lifting up another piece. "That's the last thing on my mind."

It takes me a second, but I can feel the blush stealing up my cheeks, closely followed by an idea.

When I lean in next, I take my time, pushing my lips up and dragging my teeth back slowly. I follow it up with the most wanton fucking moan I can come up with, my eyes half-closing, and I'm rewarded by the sight my Soul Bonding choking on air.

Swallowing, I give him the sweetest smile I can. "Problem?"

"No," he chokes out. "No problem."

"Good. Because this is *delicious*."

Picking up a piece of strawberry from the plate, I slide it between my lips, taking in the way he follows my motions, his blue eyes dark.

He looks ravenous, and I swallow down the fruit, my amusement fading and replaced by something *else*. Maybe this wasn't such a great idea.

"I – I think I'm full," I whisper, and he closes his eyes, taking a deep breath.

"One more for me," he says slowly. "Just like that, Bonded."

Oh. Ohhhh. His voice is dark, raspy, sending a shiver down my spine that has nothing to do with the cool morning air.

My heart thuds against my chest as he holds out the last forkful, my eyes staying fixed on his as I lean forward slowly, taking the food he offers.

His eyes don't move from mine as I chew, swallowing the food down in a lump without tasting it. The only thing I'm aware of now is the way his scent is filling the room, twisting around me in smoky waves.

"Perfect," he murmurs. His hand reaches out, his thumb swiping gently against my lower lip. I stare at him as he brings it to his lips, sucking off the syrup.

"Syrup and raspberries. Delicious, Sienna."

There's creaking outside, and my head shoots to the door, breaking the moment. I hear the bathroom door open, and I shuffle back from Gray. I need distance, before I do something I regret.

His face softens, and he grabs my hands. "Wait."

"Gray—" My words cut off as he holds my hands together, turning them over and tipping something into them. My heart skips a beat when I look down.

Three little wooden baby bear cubs sit in my palms. One is curled up as if asleep, another up on its rear legs doing an adorable baby roar. The other is sat, back legs out and front paws placed between so he's a little lopsided.

I *love* them. I can feel the smile spread across my face, almost painfully unfamiliar.

"They're nothing special," Gray murmurs, "but I'm making do."

My head jerks up, my hands curling protectively around them. "I think they're amazing. Do you have any more?"

His cheeks pink. "I'll make you more, if you like them."

"I do," I say softly. Turning to the nightstand, I arrange them so they're gathered around the mama bear. "You have a gift, Gray."

My smile slides away when he moves off the bed. I'm not ready to say goodbye to this Gray yet.

Angry, harsh Gray? He can fuck all the way off.

But this Gray, with the subtle dominance, the shy smiles and the care? I want to know more about him.

He shifts on his feet. "I was wondering… you want to go out, today? We could go for a drive. Should be safe enough, with your hair covered. Only if you want to."

I hesitate. This feels like a safe space, my own space, even though we're still in Emmett's home. Like there's a spell on it, and the moment will shatter the second I go outside with them.

"Okay," I whisper, tucking my hair back. "Just a quick drive. I'll need to get ready."

Gray moves to the door, shaking his head. "Come as you are. You're beautiful."

Okay, he needs to stop now.

I'm still angry at him.

Furious.

But… I'm a little hopeful, too.

29

# TRISTAN

I wait outside Sienna's door.

And I wait. Maybe she's sleeping. She went for a drive with Gray earlier, and maybe it sapped some of her energy.

I'm not burning with envy over that *at all*.

Fifteen minutes later, I'm still waiting. Cautiously, I knock. "Sienna?"

The door opens slowly, and I'm face to face with my Soul Bonded, alone, for the first time in days.

"You look better." There's relief in my words. She looks healthier, more *vibrant*, color flaring in her cheeks.

She hesitates. "Tristan...,"

I pick up on her discomfort. "You want me to leave."

My chest deflates, the anticipation and hope that's been sitting in my stomach all day draining away. Sienna shifts on her feet.

"It's just... I've had a *nice* day, Tristan. The first nice day I've had in a long time. And I just – I want to hold onto it, for a little bit."

*Before I ruin it.*

"I understand," I say with a nod. I dip to meet her eyes, wanting her to understand. "It's not a problem, Sienna. Maybe tomorrow."

"Maybe." She swallows, before she moves to shut the door. "Goodnight, Tristan."

"Wait." I just want to drink her in for a little while longer.

"I'm glad you had a good day," I say quietly. "You deserve nothing but good days, Bonded."

She swallows. "See, you say things like that," she whispers, "and it makes what happened in the Trials feel like a bad dream. It makes me want to forget. But I can't, Tristan. I have to have some respect for myself, because you've proved that I'm the *only* one in this Soul Bond who does."

Her words twist in my chest.

"I never, ever wanted you to feel that way," I say hoarsely. "I tried so hard to fix everything, and I broke it instead. You deserve better than me as your Soul Bonded, Sienna. But I swear to you, you are my first and only priority."

She sighs. "Until the next time, Tristan. You have a life in Navarre. A career. All of you do. How long before you decide that a life on this side of the wall isn't enough? Until you leave again? What happens to me then?"

Shame curdles my stomach, crawls up my throat. She thinks we're just going to abandon her?

"I will never, ever leave you again." The words leave my lips on a growl. "Never. I will go wherever you are, Bonded."

And as I say it, I realize that there's no way I can leave her. Even if she despises me for the rest of our lives, I'm never going to stop working to make amends.

"Until—"

"I am *yours*, Sienna. I was yours the second I saw you on that stage."

I take a deep breath. "I took what should have been perfect, and I broke it into pieces. Not just once, but over and over again. And I told myself that it had to be done. To keep my family safe, my pack, *you*. I didn't know how to ask for help, didn't trust anyone else to get involved in case it fell back on one of you. I know what my choices have cost. I see the consequences every time I look at you. And I will spend the rest of our lives atoning for them."

I meet her eyes, the bright blue of her gaze muted. "I'll let you rest. But I'm not giving up, Bonded. I'm fighting for you, the way I should have done all along."

Her eyes squeeze closed. "Goodnight, Tristan."

The door slowly closes with a click, and I swallow back the rest of my words. There aren't enough apologies in the world, but I won't stop giving them.

Turning, I settle down with my back against the wall, pulling out the notepad and pen I've been carrying around. I'll respect her wishes, but she's still not well. I'm not going anywhere and leaving her alone.

*Never again.*

30

# SIENNA

**M**y eyes fly open, hands flying to my throat.

Just a dream. But I can still feel the burn of my heat, the lingering embers of pain and lust and straight-up fucking *need*.

Sitting up, I reach for the water on my nightstand, downing the slightly stale glass until the dryness in my throat dissipates.

As I set the glass back down, there's a creak from the hall. Frowning, I glance up.

When I don't hear anything else, my eyes drop down, catching on a pale square on the floor. I creep out of bed, my hand reaching down to scoop up the sheet of paper and turn it over.

*Bonded,*

*What did you want to be when you grew up?*

*I always knew I'd take my father's seat on the Council, but when I was a kid, I wanted to be a singer, just like Jax. We were going to form our own band and call it The Trix – so it's probably for the best that it didn't work out.*

*T*

My hands tighten on the paper. Turning, I open the drawer of my nightstand and grab a pen.

*I was a little girl dreaming of dresses and handsome alphas.*

*Then I learned that dreams are just disappointments waiting to happen.*

*You didn't want to be Council Leader?*

Carefully, I feed it back under the door. My suspicions are confirmed when I hear another creak.

Grabbing my green blanket from the bed, I settle myself in the small gap next to the door. I wait for a few minutes, and a tendril of disappointment snakes into my stomach when there's no response. I'm about to give up and go back to bed when the rasp of paper on wood sounds, and another sheet slides under to land next to my feet.

*I didn't want my life to be chosen for me. It took me a long time to realize that it was where I wanted to be.*

*Tell me more about these dreams, Bonded. Maybe they won't all be disappointments.*

I flip the paper over, a spark of temper lighting inside me as I scribble.

*I dreamed of a pack, family. Somewhere I would be loved.*

*Tell me again about disappointments?*

The pause is longer again this time.

*I'm making you a new promise, Bonded.*

Frowning, I check the other side of the paper, but there's nothing.

Aggravating alpha.

My fingers tap impatiently on the floor until a new piece slides under.

*Bonded,*

*I promise that I will never let another day pass without building new memories to replace the ones I lost us.*

*I will give you your dreams back.*

*T*

I hunch over the paper for a long time, before I slowly pull myself up and walk back to my bed. I don't have any more words for him.

But I fall asleep with his promise in my hands.

## 31

# SIENNA

I'm gritty-eyed and grumpy the next morning when I drag Jessalyn into Emmett's tiny but immaculate kitchen. I haven't been in here before, but Jess wanders around, pulling out cups and opening the cupboards like it's home.

It's when she's leaning into the refrigerator looking for milk that I notice what she's wearing.

I cough into my fist. "Jessalyn. Whose shirt is that?"

"Ow!" Jess grunts as her head bangs into a shelf. She spins to face me, crossing her arms against the oversize white shirt in a defensive position. "I don't know."

"Hmmm," I say thoughtfully, enjoying the flash of panic on her face. "It looks *awfully* like the shirt Emmett had on yesterday."

She swallows. "Does it? Huh."

"Jess." I lean forward, giving her the stink-eye. "Spill. I want to know everything."

I've been far too wrapped up in my own little tit-for-tat with the Cohens to grill her, but something is definitely going on.

She shifts on her feet. "Si... there's not much to talk about."

Now my senses are definitely tingling. With Jess, there's *always* something to talk about.

"You like him?" I ask gently. "Emmett?"

She swallows before she nods. "I... it's stupid. Right? An omega and a beta?"

I tilt my head. "Just because something's always been a certain way, doesn't mean that's the way it always should be. And if anyone's gonna lead the way, it's you."

"You give me too much credit," she mutters. "The baking stuff is over here."

Following her pointing hands, I find a few of the basics I need for cookies, and start piling everything up on the counter haphazardly. I need to think, and I always think better in the kitchen.

"Your turn," Jess turns the tables back on me. "What's going on with you and the Cohurts?"

I choke. "The Cohurts?"

She clicks her tongue. "Don't change the subject."

I frown into my dough. "Nothing. I haven't forgiven them."

Sneaky alphas. Sneaky alphas and their little sneaky gifts and sweet words.

I'm starting to waver. Not that I'm ready to forgive them, or to forget.

But for the first time, I'm starting to think about the longer-term.

Plunging my hands into the bowl, I yelp as a cloud of flour envelops me. "Shit!"

"Shortcake. What are you making?"

I jump at the sound of the throaty purr. Waving my hand to dissipate the cloud, I look around, my heart pounding as I catch sight of a violet-eyed alpha with messy black hair leaning through the low, open window.

"Jax." Swallowing, I give him a nod. "Good morning."

"You look better." His voice softens, his eyes scanning me. Turning away, I start shaping balls of dough. "I feel better."

I do. Stronger. More myself.

"Well, you look like perfection."

Damn it. I'm blushing.

I'm not falling for it.

I cast around desperately, and my eyes land on the bag of flour.

What did Jess say?

*Vengeance is a dish best served to alphas who have royally fucked up.*

My lips curve as I grab the open bag. "Jax?" I ask, swinging my head around with a woeful look. I even throw in a lip wobble for good measure. The sensual expression slides off Jax's face so quickly it's almost comical, replaced with concern and more than a tinge of panic. "What's wrong?"

"There's something wrong with the flour," I sigh dramatically. Jess coughs in a really obviously-trying-not-to-laugh way, and I purse my lips.

Maybe subterfuge isn't my strong point.

Jax doesn't know that though, because I can see him trying to look genuinely concerned over my flour. "Uh – do you want me to go and get you some more?"

"Have a look," I say, biting the inside of my cheek. "See what you think."

As he peers into the open bag, I smack the bottom, sending a massive cloud of flour directly into his face.

He's covered. His hair, his eyes, his nose…

Oh, wow. There's quite a bit more flour than I expected.

The laugh bubbles up my throat and out into the air, helped along by Jax's stunned expression as he blinks owlishly. Jess cackles behind me.

"You look like a floury snowman," I gasp. I shriek when he leans forward, shaking his head so flour lands on me.

"You," he rumbles, "are in *trouble*, shortcake."

His eyes track me as I move backwards. "Keep going," he rasps. "I like the chase. It'll make it all the sweeter when I catch you."

Oh, *shit.*

*Did not think this through.*

I break into a run as Jax pushes himself away from the windowsill. I can hear Jess laughing hysterically behind me as I skid out of the kitchen, my hair flying everywhere as my head swivels. I'm not completely familiar with the downstairs layout, so I make a mad dash down the hall, grabbing at doors until I find a small closet.

Sliding inside, I yank the door shut and shove a hand over my mouth, trying to quieten my breathing as footsteps sound from outside.

"Sienna," Jax calls, a laugh in his voice. "I'm going to catch you."

There's a creak right outside the door. "Especially when you leave me a trail."

My eyes round as I stare down at my hands. My flour-covered hands.

The door flies open and I squeak as a strong grip closes around my upper arms. Jax tugs me into him, getting even more flour over my top as I find myself pressed against him.

His nostrils flare as he dips his head and breathes into my neck. "Sweet Sienna."

"Jax." My eyelids actually fucking flutter as his stubble rasps over the sensitive skin at my neck.

Somehow, I find the damn near fucking superhuman strength to push him back.

"*No,*" I warn him shakily, pointing my finger for good measure. "Bad alpha."

"Only for you." His eyes are dark as he takes a step forward. "What's my reward for catching you?"

I fend him off with wavering hands. "I don't know. What do you want?"

"A kiss."

*Oh, hell.*

Jax giving me puppy eyes and apologies is pretty hard to resist. Jax with smouldering eyes and flour-spattered hair is fucking *devastating.* My back meets the wall as he stalks me, his hands caging either side of my head as he brings his face close to mine. His scent washes over me, slightly musky and all Jax.

"Let me kiss you, Sienna," he whispers against my lips. "Let me kiss you the way I should've all along."

I mean…just a *little* kiss won't hurt.

My lips part under his, and my eyes close as I wait. Instead of the fire I expect, Jax presses the softest kiss to my lower lip, before he does the same to the top.

I blink at him as he withdraws, and he gives me a small half-smile.

"You deserve to be treated like you're precious, shortcake."

*Yeah, that's cute and all, but I want the damn fire.*

He closes in on me again. "And now, I can do what I've wanted to since I saw you in that bar."

*Wha—*

His lips crash against mine, almost bruising in their intensity as I melt underneath him. Jax's arms slide around me, his hand splaying across my back, the other cradling my head as he holds me against him and *takes*.

My back slams against the wall, Jax taking the brunt of it as his body sinks into mine. He breaks away from my lips on a ragged breath, pressing rough kisses down the side of my neck that make my knees weaken underneath him. My hands slide into his hair, gripping it tightly.

"Jax." My voice sounds woozy, almost drunk.

I lick my lips, tasting him. I'm drunk on Jax Cohen.

He softens his kisses, tracing his path back up to my lips and catching them for one last, lingering kiss before he pulls away. My breath heaves as we stare at each other.

His tongue darts out, chasing the taste of me across his lips. "Knew you'd taste like sin, shortcake."

Holy smokes. I stay where I am, very much aware that if I try to move right now, my knees will collapse.

He takes a step towards me, his hands cupping my face as he searches my eyes. "You okay? Too much?"

I manage to shake my head.

It doesn't feel like enough, every part of me straining to reach for him. But it's enough for now.

He rubs his thumb across my cheek. "You've got a little something here."

I give him a look. We're both covered in flour. I wince as I glance down the hall, seeing the trail of white we've left behind us. "Emmett won't be happy."

"I'll clean it up," Jax promises.

He darts in to steal another kiss, and I narrow my eyes at him. "Woah there, stud. You've had your reward."

"Not enough," he says promptly. "I'll never get enough of you, Sienna Michaels."

Smooth talker. I kind of like it. Chewing my cheek to keep the blush off my cheeks, I start making my way back down to the kitchen.

"If you're good," I call casually over my shoulder, "I might give you a cookie."

"Baby, I want all your cookies. Every single one."

Why does he make that sound filthy?

## 3 2

# LOGAN

My fingers pause in their sketching, my hand clenching around my pencil as a twig snaps ahead of me.

I'm fairly far out from the bar, my back resting against a tree as I sketch on the tiny pad Gray brought back amongst the art supplies he managed to find in town. My body stills as I hear another crack, and then I catch the simmer of smoky campfire.

Home. That's what Gray smells like to me. Sienna gives me the same feeling. It's hard to describe, but I can feel it coming out in my art, even though what I can do is limited out here. I flip the sketchbook closed as Gray appears, his eyes finding mine.

He looks tired, but he smiles. "Hey, you."

"Hey." I set the book aside as he comes to crouch in front of me, balancing himself with his hands on my knees. "Everything okay?"

Gray nods. He looks more rumpled than I've ever seen him, dressed in a crumpled tee that I'm pretty sure might be mine, his hair glinting copper in the sun and falling over his forehead in a lazy curl.

His hands tighten on my knees. "Stop looking at me like that."

I grin. "Like you're edible, you mean?"

He snaps his teeth at me playfully, so I take it ten steps too far and just launch myself at him. The sudden attack takes him by surprise, and by the time he's caught his breath, I have him pinned, his hips snug against the inside of my thighs.

Leaning down, I snap my teeth right back into his stunned face. "I win."

The laugh rumbles from his throat. "You think?"

The sudden push sends me rolling, Gray pushing me down into the leaves and following the line of my body with his own, pressing against me until my breath catches.

He gives me a self-satisfied smirk. "Looks like I win."

I wriggle beneath him. "You sure about that?"

His cock is a solid length between us, his breath catching as I lean up and capture his lips. Gray groans into my mouth as he cups my face, tasting me leisurely before he pulls away.

"I can't," he whispers, his eyes searching my face. "I want to, Lo. But it doesn't feel right."

"I know." I get it. What kind of mates would we be if we messed around out here whilst Sienna sits a few paces away from us, suffering for our shitty fuck-ups?

Gray shifts down until his ear is pressed directly against my chest, listening to my heartbeat. Leaning back, I watch the sky as my hands drift into his hair, pushing the growing strands back and letting them spring back into place.

"That feels nice," he murmurs.

I hum in acknowledgement, but before I can respond, I pick up the sound of footsteps heading our way.

A muted curse filters through the trees, and my lips press together as Tristan stalks out of the trees, covered in forest debris. He freezes when he sees us, the limp flowers in his hands drooping almost as much as his shoulders.

"Uh… hey," I try. "Out for some flower picking?"

Gray shakes against my stomach as he tries to hold in his laughter.

"Fuck off," Tristan grunts. "There's no damn florists out here."

127

"Tris, those are the saddest looking daisies I've ever seen," Gray points out, his voice choked. "You can't give her those."

Tristan stares down at his hands. "It's bad."

It's not a question. Nudging Gray, I sit up, squinting. "If we use some of the foliage, we could probably make it a bit better."

Tristan looks slightly desperate. "Yeah? I'm not... I'm not great at this stuff."

"I'll help." Getting to my feet, I hold out a hand for Gray and pull him up. We work our way into the trees so I can grab some of the longer, thinner leaves, and I strip them off to create a frame for Tristan's flowers.

"Have you heard anything?" I ask him as we look around a clearing. "From home?"

He shakes his head. "We might not," he says quietly. "Not for a long time. I have no idea what's going on, but it was chaos when we left."

"If we don't hear anything," Gray says slowly. "Then we need a plan, Tristan. We can't stay here forever."

"I know." Tristan leans down to grab some orange flowers, adding them to the growing bundle in his hands. "But we'll work it out."

He sounds so relaxed about it all. Catching my skeptical look, he sighs. "I can't control everything around me, Lo. It only causes more damage. So we'll wait, and if we need a plan, we'll make one. I'll follow Sienna's lead. But my focus is her."

Nodding, I take the flowers from him, sitting down and tying them into a small but better bouquet. Tristan exhales with relief when I hold them up.

"Thanks," he mutters, taking them. "I'm going to head back."

"We'll walk with you." Brushing off my hands, we head back to the house, and I scoop up my pad as we walk past. As we reach the yard, the door opens, and we all pick up our pace as our Soul Bonded emerges with a tray. Jax is right behind her, trailing her steps and looking like he's won the damn lottery.

"One," I hear her saying as we get closer. "You can have *one*, Jax."

"But I want cookies," he pouts. "All the cookies."

My eyes widen when his arms slide around her waist. She can't shove him off with the tray in her hands, but to my shock, she doesn't move away, although her brows crease in a frown.

"Honestly," she mutters. "I give an inch. One single little inch, and you take a damn mile."

"Shortcake, I'll give you all the inches you want."

Sienna's cheeks flare scarlet as we reach them. She half widens her eyes, half glares at Jax before she turns to us.

"I made cookies," she says through gritted teeth. "You want some?"

"She made a lot of cookies," Jax interjects. "Like four batches."

"I like to bake when I'm stressed."

"Do you feel okay?" Tristan asks, his mouth turning down as he looks at Jax. "Stop bothering her."

Sienna raises her eyebrows. "He's not bothering me. Much. You want these, or not?"

It feels like another small step, and I'll take every bit of movement I can. Eagerly, I step up and take a cookie from the tray, looking up to meet her eyes. "Thank you."

She bites her lip as Gray and Tristan grab one too, and we all bite into it.

It takes me a second or two, the first delicious burst of vanilla in my mouth rapidly changing to a... burning?

My choke closely follows Gray's, and my eyes start to water as I stare down at the cookie.

*What in hell's name is in this?*

I need water. Liquid. Anything.

But I don't want to hurt her feelings, so I swallow down the burn and force a smile through gritted teeth. "These... something."

She starts to look suspicious when Gray hides his gag in his fist. "What?" she demands. Her eyes dart between us. "You don't like them?"

I sense that we're walking a very, very thin line with our Soul Bonded.

I swivel to Tristan, and I can *see* his eyes streaming. But he takes another bite, chewing it like it's the best damn thing he's ever tasted. "Delicious."

He doesn't bat a fucking eyelid, even as his face turns bright red.

Sienna looks at me before her eyes drop down to the tray, and I catch a flash of hurt on her face.

*Oh, no. No, no, no.*

I shove the rest of the cookie into my mouth and brace myself.

"Mmmm. 'S good." I nod frantically.

Oh fuck. I can't swallow. It feels like my throat is on fire.

Gray whacks me between the shoulders as I bend over, wheezing as the cookie crumbs get caught in my throat.

"What the hell?" Sienna mutters. "They can't be that bad."

Tristan moves past me as I wheeze. "They're perfect, Bonded. Can I have another one?"

*What the fuck? Is his throat made of fucking titanium?*

I'm saved from my humiliation by a loud burst of laughter from the doorway. Jessalyn is leaning against it with a smirk.

"How're those cookies, Cobutts?"

We all stare at her, even Sienna. "Jess? What did you do?"

Jess cackles like a damn witch. "I might have added something special. Just for them."

Sienna swings her gaze across us. "Like what?"

Oh god. She has actually poisoned us.

"Just a bit of chili." Jessalyn rolls her eyes. "Honestly. Bunch of babies."

"*Jess.*" Sienna spins back to us, squinting at Tristan. "And you just ate it?"

"You made us cookies," he says, his brows lowering. "I'd eat whatever you made me, Bonded, and I'd be grateful for every bite."

Jess retches, but Sienna's cheeks pink as she turns away. "Come inside," she says, a huff in her voice. "Just for a minute. I'll get you some water."

I cough as I follow them inside, taking a seat at one of the tables. Emmett wanders over to us, grabbing a cookie from the tray. Jessalyn smacks it out of his hand, and he turns to her incredulously. "Am I not allowed one?"

"Not these." Jess purses her lips. "There might be some more in the kitchen. Edible ones, I mean."

Jax leaps up. "I volunteer as tribute."

"Not a chance, asshole." Jessalyn chases after him as he heads down the hall, their argument floating back to us as Emmett swivels his head to watch them.

Massaging my throat, I lean back, taking in the bare walls of the bar. An idea hits me.

"Hey – Emmett?" I rasp. When he turns to me, I motion at the blank space. "You mind if I do something with the walls? I'm a painter."

Emmett looks dubious, but Gray leans in. "You definitely want him to decorate your bar."

Sienna reappears, and I slide out to help her hand out bottles of water. I glug mine down in one, finally relieving the burn in my chest.

"You know, they were really nice cookies," I say awkwardly. "Besides the chili."

She shrugs. "Don't read into it. I made too many."

But she still brought us some.

"It means something to me."

At that, she glances over at me, a smile playing around her lips. "Like… heartburn?"

My laugh shakes my chest. "Nah, that's just a bonus."

Jax and Jessalyn reappear, squabbling over the tray as Sienna wades in, confiscating it. We all take one as it's passed around, settling into a strangely comfortable silence. Sienna takes a seat on my right, nibbling on a cookie of her own. She's starting to fill out some, the sharpness of her cheekbones regaining some of their softness.

"Emmett," I call, and he looks over. "What do you say? About the bar?"

He shrugs. "Have at it. But you're painting it back if you fuck it up."

Fucking *deal*. My hands itch as I look around at the blank canvas.

Sienna looks up at me as I stand. "Want to help me paint a bar?" I ask her with a crooked smile.

It's not the most romantic proposal. But, an idea is forming in my head.

Her eyes widen a little. "Right now?"

"You don't have to," I assure her. "I just thought, maybe…,"

"No." She stands. "I can help. I haven't really been doing much. Hence the baking."

My grin stretches across my cheeks. "Okay. I'll go and get my stuff."

I don't have enough paint to do the whole bar, but I have enough for the first wall. That's all I need.

Sienna watches me as I set up, tying her hair back into a braid. "You're not just using one color?"

"Ah," I glance down. "No. I think we can do better than that."

She scoots closer, glancing into the pots. "What can I do?"

"Whatever you want." I join her, both of us leaning over to look at the colors. Her arm brushes against mine, the sweetest tinge of raspberry dancing on my tongue.

*Edible. Our Soul Bonded is definitely edible.*

Shoving a lid over those thoughts, I sweep my hand out. "I'm thinking… we could do a mural on that wall. Maybe music-themed?"

Jax ambles up to us. "Did you say music?"

"Yeah." Rubbing the pack of my neck, I notice Sienna

watching me from the corner of my eye. "Like… instruments? Music notes, mics… that sort of thing."

And a little message for my Soul Bonded, but I don't mention that.

"How are you with music notes? Think you can paint some?" I ask her, and her brow furrows. "Maybe."

She doesn't sound sure, but I grab the small tin of black paint and a paintbrush in one hand, and her hand in the other. Leading her over to the wall, I show her the area I'm thinking of.

"We can put a trail of notes along here," I suggest. "And then build everything else around it."

Her hand still in mine, she reaches the other up to trace an invisible line. "Across here?"

"That's it."

I'm reluctant to drop her hand, but I need both of them to paint. Taking the brush, I dip it into the paint, leaning in and swirling a small note onto the wall.

Sienna lets out a small laugh. "It looks cute."

Mock frowning, I wiggle my eyebrows at her. "Art is not *cute*. Art is majestic."

She smiles at me as she steps forward. "Can I try?" she asks, a tinge of excitement in her voice. Our hands touch as I hand over the brush, and I step back to watch her work. Her tongue darts out in concentration as she carefully paints a treble clef and steps back, looking to me with uncertainty in her eyes.

"Cute," I tease softly. "And perfect."

Her face lights up as she turns back to the wall. "Another?"

"However many you want."

33

# SIENNA

## 3 - Sienna

Logan's hand brushes against mine again, his fingers closing over to guide my hand across the wall, leaving sweeping, swirling lines of black behind that definitely wouldn't look that pretty if I did it on my own.

His heat burns into my back as he gently tugs my braid. "They're looking really good."

*You know who's looking really, really fucking good? Logan.*

I keep my eyes very firmly focused on the wall as he stops to yank his shirt off, hanging it over a chair. "Don't want to mess it up," he explains with an apologetic smile.

When he comes back to stand close to me, I could catch on fire from the heat coming off my cheeks. His skin is more tanned now after all the time he's spent outside, highlighting the golden strands in his hair. He pushes it back absentmindedly as he studies our work, and I swear the muscles in his stomach flex.

Oh holy fucking god.

I need to give myself a stern talking to. I'm having way too many indecent thoughts right now.

"It's coming together." He grins when he turns to me, and the carefree expression in his eyes takes my breath away. He pauses, his eyes scanning my face.

"You okay?" he asks me anxiously. "You look hot. Is it too much? Do you need to sit down?"

I seize on the easy out, nodding and backing away. "You know, I do feel a little warm. I'll sit down for a minute."

To my horror, he follows me. There's concern on his face as he presses me into a chair, his hands heated on my skin as he cups my shoulders. "I'll get you some water."

"I'm fine," I protest. There's movement across the room as Jax, Tristan and Gray spin in their chairs, taking in Logan bent over me like some muscled blonde god with a nursing fetish.

*Oh my fucking god.*

Not *one* of them is still wearing a top. I mean, I know it's warm, but honestly. Do they have a thing about wearing clothes? There's so much male flesh on display I feel like I'm letting the side down. I might need to get my tatas out to even the playing field.

And now they're getting up.

*No, please—*

Here they all come. God, if they'd been this attentive to start with, I wouldn't be sitting here with a hot flush over a little bit of skin showing from my Soul Bonded.

Tristan reaches me first as he drops down, crouching to see into my face. "Do you have a fever?" he demands. His hand reaches up to cup my forehead and I bat him away. I might be having a moment, but I haven't completely lost my senses.

"Back off." My voice comes out a little too high-pitched. "Personal space, Tristan!"

He rocks back on his heels as Gray leans in, studying my face. "Did we get anything from the pharmacy for fevers?" he asks Tristan.

"I don't have a fever," I snap irritably, losing my temper. "I'm fine. And would you *please,* for the love of freaking god, *put some damn clothes on!*"

135

The silence is deafening, and I just want the ground to open me up. Tristan and Gray both stare at me, their eyes darkening.

A warm breath huffs in my ear. "Shortcake," Jax murmurs, making me jump. "Your scent appears to be leaking."

"Hormones," I croak out. "Just ignore me."

"But we could make you feel better," Jax coaxes. I shiver as his hands land on my shoulders, sliding down my arms in a caress that *feels* indecent, even if the touch is innocent.

Footsteps sound behind me, and I jerk away from Jax to look.

Emmett and Jess freeze against the wall. They're creeping towards the door to upstairs, and Emmett flushes a deep red. Jess has her hands pressed over her mouth as she tries not to laugh.

"Don't mind us," she manages to gasp out, flapping her hand. "We're just going to... pretend we're not here!"

I bury my face in my hands in mortification. "Please go away. *All* of you."

My voice is muffled, but I jerk when hands land over mine, carefully tugging them away from my face and revealing Tristan. His mismatched eyes are still dark, his voice low as he runs his thumbs over mine.

"What do you need, Bonded?"

I shake my head frantically. "Nothing. I'm good. Spiffy, actually."

*Spiffy? I don't even know what that fucking word means. Is it a word?*

Jax's fingers slide around the back of my neck, cupping the skin there possessively and squeezing. "You sure about that, shortcake?"

I press my knees together. "Absolutely. One hundred percent confidence here."

His fingers trace my skin before he slowly withdraws, and I actually have to bite back a whine as they all shift back, giving me the space I asked for.

*Fucking hormones.*

"In that case," Jax murmurs. "I have a surprise for you."

"You do?" Shaking off the weird little omega moment and seizing the change in topic gratefully, I spin around in my chair.

My gratitude lasts a split second before it drains away, and I give Jax a flat stare. "No."

"Oh, come on." He shakes the neck of the guitar he's holding carefully, a black painted, wooden, slightly musty looking instrument.

"Where did you even get that?"

He beams. "Emmett has a lot of shit in his storage shed. Come on, shortcake. Sing a little song with me."

I stare at it. God, I want to. My fingers itch to reach for it, to run my fingers along the familiar feel of strings, to play for them like I always wanted to.

But that was before. When I had my dad's guitar.

And it's the reminder of everything I've lost that throws a bucket of cold water over my warm and fuzzy feelings.

Because of *them*.

"I'm going up." I stand so abruptly that Tristan rocks back, catching his balance as I tug my hands from his without looking at him.

"Sienna." Jax's expression slides away, and he swallows. "I – I didn't mean—,"

I hold up my hand. "I know."

And I think that's the worst thing. I believe him. I believe all of them, even Tristan, when they say they're sorry.

But it still doesn't change anything that happened.

And I don't know how to get past it, or if we even can.

I force a smile. "I'm just tired."

"No, you're not," Tristan says quietly, his eyes meeting mine. "But that's on us. Who do you want with you tonight, Sienna?"

I shake my head, my feet already turning towards the stairs. It's technically Jax's turn, but I hate how fucking sterile that sounds. Like they have to have their regular slot with me to keep my heart pumping. "I'm good for tonight."

Tristan follows me, his hand landing on mine as I place it on the stair rail.

"Please," he says softly. "It doesn't have to be me, Sienna. But have one of us with you. You're still recovering."

I draw in a breath. "Can we just stop for a minute? This is... it's a lot, Tristan. We've gone from one extreme to the other, and I can't just – I need *time*. You need to give me space when I need it."

His hand drops slowly. "Sienna—"

And then, of course, it all goes to shit.

An unfamiliar voice cuts into our space. "Hello?"

The low, male call makes me flinch back against the wall. Matching growls ripple out around me, and my view is suddenly taken up by a broad, muscular back as Tristan physically twists, keeping me behind him.

My hands start to shake as I unashamedly hide behind him.

*This is it. They've found me—*

Tristan is frozen in front of me. I don't think he's even breathing, and my hand rises of its own volition, settling against his back.

"Tristan?" I whisper. "Who is it?"

His hand snakes back, and he wraps his fingers around mine. "It's alright, Bonded."

At his nudge, I step out from behind him, peering around his frame to the person standing in the bar doorway.

And then I blink. Because it's probably the last person I would have expected to be standing in Emmett's little bar in the forests of Herrith.

Tristan lets out a raw breath, his fingers tightening around mine. "Dad."

34

# TRISTAN

"Tristan." My dad looks around at the bar, taking in the surroundings. His eyes dart to Sienna when she steps out next to me, and he sucks in a breath.

"Sienna Michaels," he says, his eyebrows drawing together. "I'm glad to see you. You're unharmed?"

My Soul Bonded is frozen next to me, but I can feel her hesitation. I take a small step, sheltering her. "That's relative," I say quietly. "What are you doing here, Dad?"

Not that it's not good to see him. Truthfully, I wasn't sure that I'd ever see him again when we left Navarre.

"All is well," he assures me quickly. "Well, as well as it can be, given the circumstances."

He looks around, and my pack give him nods, all of us framing ourselves around Sienna where she still lingers uncertainly behind me.

"Is Jessalyn Rogers here?" Dad asks. "Your parents reported her missing, Sienna. They received a note saying she was leaving Navarre to come after you."

Sienna nods. "She's upstairs."

My dad's shoulders relax, and he swipes a hand over his face.

He looks exhausted. "Thank goodness for that. Shall we sit? I have some news for you."

Sienna's hand is still in mine, and I keep it in mine as we move towards the table, everyone settling in. My dad looks older than I've ever seen him, like he's aged a decade or more in the days since the Bonding Ceremony.

He clears his throat, and Jax jumps up, returning with a soda that my dad takes gratefully. "Thanks. It took me a few days to find you. Followed another trail."

I lean forward. "Dad, what's happening? Did you find Erikkson?"

Sienna is still and silent next to me, and I pick up a tremble in her fingers as my dad shakes his head. "There's no sign of him. I'm sorry, son. We're still trying to work out if he's crossed the wall, but that seems the most likely option. Alicia Erikkson is still in custody."

"My parents," Sienna whispers, and we all turn to her. "How are they, Councillor?"

"Please call me David." My dad smiles at her, but it's tinged with sadness. "They're very angry, Sienna. Your father wanted to come with me today, but he couldn't leave your mother."

I catch the tremble of Sienna's lip as she drops her head, and it tugs at my chest. "I understand."

Leaning forward, I draw my dad's attention. "You mentioned news."

My dad clears his throat. "I did. Through some rather complicated research by Justice Milo, we found a way to remove Erikkson from his position as Beta representative in his absence."

Jax snorts. "About damn time."

Dad gives him a chastising look. "It's caused us some issues, but it helps that Erikkson wasn't a popular beta leader. It does mean that whilst the Council does not have the authority to change the laws, we have created some… gray areas. The Trials have been suspended."

"What?" Sienna sits up straighter. "Suspended?"

Dad nods. "None of us were happy with how your Bonding experience ended, Sienna. And we're sorry for it. Ollena in particular will not countenance any future Trials going ahead until they're reviewed, and the Denied law revoked."

Sienna shrinks in her chair. My hand raises to clasp the back of her neck gently, my fingers massaging her skin. "So… I'm still Denied. I can't go home."

"Technically," my dad admits, and Gray curses. "But we seem to have found a loophole."

The tension in the room ratchets up as everyone stares at him. But my eyes move to Sienna's face, watching her expression.

"Whilst we cannot legally revoke your status until a new beta representative is appointed," my dad explains, "every citizen of Navarre is entitled to an appeals process in law. It has never been applied to the Denial process because no omega had ever been Denied, until you. But you're also entitled to it, Sienna."

I watch as Sienna's eyes fill. "She can go home?" I ask, just to make sure I'm understanding correctly.

My dad nods. "Yes. Whilst the appeals process is underway, you can return to Navarre."

My heart clenches as Sienna leans over. Her body trembles under my hands as she drops her face into her hands.

She can go home. She can see her family again.

But it might be temporary, if another vote doesn't go in her favor.

"Who will the new beta representative be?" Logan asks, his thoughts clearly following mine.

My dad shrugs. "We don't know. A few have put themselves forward, but nobody meets the eligibility requirements."

I frown. "The Herrith connection?"

When my pack looks confused, I elaborate. "It's a difficult position because the beta representative should also act as the link between Navarre and Herrith. They need to have spent time in both places to be eligible for the role."

Gray raises an eyebrow, giving me a considering look. "If only we knew someone who could be a good fit."

Pursing my lips, I nod at him but don't say anything. I had the same thought. But it's not a discussion for now, not when our Soul Bonded is curling into herself next to me, her arms wrapped around her waist as if she's physically holding herself together.

Getting up, I give my dad a nod. "We need a minute."

His brows lower. "Take all the time you need."

Not asking for permission, I bend down and lift Sienna into my arms. She doesn't push me away, burying her face in my shoulder as I carry her towards the stairs. Dampness soaks my skin as I carry her up and down the hall to her space.

I pick up on heated discussion coming through one particular door, keeping my footsteps light as I slip through into her bedroom.

Sienna is still pressed against me, so I sit down on her bed, keeping her on my lap and running my hand over her hair. "Talk to me, Bonded."

It takes her a minute, but she lifts her face to mine, tear-stained and pale. "I can go home, but I might not be able to stay."

I carefully wipe away the dampness from under her eyes. "We'll fight it."

"I can't go through that again," she whispers. "I can't, Tristan. And I don't just mean being Denied."

My ribs feel too tight against my chest as I read between the lines.

"I can't offer you proof," I say quietly. "All I can offer are words, and I know you don't have any reason to believe me. But whatever happens, we will not leave your side, Sienna. If they refuse to overturn it, then we will be leaving with you. But we can *fight* in Navarre. We can put a case forward. We can't do that here, on the other side of the wall."

My hands are tied here. I can't help her. I have to sit and watch my mate suffer from the choices I made, and it hurts to feel so powerless.

"And what about us?" she asks me, her blue eyes wide on mine. "We're not even close to figuring things out, Tristan. If we go back, that doesn't mean everything is forgiven."

"I know. You have choices now. The Trials are over."

It hurts to say it. "You don't have to come back with us if you don't want to. We can carry on working things out, even if you're with your parents."

She looks away from me. "What would you prefer?"

My fingers are firm on her chin as I turn her back to me. I want her to see that I mean every damn word of what I'm going to say.

"I want you where you belong," I say honestly. "With us. In your home, with your pack. With *me*. Where we can make new memories. Take a chance on us, Sienna. One more chance for us to prove that everything we've said here is the truth."

She sighs. "That house doesn't feel like my home, Tristan."

"Then we'll find somewhere else." She looks at me, her eyes widening. "I mean it, Sienna. If you can't settle there, then we'll look until we find somewhere that does. We could even design our own home, together."

"You would do that?" she asks, surprised. "That's your home, Tristan."

"It's not my home unless you're there with me, and the pack will agree." Drawing her hand into mine, I turn it over and press a kiss to her wrist, her pulse light as butterfly wings under my lips. "But I understand if you need space, Sienna. We'll wait until you're ready, no matter how long it takes."

She chews on her lip. "I need to think. You should go and see your dad, Tristan. You missed him."

"I did. But you're missing your dad too, Sienna. And you're my priority."

"I...," she closes her eyes. "I'm alright now. I just need to think things through."

She slides off my lap, and I reluctantly get to my feet. I don't want to leave her.

"Call me if you need me. I'll be back soon."

She starts to shake her head, but I give her a firm look. "Just to sleep. You're still recovering, and there's a lot going on." I'm not going to forget about her health in the middle of all of this.

My Bonded concedes with a small smile. "Pushy."

Leaning in, my lips brush her forehead. "It's a character flaw. Probably a fatal one."

## 35

# JAX

David looks around at us as Tristan carries Sienna upstairs. All of our attention is firmly focused on the omega that's just left, and he coughs a few times.

When I finally look at him, he tilts his head. "Things seem... a little better, with you and your omega."

"Our Soul Bonded," Gray corrects him, and David nods. "How is she?"

Our relationship with our Soul Bonded is nobody's business but our own, but the last time he saw us, Sienna was broken almost beyond repair and we were reeling from finding out our omega had been sent across the wall to face traffickers.

I give him a rundown, including the trio who've been asking around, looking for a pink-haired omega. David goes pale.

"So, it's definitely true then," he says with a sigh, leaning back in his chair. "I had hoped... but this confirms it."

I lean forward. "Denial has to be revoked, David. The omegas can't have this hanging over their heads. Do they even realize how serious it is?"

"They do now." David rubs his hand down his face. "Things are... chaotic over there, to say the least. Parents are refusing to let their omegas join the Hub, and the alpha population is demanding answers. There are a lot of rumors floating around about your pack. Most of them true, it would seem."

He glances at Gray and Logan. "News of your relationship has also spread."

Logan rolls his eyes, his arm spreading out across the back of Gray's chair. "I couldn't give a shit, to be honest. They can say what they want."

David frowns. "It's not bad. You have a lot of support, it would seem."

Gray looks surprised. "We do?"

"The Michaels family are well-known, and popular. Helena Michaels in particular has been campaigning on your behalf. It seems she wants to make sure her daughter returns to a welcoming reception, along with her pack."

That's kind of her. Unexpectedly so. My face must say so, because David lifts his eyebrows.

"I wouldn't expect that reception to be so welcoming in private," he warns. "Helena and John are furious, and rightly so. I still don't know what the hell you were all thinking."

I look down at the table. "We weren't thinking. We panicked, and we fucked up. We're working on it."

It's a reminder that if Sienna chooses to go back, we won't just need to prove ourselves to her, but to her parents and family. In fact, everyone in Navarre. We humiliated her at our first Mating Ceremony, and society doesn't forget. They whisper, and gossip, and taunt.

My fist curls. I don't want her exposed to that. I never did. But this is just one of the many consequences my Soul Bonded has to face for our choices.

I can see the same realization reflected in Logan and Gray's faces. Gray in particular looks furious, his jaw clenched.

Footsteps sound behind us, and Tristan slides back into his chair. "She's going to think about it."

If we go back, we'll be hit at every stage by judgment and whispers, and Sienna will take the brunt of it.

I'm not entirely sure I even *want* to go back. But I'll follow her lead.

I always will.

## 36

# SIENNA

I shake out my hands as I pace up and down the small space in my room. I've got my green blanket wrapped around me for comfort, but it's not providing much.

I can go home, but I might just have to leave again.

And if I go home, then the little bubble, that wall of protection that I've put up between me and the Cohen pack might just burst.

Everyone will be watching us. *Everyone* will have an opinion.

My eyes scan my surroundings, landing on the nightlight that Tristan slipped into my room. The little wooden figures that sit on my nightstand. These men are starting to slip back inside that wall, but if we leave here now, it might crumble altogether.

And I'm not sure I'm ready for that.

And then there's the secret fear that I keep hidden, pushed down so far inside my heart that the Cohen pack can't see it.

What if it happens again? What if I go back, and things just... slip back, to the way they were?

Alone. Abandoned. *Neglected.* Maybe they'll just leave me to it and go back to their lives, and I'll shrivel away in that horrible, open excuse for a nest, waiting for comfort that never comes.

The whine slips out, anxious and high, and I tug the ends of the blanket around me until it's pulled tightly across my shoulders. Taking a deep breath, I work through my options.

The traffickers are still out there looking for me. Navarre would offer more protection and they won't be able to get to me on that side of the wall. But Erikkson is out there somewhere, and we have no idea what he's planning or if he'll turn up.

Alicia is in a cell, but I have no doubt that she'll be trying everything she can to get to the pack. I saw enough of her true colors to see that she won't let go of them, especially Tristan.

My fists curl, and I keep going.

Everyone I know saw me humiliated at my Mating Ceremony. I was sheltered from it during the Trials for the most part, but I'd have to face them, their reactions and smirks. I know how this shit works. People delight in others misfortune.

We can't stay here forever, even if Emmett is happy to have us. It's not sustainable. We need a place of our own, no matter what happens with the pack. I want a home.

My throat aches, and I drop down onto the bed.

My family is in Navarre. Mama, Dad, Elise. All of us separated. But if I go back, there's no guarantee that I wouldn't have to leave again if the Council rejects my appeal.

I chew my lip. And this isn't all about me.

My feet pad on the floor as I make my way down the hall. I hear a throaty laugh as I knock on a door, and I really hope I haven't interrupted anything.

Jess only looks mildly flustered as she answers. "Are you okay?" she asks immediately. Her eyes sharpen. "What's happened?"

I wet my lips. "Tristan's dad is here," I say numbly. "We might... we might be able to go home, Jess."

I don't know what I expected, but it wasn't for her to lose the color in her face. "W-what?"

Emmett comes up behind her, his hands settling on her shoulders in an easy familiarity. My eyes meet Jess's as she closes them briefly.

*Oh, Jess.*

"I can come back," I say quickly, but she shakes her head.

"No… we need to talk about this, Si. Come in."

We take a seat on the chairs, Emmett joining us as I talk them through the conversation with Councillor – *David* Cohen. Emmett's face drops until he's almost as pale as Jess, his eyes sliding over to her.

"So… you're leaving?" he asks quietly.

It's not a question for me.

Jess pushes her hair back, her eyes dropping to her lap. "I need to think."

"Right." Emmett unfolds himself carefully from the chair. "Let me know, once you decide?"

Jess's head shoots up. "Emmett—,"

He holds his hands up. "It's okay," he says, with a quiet, sad smile that makes my throat hurt even more. "I get it."

As the door closes, I turn back to Jess. "Jess—,"

"Don't." She shakes her head so forcefully that her curls bounce everywhere. "I'll talk to him, but this is a decision for us. Maybe he gets a say. But this is our life, Si, and we have to make the right choice for us. Not for them. Right?"

I'm about to agree, but something stops me.

On one hand, Jess is right, and we absolutely do have to make the right choice for us. But our choices affect them, too.

Isn't that the point of having mates? Especially Soul Bonds. We have to talk to each other. We have to communicate, and we've been especially lousy at that part so far.

Going back won't just affect me. It'll affect them, too. Gray and Logan—

"We all need to talk, Jess," I whisper. "If he matters."

Jess looks at me, and her face crumples. "I think… I think he might. Matter."

"Okay. So we'll talk it through, and then we'll go and talk to them."

She nods. "How do you feel about it?"

I run through my pros and cons list as Jess listens, her head cocked to the side.

"All valid," she nods. "But I think the question here is… what do you want, Si? In the long run? Do you see them being part of your future?"

"They kind of have to be," I point out.

"Pssht. There are ways around that," Jess waves her hand. "But do you *want* them?"

*Do I want the Cohen pack?*

"I want the pack I know here," I say, biting my lip. "But I'm scared that we'll go back and just end up in the same cycle. Like we'll fall back into the same pattern of behavior, and it'll ruin me, Jess. It'll ruin all of us."

"Then that's the question you need to really answer," she says. "Do you trust them enough to take the chance?"

There it is. And I don't know the answer, not enough to be one hundred percent confident.

"Nothing is certain, Si," Jess says softly. "But I think they're genuine."

Wow. My eyes fly up in shock, and she laughs.

"I mean, I'm not gonna tell them that," she says, rolling her eyes. "I have far too much fun ribbing them. And I don't think they've crawled *nearly* enough yet. But I do believe they're sorry, and they've taken their heads out of their asses long enough to focus on you."

Sitting back in the chair, I blow out a breath. "I need to talk to them," I admit. "I can't… I can't make this decision on my own."

She waves her hand. "Go on. I need to find Mr. Grumpy and have a few words."

"What about you, though? Where's your head?" I ask.

She shrugs. "I mean, I don't really have a family to go back to. Only Monty. But he's getting older, and honestly, I've been helping him more than the other way around lately."

She twists her hands, worry for the old man who basically raised her after her parents died bleeding through.

And she left him for me.

"I'd say you do have family to go back to," I say quietly. "And maybe you should tell Emmett that. He could always come with us, Jess."

Her face twists in uncertainty. "I don't think he will."

"Have you asked him?"

Her mouth opens, but nothing comes out.

"Think about it," I urge, getting up. "Because I think he's somewhere up here panicking that you're gonna leave him, Jess. Go talk to him."

I need to have the first of many conversations with my pack.

37

# GRAY

Logan knocks my knee with his under the table. "What do you think? About going back?"

I hesitate. "I... I don't know, Lo."

I really don't. My thoughts are all over the place, worry about Sienna, worry about Logan, about how we fill in the deep as fuck cracks in our relationship. It's hard enough here, but with the eyes of Navarre on us?

I'm saved from answering by soft footsteps. Everyone straightens when Sienna appears, and she offers a small smile to David. "I'm sorry to interrupt, but can I have some time with my pack, please?"

*My pack.*

God, those words sound good coming from her lips.

David gets up immediately. "Of course. Is there somewhere I can rest? It was a long few days."

Tristan gets up. "We're staying out back. I'll show you."

"Thanks." He turns to Sienna. "I'm glad that you're safe, Sienna. And give them hell."

Sienna's lip twitches. "I intend to."

Tristan rolls his eyes. "Come on, old man. Before you get us into more trouble."

Sienna settles at the table. "Can we wait until Tristan gets back? I'd like us all here."

Nerves jingle in my stomach at her words, but we all wait until he comes back in a few minutes later. His hand drops to Sienna's shoulder, squeezing it gently. "Sorry."

She shakes her head. "He's your father, Tristan. No need to apologize."

Our Soul Bonded takes a deep breath, clasping her hands in front of her on the table.

"This isn't a decision I can make on my own," she says slowly. "I appreciate that given what happened, you're trying to show me that I can trust you. But if this is going to work, we need to communicate. We need to talk, and discuss things properly. I'm not the only one with an opinion, and for something like this, we need to act like the pack we're supposed to be and talk it through, *together*."

Tristan leans forward, and I can see the surprise on his face. "But you're the one who's had to suffer for decisions we made, Sienna."

She shakes her head. "Not just me, Tristan."

She locks her gaze with mine, moving over to Logan. "A decision that you should have had the freedom to make was taken out of your hands," she says softly. "That should have been your choice, and it was stolen from you."

My mouth dries, and Logan shifts in his seat. "Sienna…"

"No." Her voice is firm. "We're pack. Maybe we're not there yet, and maybe we're working through our issues, but we're all equally important, Logan. That includes your relationship."

Sienna drops her gaze to the table before she looks at me. "That day… when I saw you together. I didn't respond in the best way, and I'm sorry if I made you feel that your relationship is in any way inferior. You offered to hide who you are if it made me uncomfortable, and I hate that you felt you needed to do that."

"It was a hard day," I say, my voice hoarse. I don't have any words.

Sienna gives me a wobbly smile. "I was jealous," she admits. "I saw the two of you together, and it was so... you had so much love for each other, and I so desperately wanted to feel the same way."

There's a prickling sensation behind my eyes, and I swallow hard. I can't even look at Logan. "But we made you feel that way."

She shrugs. "You did, but not because of the two of you being together. It was everything else, and that's something we have to work through. But we *don't* need to work through your relationship, because it's not something you can work through. You're not side characters in your own damn story. I don't want you to feel like you have to hide it from us, or spring apart when I walk into a room. I think it's beautiful, Gray. And I'll tell everybody in Navarre to fuck off if they're stupid enough to not see the same. If we decide, *together*, that going back is the right thing to do."

She takes a deep breath, and I glance over at Jax and Tristan. Both of them are silent, staring at Sienna. It's Jax who looks over at us first. He looks a little lost.

"Did...," he stops, clears his throat. "Did we make you feel like that? Like it was something you needed to hide?"

Logan shifts. "It... I mean, when you found out, you were angry. I get that you were annoyed we didn't tell you, but can you understand why we didn't? And maybe we would have, if the whole thing wasn't taken out of our hands."

Jax looks dismayed. "Shit, Logan. Gray. Yeah, I get that. I guess I never really looked at it like that before. I wasn't angry because you're *together*. God, it feels fucking obvious now. You two look good together. I agree with Shortcake. Fuck anyone who doesn't think the same."

"It was me who held us back," I say quietly, and everyone turns to me. "I was scared of what people would think. Scared of the impact it would have if people reacted badly. Logan would have told you a long time ago, but I stopped him. I'm not... I'm not scared anymore. I wish it hadn't happened like that, but I'm not scared of people knowing."

Logan's hand slides onto my knee, but I grip his fingers in mine, locking us together and pulling it up onto the table.

"This is who we are," I say, a smile tugging at my mouth. "And it feels good to be able to say it out loud."

Sienna smiles when I look at her. "I'm glad for you. Both of you."

Tristan still hasn't said anything. Straightening my back, I look over at him. We've talked it over, mentioned it in the truck when we went to get Sienna's things for her room, but this is the first time we've talked about it as a pack.

It's the first time we've really talked about anything as a pack in a long time.

He swallows. "I told Gray before that I hadn't been a very good pack leader. And listening to all of you... I really haven't. Sienna is right to call us out on it."

He turns to me and Logan, pinning us with his eyes. "I'm going to say this as clearly as I can. There is nothing more important to me than you. *All* of you. This pack. And I don't give a fuck about the rest of it. You think that I care more about shit like our social status than I do you? You think I'd choose any of that over you, and you being who you're supposed to be? Family first. Always."

He moves his eyes to Sienna. "I once made the mistake of thinking that family first meant I had to choose. I know better now. We lean on each other. And I need you to call me out if that's not happening. I'm not going to magically change overnight. I don't always make the right decisions, but I'll do better."

I watch as they lock eyes. "For once, I'm starting to believe you," Sienna whispers. Then she raises her eyebrow. "Just don't fuck it up."

Jax barks out a laugh, and Logan grins. My chest feels so damn full I'm afraid to speak, so I just squeeze Logan's hand.

"So...," Logan starts, looking around at us all. "Navarre."

We all look at Sienna, and she balks. "Guys, we *just* talked about this."

"We all get a say," I force out, "but on this one, you get the first say. We'll go next."

Tristan nods. "Gray is right, Bonded. We're not going to budge on this one."

Sienna takes a deep breath. "Okay. Well. I thought about it, and I ran through the reasons why we might go back, and why we wouldn't. And – seeing as we're putting all of our cards on the table…"

She swallows, looking down. "I'm scared," she confesses. "I'm scared that it feels like we're at the beginning of something real, and if we go back now, then… it sounds stupid, but I'm scared that we'll go back, and things will be exactly the same as they were. And I don't think I could survive that a second time."

Her voice is raw as she voices her feelings to us, and it hits me straight in the middle of my chest.

"Sienna," I say, and she turns to me. I open my arms. "Come here? Please?"

Hesitantly, she gets up, moving around the table and hugging her elbows. Carefully, I tug her down until she's settled on my lap, and I relax a little at the feel of her warm weight against my chest.

"Do you think I could give this up?" I murmur in her ear. My hands stroke down her back as she fits her head under my chin, a perfect fit. "Give you up? We're not going back, sweetheart. We're moving forwards. Here, there, it makes no difference to me."

Logan cups her cheek. "We're still proving ourselves to you. Hell, we will be for a long time yet. And I can't think of a better way for us to do that than to show you just how different it will be."

Tristan leans forward. "You know my views. We'll do whatever it takes to make this work for you. And if you don't want to stay at the house, you don't have to. If you want somewhere new, we'll design something that works for all of us."

My hand clenches against Sienna's back, and I look down at her. "Do you want that?" I ask. Ideas flood into my mind, plans and dimensions and possibilities. "Because I'd love to design a home with you."

She glances up at me. "You would?"

"Hell, yes. Let's do it."

"That'll have to come later," Tristan interjects gently. "The decision we need to make is immediate, but we can start looking at it as soon as we're back."

Jax whoops. "A music room, please. One big enough for both of us to use."

Sienna bites her lip, but I can see the smile hovering. "You're incorrigible, Jax."

"Damn straight I am," he announces proudly. "I've got all sorts of ideas, shortcake. And you'll enjoy every single one of them."

Sienna flushes, her cheeks pinking and a tantalizing tendril of raspberry snaking up into my nose. Clearing her throat, she waves her hand.

"I do want to go back," she says, after a pause. "I want to see my family. I'm not so keen on the rest, but I'll take it if I have to. But I don't want to lose this. And it doesn't mean that everything is just fine and forgotten, either. We still have to work things out. Just because we're changing location doesn't make everything okay."

Her words remind me, and I dig a hand down into my pocket, jostling her slightly. Taking her hand in mine, I unfurl her fingers and place the wooden figure inside.

"For you," I murmur, dropping a kiss into her hair and taking a second to just breathe her in.

She gasps under me as she reveals the little baby fox, curled up with its tail in the air. "Oh, I love this one."

"How come you've never made me a cute wooden forest creature?" Jax leans across the table, eyeing the fox with fascination.

"Ask me nicely," I say smoothly, "and I just might."

"All right," Tristan says, but he's grinning as he looks at Sienna. "Are you sure, Bonded?"

She nods, looking up from the fox. "But I mean it," she warns, looking each of us in the eye. "I'll move back in, but I need this to move at my pace."

I swear all of our tension sucks out of the room, each of us letting out a collective breath of relief. I think we were all afraid she'd choose to leave us, to be with her parents or Jess.

This... this is good. We can work on building our pack, our family, and on getting Sienna's Denied status revoked.

Everything else isn't even a blip on the radar in comparison.

## 3 8

# SIENNA

P lacing the last of my candles into the box, I stare down at the things I've accumulated during my stay and blow out a breath.

*Here we go.*

I can't believe I'm actually going home. In a few hours, I'll see my family again. It feels a little surreal, like it might not actually happen.

My hands twist into the cotton of my top, tugging at it.

I still don't know if Jess is coming with me. Even now, I can hear Jess and Emmett's voices from down the hall, going back and forth as they debate their options.

Everything feels so... *unsettled.* I don't know what we're going to walk back into. And even though I'm making progress with my Soul Bonds, I'm still keeping them at bay. Going back into that house, into the same space where they broke me into pieces and where Alicia played her games... I don't know what that'll do to the tentative relationship we're starting to build as a pack.

It might be the making of us – or it might break us completely.

As I move to lift the final box, arms slip around my waist and gently tug me away.

"I've got this." Logan grabs the box and lifts it, and I frown at him. He's done the same with every box I've packed.

"I'm not entirely useless, you know. I can carry a box."

He shrugs, his hands full. "I know. But I want to carry them for you, Bonded. Indulge me."

I take a last look around the little room that's been my haven. It looks as empty now as it did when I arrived. The bed has been stripped, the fairy lights untangled and packed away along with the blankets and pillows, all placed carefully on the truck for me to take home. My little wooden figures from Gray are safe in my pocket, along with the notes from my pack.

Logan is watching me when I turn around, his brown eyes soft. "You okay?"

"Nervous," I force myself to admit through the dryness in my throat. "There's a lot to work out, Logan. So much that can go wrong."

"Hey, now." Logan sets the box back down and approaches me slowly, pulling me into him into my face is pressed into his chest, his heartbeat reassuringly steady in my ear. The tightness in my bones relaxes as I take greedy inhales of his scent, filling my head with fresh lemon until I'm loose against him.

"That's it," he whispers, his hand stroking over my hair. "It's going to be okay, Sienna. We're going to lean on each other, and whatever happens, we stick together."

I nod against the warmth of his shirt, my fingers tangling in the material.

Whatever happens, we stick together.

When I step back, Logan gives me a small smile. "You ready?"

Nodding, I take a final look around. It's time for the next step, whatever it may bring.

Following him downstairs, my feet come to a stop as I take in the wall we started decorating a few days ago, my head swiveling to Logan.

He grins at me. "What do you think?"

"It's amazing," I breathe, taking a step forward. Logan moves with me as I approach the mural. Hundreds of music notes spread across the wall, the backdrop to a bright, varied selection of instruments. A guitar, drums, bass, all spread out as if they're waiting for someone to come and play them. A microphone sits front and center, even the wire trailing from the stand disappearing behind the tables. It looks so *real.*

"Take a closer look," Logan coaxes, placing the box on the table. "You might have to go right up to it."

Glancing at him, I do as he says, until I'm within touching distance. Squinting, I bend down to take a closer look, and my eyes fly wide as I see it.

At first glance, the swirls of paint between the instruments look random. But they're not.

"It's me," I whisper. My fingers reach out to trace the small figure with pink hair. And then I see another. And another. Standing, kneeling, dancing, but all spread between the art that you see at first.

Logan built his whole mural around me. I see more and more as I step back, until it feels impossible that I missed it the first time. I can't stop the smile from spreading across my face as I look at him. "But we're leaving! How – when did you do this?"

"Last night." Wrapping his arm around my shoulders, he tugs me into him, resting his chin on my head. "You like it?"

"I love it," I say softly. I'm sad that we'll be leaving it behind.

Logan reads my mind. "I have many, many plans for all the art I want to create around you, Sienna. And I kind of like the idea that we're leaving a little piece of our story behind in Herrith."

I... kind of agree with him.

## 39

## JAX

As I exit the bathroom, I run straight into a pissed-off wildcat.

"Careful, asswipe," Jessalyn snaps as she bounces off me. But her words lack their usual fire, and I catch tears before her head drops.

"Hey – woah." I steady her. "You okay?"

She sniffs. "Fine. What do you care?"

"You're shortcake's best friend," I say softly. "Of course I care."

I won't forget that Jessalyn gave up her entire life to follow Sienna out here. My eyes dart to the living room door, and I catch a glimpse of a pissed-off looking Emmett. Our eyes meet, and he turns his back to me.

"You want me to talk to him?" I offer.

She looks at me askance. "Why would you do that?"

I shrug. "You want him to come back with us, yeah? Maybe he just needs someone to talk it through with. We have each other. You have Sienna. Emmett… he doesn't have anyone."

And that's the thing. We've been here a while, and I've never seen a friend, a family member. The only people we've seen here are the handful of regulars that come into the bar, and Emmett even keeps his distance from them.

Jessalyn hesitates, but her shoulders slump. "That... yes. Please. If you don't mind."

I think that's the most polite thing she's ever said to me. Nodding, I pat her shoulder. "Sienna's downstairs," I call, before I jog down the hall and push the door wider.

I clear my throat as I step into the room. "Hey."

Emmett turns, rolling his eyes. "You here to try and sell Navarre to me too?"

"Not really." Throwing myself into a chair, I look up at him. "Figured you might want someone to talk it through with, though."

He runs his hand through his hair, the curls bouncing as he sits opposite me. "She's asking me to give up everything," he says quietly. "My whole life, to move somewhere where it sounds like betas aren't all that well thought of. I moved here to get away from people, and I'd be walking right back into everything I wanted to leave behind."

Curious, I sit forward. "What made you move up here? You're not from here originally?"

He swallows. "No. Moved up a few years back. There was... an accident. My family, my partner, they were traveling for a wedding. I was working, supposed to travel down the next day. But the plane went down. Engine failure."

His face is pale, and my heart constricts in my chest. Fucking hell. I can't even imagine it.

"You lost everyone," I say quietly, and he nods.

"Few cousins left on the other side of the country, but we're not close. Everyone who mattered was on the plane. My parents, my sister, my brother, his wife and kids. And Liv—," his breath catches, and he looks down at his hands.

"When something like that happens," he says softly, "You become a commodity. Almost like public property. Everyone wants to talk to you, to say they're sorry. Empty fucking platitudes. I lasted a month before I got in the truck and just started driving. Found this place, tracked the owner down and bought it outright. It was quiet, peaceful. Exactly what I wanted."

His lip twists. "Then I found Sienna burning up in my shed. And Jessalyn followed her. You know she pointed a damn gun at me when I found her in Sienna's room?"

I bark a low laugh. "Somehow that doesn't surprise me."

Emmett shakes his head, a smile tugging at his lips. "Me neither, now."

He sighs, looking at me. "What would I even do, over there? I know so little about how your society works, Jax. I'd just be dead weight for Jess, and that's the last thing I want."

I frown. "You need to speak to Gray. There's a whole lot of stuff he was working on for the beta population… before. Stuff he could use help with. He was looking at housing, better standards, that sort of thing."

I catch a gleam of interest in Emmett's eyes, and he sits forward. "I was a builder. Before."

I raise an eyebrow. "Sounds like the last thing you'd be is dead weight to me."

Emmett blows out a breath. "I mean- can I even just do that? Cross the wall? Don't you need, like, a visa or something?"

I chew it over. "Well, we've got the current Council Leader with us, so that won't hurt. And if he's bringing someone over who could be a potential candidate for the open Beta representative position on the Council, that they've been struggling to fill… hard to argue with that one."

Emmett stares at me in horror. "Politics really aren't my thing."

Shrugging, I stand up. "Don't need to tell them that," I point out.

He follows my lead. "I need to talk to Jess. You're leaving soon, right?"

"We'll wait," I say. There's no way my Soul Bonded will be leaving Jess without knowing what her plan is, and honestly, I'm not about to drive off and leave her here either.

"Okay. Good. Thanks, Jax."

"No problem. Want me to braid your hair next?"

"Oh, fuck off."

## 40

## SIENNA

"There it is."

Tristan reaches over, placing his hand on my leg and stilling the nervous jiggling I've been doing for the entire drive. "Breathe, Bonded," he says quietly. "We're nearly home."

*Home.*

Shading my eyes with my hand, I look up, taking in the huge expanse of the wall, the sandstone shadowed in the afternoon sunlight.

It makes me flinch. Memories of the Bonding Ceremony, the sheer, blind fear and panic as I was dragged through the streets of Navarre, dumped through the gates in bare feet and a dress and nothing else.

My whine is quiet, but Tristan brakes, pulling to the side of the dirt track.

"Sienna?" Gray says my name, but I'm spiraling, my breathing speeding up. Tristan undoes my belt, lifting me over the space between us and pulling me onto his lap.

"Listen to me," he says fiercely, his hands cupping my cheeks. His thumb strokes across my skin, over and over again, and I focus my panicked eyes on him.

"Never alone, Bonded," he whispers, pressing his forehead to mine. "Never again. I swear to you."

I breathe him in, that warm, smoky scent of whiskey. "I don't think I can do it," I admit brokenly. The sight of the wall has triggered something in me, and I feel that if I take even one step towards it, I'll crumble.

"Your family is waiting for you," Tristan murmurs. "Your mother, your dad, Elise. All there, all waiting to welcome you home, Sienna."

I take a deep breath. "And I won't be alone."

I raise my eyes to his, and he shakes his head. "Never," he says quietly. "We will be with you. And if we leave, we leave together."

I nod. Together.

I climb back into my seat, Gray's hand sneaking through the gap as he sits forward in the middle seat and taking my hand. Tristan keeps his hand firmly on my leg as we pull off. Emmett pulls out behind us, he and Jess and David following as we approach the gates that will welcome us back to Navarre.

For a second, I wonder if they'll open at all, but there's a screech, the doors sliding apart enough for us to move smoothly through.

It happens in an instant, just as quickly as I went through the first time. The dark greenery of the forest gives way to paved stonework, the truck gliding smoothly to a stop in front of the group waiting for us.

As I see them, the tears I've been holding back start to spill, and I grab blindly for the doors. There's a slamming sound, and then Jax is there, his hand out as he smiles crookedly.

"Here we go, shortcake. You ready?"

With a sob, I grab his hand, allowing him to lift me out of the truck. There's a cry, and I turn away from my pack as I stumble forwards. My knees are about to give out, but I'm caught in strong, familiar arms.

"Sienna." My dad is crying, heaving sobs as he reaches me. "Sienna!"

My dad wraps his arms around me, both of us going down in a laughing, crying pile. My mama drops down next to us, her hands cupping my cheeks.

"Oh, sweetheart," she sobs. "There you are."

Elise is burrowing under my arm, and I'm surrounded in so much love and emotion I can barely breathe for feeling it.

"I'm sorry," I gasp. "I'm so sorry – mama—,"

"Don't be silly," she breathes. Her hand smooths back my hair shakily. "You have nothing to apologize for, baby. *Nothing*."

I pull back, wiping my eyes as I look behind me. Emmett and Jess are out of the truck, and Jess has her arms wrapped around Monty. Tall and impeccably dressed as always in his suit, the butler closes his arms around her gently, but I catch him giving Emmett the side-eye, and I snort out a teary laugh as my pack comes to stand behind me.

My father helps me up, his hand staying in mine and his mouth turning down as he turns to Tristan.

"Sir." Tristan nods respectfully, his eyes sliding to me.

This feels… a little awkward. My dad's hand tightens in mine, before he turns away, dismissing Tristan completely.

"Come on, sweetheart. We're taking you home."

*Wait. What?*

I dig my feet in, pulling gently on my dad's hand. "Dad… I have a house."

It's not a home, not yet, and maybe it never will be. But I'll never resolve things with my pack if we're on opposite sides of the city.

My dad's mouth firms, but my mama interjects, her hand laying on his arm as she gives him a look. "We talked about this," she reminds him. "Sienna needs to be with her Soul Bonded, John."

My dad gives Tristan a look filled with utter contempt. "They are *not* her Soul Bonded. They nearly killed her!"

I flinch, and Tristan takes a step towards me. "Mr. Michaels," he says quickly, lifting his hands up as he moves closer. "I know that I can likely never make up for what has happened, but we are committed to giving Sienna everything – and more – that we should have from the day we met."

My dad looks furious. "I don't like you," he says plainly, looking around at the rest of my pack. "Any of you. If it's Sienna's choice, then I will respect it. But you better remember that the Trials are over now. So I will be making regular checks on my daughter's welfare, and if I find a single hair out of place, I will end you. Tell me that you understand that, Cohen."

"You wouldn't have to, Sir," Tristan says, but his eyes are on mine. "We'd end ourselves before we let any further harm come to Sienna."

Dad humphs, but he steers me a little way away from the pack. My mother follows us before his hands move to my shoulders. His eyes still look damp.

"Tell me they're treating you right," he says brokenly. "Sienna – when we last saw you – I know I can't interfere. But it kills me that they let that happen to you."

Wrapping my hands around his waist, I sink into him just the same as I did when I was a little girl, and it's just as comforting now as it was then. "I'm alright, Dad. We're working it out. And they're not forgiven, not yet. We're just… a work in progress. But I can't come home right now."

"I don't like it," he grumps, and my lips pull into a smile at the familiar tone. "But I don't have much of a choice, I know."

Cupping his cheek, I smile. "I'll come and see you."

"You'd better," he warns, taking a step back and letting my mother in. She pulls me into her arms, her grip fierce as she hugs me.

"I cannot imagine what you have been through, sweetheart," she says, letting me go and wiping her eyes. "But I can see that it's changed you. And not just on the outside."

My mother is possibly the only person who could truly understand, and my eyes grow damp again.

"It was so hard," I tell her, keeping my voice to a whisper so my dad doesn't hear. "And it hurt so much, mama."

Her hand traces my cheek. "We'll talk about it," she promises. "Do you need the Healer's Center?"

"I don't think so. Not now."

I should probably go and get myself checked out, but I do feel much better. I give my family another hug, breathing them in, before I move over to my pack. They're waiting patiently, Tristan's eyes soft as I stop next to him.

"Do you want to go back with them?" he asks. "We can take you, or wait for you, if you want more time."

"No." My mind is made up. "I'd like to go back to the house."

I need space to think, to get my head straight and to work through everything that's happened. And as much as I love them, I can't do that with my family around. Turning, I look for Jess, but she's already making her way over to me, Emmett following behind her.

"Everything okay?" I ask her, and she grins.

"Yeah. We're going to head back now, but we'll check in tomorrow, see how things are going."

Jess turns around to face my pack, giving them a very clear warning look. "Just because I'm not there, doesn't mean I'm not watching you *very* closely, Cohumps. You've managed to scrape back about half an inch of kudos, but you have a long, looooong way to go."

"Noted." Tristan grins at her. "You need anything from us, you know where we are."

Jess humphs, but I catch the small smile on her face as she hugs me. "Call me anytime," she mumbles into my neck. "I don't know how the hell this is gonna work, but I guess we'll find out."

I wave at Emmett, and he nods at me. "You sure you're okay?" he asks, tilting his head. "Because you can come with us."

Smiling, I shake my head. "We have things to sort out," I say, glancing at Tristan when he comes to stand next to me. "But I'll see you both soon. And, Emmett... thank you."

He nods, but his eyes are already focused on Jess, who's whispering something to Jax that's making him go very, *very* pale. "Pretty sure I'm the one who might need to thank you, Sienna."

My pack all look to me as Jess and Emmett make their way back to Monty. "You ready, sweetheart?" Gray asks.

Looking around, I take a deep breath. "I am."

Let's do this.

It's a good forty-minute ride to the house, and we're all quiet, lost in our own thoughts, but it's not an uncomfortable silence. Not with Tristan's hand reassuringly heavy on my leg, Gray's fingers tangled with mine. Jax's hands play with my hair as he whistles, twisting and tugging the strands.

*I'm not alone.*

When we pull through the gates, Tristan frowns. "We need a security system sorted as soon as possible. Today, preferably."

"I'll make some calls," Gray offers. "I don't want any more unexpected visitors."

Definitely not. There's sounds of agreement from everyone as Tristan turns off the engine. As I get out, I take in the pale, majestic stonework, the wide-set windows. It's still a beautiful house. Everything that made excitement curl inside me the first time I saw it, even after the initial hell of the Mating Ceremony.

I was so *hopeful.*

I'm still studying it when my feet leave the ground in a sudden rush, and I squeal. Jax grins down at me as he holds me tightly.

"What are you doing?" I ask him breathlessly.

"Carrying you over the threshold," he says, gravity entering his eyes as he looks down at me. "I want to do this right, shortcake. Right from the start. And that means you get carried inside."

Tristan, Logan and Gray follow us as Jax carries me, Gray jogging past us to unlock the doors.

"Welcome home, Sienna," he murmurs as we pass him, his blue eyes bright on mine.

Home.

I look around, taking in the bare walls and floors. "It feels like it should look different, somehow," I note. Everything else feels different, but the house feels the same. Like it's been holding its breath, waiting for us to come back.

Tristan comes in with a stack of boxes in his arms as Jax lowers me carefully to the floor, keeping my back against his chest and shamelessly wrapping his arms around my waist so I can't move. "Did you ever wonder why the walls were so bare?"

I tap on Jax's arm, but it doesn't budge, so I resign myself to staying where I am for a little while.

*Oh, the hardship.*

Frowning, I look at Tristan. "I did. I asked Logan once, actually."

And he was rude as hell about it, too.

Logan's cheeks tint a dark red as he comes to stand next to me. "We left it that way on purpose," he admits. "We wanted our mate to be able to decorate it the way she wanted."

He smiles at me. "So we have plenty of space to create more art, like we did in Herrith."

I bite my lip, not wanting to let on how much I like that idea. I spent a long time poring over coursework during my training at the Hub, creating my dream home through fabric and paint. I can already see some of the tweaks I'd like to make, but I hold the words back on my tongue.

Not yet. Not until I'm sure I'm staying.

And I'm not even talking about the Denied appeal.

Jax nuzzles into my hair, and I bat him away, twisting out of his hold half-heartedly. "Jax."

"Shortcake," he rumbles. "Are you gonna keep the brunette look? Because I'd love whatever color your hair was, but I'm especially partial to the pink."

173

My hand jumps to my hair. I can take the brown out now. God, I miss my hair.

Pursing my lips, I tap them with my finger. "I actually quite like the idea of experimenting," I say casually. Moving over to the mirror, I tweak some of the strands, pulling them down as I watch the pack's reactions from the corner of my eye. All of them turn towards me, Tristan stopping mid crouch to put down a box as their eyes follow my movements.

"I kind of feel ready for something more adventurous. There was this really pretty shade of lime in the box Jess got me. I think I might try it out." Spinning, I tilt my head at them. "What do you think?"

All four of them gawp at me. Jax's eyes bulge.

"Shortcake…" he says pleadingly.

"You don't like the idea?" I drop my mouth into a truly omega-worthy pout.

Tristan gives Jax a *shutthefuckup* look as he stands up. "You'll look beautiful with any shade of hair," he says weakly. "Even lime. It'll be…bright?"

I beam at him. "*So* bright. Almost reflective."

Jax lets out a tiny moan, and I can't hold back my snort. Tristan's eyes narrow as I clap my hands over my mouth.

"No lime," he guesses, tilting his head to the side. When I shake my head, still trying to hold back the laughter, he growls.

"*Tease*, Sienna Michaels."

"Wait," Jax gasps. "So you're not dying your hair green?"

"Not right now." I point my finger at him. "But it's my hair, so if I ever decide to go down the neon route, you will love it. Get me?"

He nods, relief passing over his face. "Oh, thank god for that. I mean, we would have clashed, shortcake. But, you know, whatever you want."

Logan shakes his head as he walks past, more boxes in his hands. "Sienna? I'm going to put these things in your room, okay? For now, at least, until we sort your nest out."

I frown, looking around. "But I have a nest. In that room, right?"

God, I hate that room.

Tristan steps closer to me as he swallows. "Actually... there is a nesting space here. Especially designed for an omega. It's never been touched."

It takes a minute for the words to sink in.

*Wow.*

"So," I say, trying to hold back the hurt in my voice, "you let me do all of that work, but you already had a nest sorted out?"

Tristan tries to grab my hand, but I pull it away. He is not getting out of this one with sweet words.

"It was part of the terms from Alicia," he says quietly. "That room was the only one she would accept."

"Because it was shitty, and full of dirt and broken boxes and rubbish. I nearly *died* cutting my leg open in that room, Tristan!"

He opens his mouth, but I can't even look at him right now, the anger coursing through me enough that I'm not sure I won't say something I'm going to regret. So I spin, stomping towards Logan and taking the box from him.

"Where?" I ask him tightly. He winces. "There's a door – in the bedroom you stayed in at the end. That whole space is yours, Sienna."

Fabulous. Keeping hold of the box, I stride away from them, up the hall.

Pounding footsteps race after me, all them tumbling over each other as I take the first few stairs. Tristan holds his hands up.

"Sienna. I—,"

"If you say you're sorry," I grit out. "I will scream, Tristan. Very loudly. *I get it.* I know you're sorry. But I'm still allowed to be massively *fucked off* that I worked my ass off, for *days, injuring myself,* in a room that is *not* right for a nest, all for you to tell me that *you had the perfect damn space all along.*"

Tristan's mouth snaps shut. "What can I do?" he asks me instead. Smart alpha.

"Bring the rest of the boxes up, please," I say with a sigh. "And leave them outside my door. I have a nest to build."

Nests aren't just a nice to have for omegas. They're essential. A safe, warm, cozy space for us to curl up in. And right now, I really, *really* need a decent nest.

41

# LOGAN

We wait until the door slams shut upstairs.

"Shit," Gray says, dismayed, and I can't disagree with him.

"This wasn't going to be easy," Tristan says, looking at us. "We've got a lot to work through, and she's right to be furious."

I don't respond, thinking it over.

"We're back in Navarre now," I say to Tristan. "We can get her more for her nest. Everything and anything she might need."

The Artist's Quarter is full of shops with various trinkets and soft furnishings. All tailor-made, all perfect for an omega who needs pretty things to feel comfortable.

"I'll go," I say quickly, already mapping the Quarter in my mind.

"I'll come with you," Gray offers, and I nod.

"Good." Tristan looks around. "We'll get this place cleaned up and some food sorted out."

We have a plan.

Gray is quiet as we get into the truck and I pull out, merging onto the highway and heading back towards the city.

"You okay?" I ask, and he sighs.

"I'm just wondering if this is the best idea. We know a lot of people down here, Lo. Word will have gotten around."

A pit opens up in my stomach. Of course. Word about mine and Gray's relationship will no doubt have spread by now. But resolve follows quickly.

"Fuck them all, remember?" I remind him. "We have nothing to be ashamed of."

He nods, but he's still quiet as we park up. The Quarter stretches out in front of us, jeweled lanes decorated with beautiful lights, coloured scarves and various other materials that make it almost glitter in the light. The people are just as bright, artists and musicians and creators all mixing together in perfect chaos, calling and shouting and laughing.

It never fails to take my breath away.

"We need to bring Sienna here," I say to Gray. I want to show her my studio, my work.

We start walking through slowly, and people start looking towards us. We're familiar faces, not just here in the Quarter but across Navarre, thanks to the notoriety of our pack, and it doesn't take long for someone to call out.

"Logan Cohen," drawls a rich voice. "As I live and breathe."

Grinning, I grab Gray's hand and tow him over to where Maureen is sitting outside her shop. The older woman is decked out in so much color she stands out like a firefly, even amongst the vibrancy of our background.

She purses her lips, blowing a ring of smoke from the pipe she always carries. "Thought it was you," she rasps. "Heard you left Navarre."

"I did," I say, pulling Gray until he stands next to me. "But now I'm back."

"I can see that." Maureen leans forward, her eyes flicking to Gray. "He yours? Looks like he's got a stick shoved up his ass. Handsome though."

Gray chokes. "I do not look like I have a stick shoved up my ass!"

"Ignore him," I say, giving her a wink. "He's nervous."

"Logan."

"Nothin' to be nervous about down here," Maureen says, eyeing him. "What're you here for, Lo?"

"I need to kit out an omega's nest," I say, spreading my hands and giving her a pleading look. "This is just to get her started, but I'll bring her down at some point."

Maureen tsks, getting to her feet and disappearing inside her shop. We wait, listening to the clinking and low curses before she emerges with something in her hand.

She presses it into my palm, and I look down at the perfectly crafted stained-glass star. Each point is a different color.

"That's beautiful," Gray says over my shoulder, and I smile at Maureen.

"That's because Maureen is the best stained-glass artist in Navarre. How much do I owe you?"

She waves her hand. "No charge. Bring your omega, Cohens. I'd like to meet the girl who's Soul Bonded to the Cohen pack."

Nodding, I carefully pocket the gift. "We will. Thanks, Maureen."

We continue on down the Quarter lane, and I keep Gray's hand locked tightly in mine. We get a few looks, but more and more people keep calling us over, word spreading that we're in the quarter and on the hunt for omega nesting materials.

We stagger back to the car with our arms full of bags and materials, and a few additional gifts for Sienna. My chest feels full as I glance behind me. Gray isn't looking at me, his face turned back to the Quarter.

"They were… happy," he says wonderingly. "For us."

Smiling, I add my packages to the back seat. "Maybe we're not the only ones scared of telling people who we really are, Gray. Maybe it only takes a voice to speak out."

I'm not kidding myself that everyone will be like that. But that's humanity. We'll focus on the good, and fuck the bad.

Meanwhile, we've got more than enough to hopefully tempt our Bonded.

## 42

## SIENNA

My temper flares the longer I sit on my bed, staring at the sneaky little door that apparently leads to my nest.

*Morons. Absolute morons.*

And sure, maybe they're doing their best to make it up to me, but damn it, I'm allowed to have a little moment over the fact that a perfectly functional nest space has been here this *entire fucking time.*

With a final disgruntled sniff, I shuffle off the bed and pad over to the door. The knob opens smoothly under my grip, and I step inside.

Pursing my lips, I look around.

*Well.*

This is... nice. More than nice, if I'm being honest. And that only irritates me more.

Because this nest is everything I would have chosen for myself.

Two steps in front of me lead down into a sunken space. It's split, with rustic wooden floorboards covering one half, shelving and various little cupboards built into the walls for storage. The other half is a giant, soft-looking mattress. The walls are painted a soft cream, matching the rest of the house, and there's paneling across the walls that bounces under my fingertips. Soundproof.

I swallow. Well, there's more than enough room for all of us. If I ever forgive them enough to invite them in, that is.

Slipping off my shoes, I venture onto the mattress, bouncing lightly and then collapsing down into a heap, spreading my arms and legs out to make a nest angel.

This is officially the most comfortable thing I have ever laid on. Is it made of feathers? Cloud? The hair of baby angels?

I don't know, but it's more of a struggle than I'd like to admit to get up and go back into my room. When I pull my door open, Tristan is setting down the last of the boxes outside.

"Can I help you carry these in?" he asks, standing upright.

Crossing my arms, I lift my nose in the air. "No, thank you. No traitors beyond this point."

His brows dip. "Bonded."

"Oh, no," I warn as he takes a step towards me. "No pulling that dark-eyed look on me, Tristan. I am really pissed off with you."

"I know," he says, stopping and crossing his arms. "And we deserve every bit of it. What dark-eyed look?"

I refuse to blush. "You know. That look. Where you look all angry and growly."

He raises one eyebrow. "And... you like that?"

*Why do I suddenly feel like this conversation has flipped on its head?*

"This isn't about me," I sputter. "This is about you."

Tristan smiles slowly. "Oh, I disagree."

I take a step back, plastering myself against the wall as he stalks closer. He stops a hair's-breadth from my mouth. "This is very much about you, Bonded," he breathes. "And how we can make it up to you."

My brain seems to have stopped functioning, instead choosing to focus on the way his shirt is open, showing me a smooth, tanned expanse of neck. I swallow, hard.

"Make it up to me?"

Pretty sure those words made no sense whatsoever. I jump when Tristan's hands come up, landing on either side of my head as he leans in even further. "I've had a lot of time to think about all of the ways we can make things up to you."

"What ways?" I ask, too busy staring at his mouth to notice his hands creeping down, until my hands are secured. Tristan lifts my arms slowly until I'm held in place, one hand gripping my wrists and making my body push out, brushing against him.

My lips open, but he bypasses them completely, pressing his lips to my cheek and following a loose trail down to my neck. An embarrassingly squeaky noise slips out of my mouth when he nibbles my skin, soothing the scratch of his bite with a lazy, open-mouthed kiss. "Tristan!"

I am angry at him. Furious.

But this is... this is fun.

He groans into my neck. "You taste like heaven, Bonded. Do you taste the same everywhere else?"

*Oooh.* I press my legs together, but it's not enough to stop him picking up the flare of my scent. He pulls back, meeting my eyes and licking his lips.

*Sweet baby mother of God.*

I'm almost panting, my breaths dropping into the silence as Tristan keeps me there, my body pushed out for him like an offering.

His other hand lifts, cupping my throat in a gently possessive hold.

"So many ideas," he muses. "And all of them work out very, very well for you, Bonded."

Sneaky, domineering alpha. He knows exactly what he's doing.

My eyelashes flutter as I spread my legs a little wider and *push* into him. We both groan as I feel the undeniable thickness of his cock, pressing into the thin cotton of my underwear.

His fingers tighten at my neck. "Sienna."

Shamelessly, I rub against him, watching the black of his

pupils swallow up the unusual coloring of his eyes. "What would you do to me, *Bonded*?" I whisper. His eyes snap to mine.

"Say it again," he demands.

I lean forward. "*Make me.*"

My challenge backfires spectacularly.

With a snarl, he pulls my face into him, our mouths meeting in a heated tangle of frustration and need. His hands slip down to my thighs and he hoists me up, the shirt I'm wearing as a dress riding up and giving him full access to sink his fingers into my bare thighs.

My head bangs against the wall as he thrusts against me, his thick cock hitting just enough to make my eyes cross. "Tristan!"

"Say it," he growls. He does something with his hips, swiveling them and making me cry out as he captures my mouth again in a quick, brutal kiss. "Say it, Bonded."

When I shake my head, he pushes into me again, grinding himself against me until we're both soaked in my fluids. I gasp into his mouth as he surges forward, again and again, my hands yanking his shirt up and clawing at his back.

"Damn you," I snap when he pulls back. "Damn you, Tristan."

He thrusts again, turning my anger into a whimper. "A lifetime, Bonded," he swears. "A lifetime to make it up to you."

My pussy clenches around nothing as I press my face into his neck, biting down hard and making him swear. "Say it," he threatens, "or I stop."

"You do that," I snarl into his skin, "and you will *never* come into my nest, Tristan."

He spreads his legs against the wall, giving me a perch to rest on as one arm slips behind my back, holding me upright. His other skitters along the soft skin of my thigh, moving upwards as he watches me.

"What if I play with this pretty pussy?" he presses. His finger traces over the soaked cotton, and I press my lips together. "Pinch that little button until you come around my hand, Bonded?"

"Try it and see," I croak. "I dare you."

His hand plunges into my underwear, his whole palm cupping me and making me bolt upright. "Tristan."

"You'll learn, Bonded," he says slowly. He rotates his palm against me, my clit pressing against the slightly textured skin. "I'll never turn down a dare, especially when it comes to you."

My hips pump. "Use your fingers."

It's a plea, not a demand, and the sneaky bastard knows it. He lightens his touch instead, making me whimper as he presses a hot kiss under my chin. "Say it, Sienna."

Fine.

*Fine.*

I bury my face in his neck again. "Bonded."

"What was that?"

I growl. "Fuck me with your hand, *Bonded*, or I'll go inside that room and make you listen to me get myself off."

He presses his mouth against mine. "It won't feel anywhere near as good as this."

And then his fingers are thrusting inside me, two, then three, scissoring and stretching me as I ride his hand. He soaks up my cries with his lips, drinking them down and demanding more as his hand thrusts into me over and over again until I crest, my body shaking as my release sweeps over me in a fucking wave. Tristan holds me tightly, his hand slowing to a gentle caress until my bones go limp against him, and he presses a kiss to my damp hair.

"I hate you," I grumble weakly, my face pressed against him. "Using orgasms against an omega is like… catnip. 'S not fair."

He laughs hoarsely, his hands stroking up and down my heated skin. "I'm not playing for the experience here, Bonded. I'm playing to *win*. And I'll use every weapon I have to make you see exactly what I am."

"And what is that?" I let my eyes close as I rest against his chest. Just for a moment.

"Yours."

43

# TRISTAN

Sienna lists against my chest, her face rubbing against my shirt, as I carry her into the bathroom.

I'm being greedy. I should let her go back to her room. I've taken enough of her time tonight. But I can't bear to let her go just yet, not with the feel of her riding my hand still fresh in my mind, the rich, heady scent of her arousal soaked into my nose.

She stirs as I lean down, flicking the faucets on. "What are you doing?"

"Running you a bath."

She yawns, covering her mouth with her hand as I perch us on the edge of the tub, reaching for bubbles and pouring a generous dollop in. "Anyone ever tell you you're really pushy?"

"Frequently," I admit. I look down into her face. "Is it too much? Do you want to go back to your room?"

"Now he asks," she mutters, but her lips tilt upwards. "I'll allow it. I'm not going to turn down a bath after weeks of showers."

"You prefer baths?" I want to know every single little thing there is to know about her.

"Mmmm." She stretches in my hold, the neckline of her shirt slipping down to reveal the perfect curve of her breast. My mouth dries. That small glimpse of her, her face wrecked with pleasure, wasn't nearly enough.

No matter how much I get of Sienna Michaels, it will never be enough.

When the bath is full, I set her down with regret. "I'll leave you to it."

She purses her lips. "No, you won't."

I pause. She points at the chair in the corner, her lips tilting into a grin that's definitely giving me thoughts. Many, many thoughts.

"You can sit there," she almost purrs. Her hands drop to the hem of her shirt. "And *watch*. Consider it your punishment for trying to edge me. Amongst other things."

I shake my head as I head to the chair and plant myself in it. "I was not edging you. You'd absolutely know it if I was."

Her eyes gleam in what I think might be interest, but my attention is drawn down as she grasps the hem of her shirt and pulls it off in one smooth motion.

My mouth dries as she stands before me, dressed in nothing but the thin black cotton panties I dipped my fingers into earlier.

My hands clench on the arms of the chair as she yanks her hair out of its messy bun. The brown tendrils scatter around her body, framing her still too-thin rib cage and the perfect, dusky-pink nipples that stand out in the cool air.

She spreads her arms out mockingly. "Well? Am I enough for you, Tristan Cohen?"

My chest hurts at the slightly mocking tone to her words. "You have always been more than enough. You're perfect."

Sienna sniffs, but her cheeks darken as she turns. She glances over her shoulder at me as her fingers hook into her underwear. I can't breathe as she drags them down her legs, bending over to give me the barest glimpse of dewy, pink softness.

"Bonded." My voice is dark. "If this is a punishment, sign me up for another round."

But it's punishment nonetheless. She's made it clear that I can't touch, only watch. And it's heaven and hell combined as my eyes track her, watch her extend a perfect, pale leg and climb into the bathtub. Sienna settles back until the bubbles cover her from my gaze, her toes poking out at the end closest to me.

She grins, and it's endearing as hell. "Feeling suitably chastened, Bonded?"

God, but it does things to me when she uses that word. The air thickens, and Sienna licks her lips as our scents grow stronger in the enclosed space.

I can't take my eyes from her as she takes a sponge, sniffing my body gel before squirting it until it lathers up. She cleans herself thoroughly, leisurely, with slow strokes that drive me closer to the edge.

"How's the view?" she asks conversationally.

"Stunning," I say honestly. "I'd endure the seventh circle of hell to come over there right now."

She quirks her eyebrow. "Stay where you are, and take your punishment like a good boy."

Her hands slide down, and I hold my breath as she cups her breasts, massaging them, pushing them up so I can see clearly through the bubbles I put into the tub.

Safe to say I'm greatly regretting that decision right now.

Even more so when her hands slip down, and her legs hook over the edges of the porcelain tub until she's spread open in the water, her eyes lazy and taunting on mine as she touches herself.

I sit forward, and I'm pretty sure I hear a crack in the wood my hands are gripping. "Move the bubbles."

She purses her lips. "No."

Her voice is breathy, and her eyes close as she tips her head back, her mouth falling open.

My cock is bursting inside my jeans, my knot swollen as hell.

*This* is punishment. I feel like I'm dying as I watch my Soul Bonded take her pleasure in front of me, unable to touch, to *taste*.

When she moans, I can't take it anymore. I'm on my feet in a second, and her eyes flutter open. "Sit down."

I take a step. "I want a taste."

She shakes her head, her hands still moving under the water. "This isn't for you."

Lie. I can taste it in the way she watches me, punishes me with the distance between us.

Two can play that game.

Her eyes widen when my hand moves to the button on my jeans. "Tristan."

I cock an eyebrow at her as I flick the button open. "Yes, Bonded?"

Sienna bites her lip as I draw the zipper down, slowly.

I'm not wearing any underwear.

My cock jumps when I pull it out, straining towards the omega tormenting me in the tub. "See this?" I give it a pump, the head already swollen. "This is all for you, Sienna."

Her breathing speeds up as she watches me, her eyes focused on my hand moving up and down as her fingers keep moving.

"You'll look so perfect, stuffed with my cock." It's a struggle to keep my voice even, my eyes fixed on her movements. "I can't wait to see how you writhe on it, Bonded. How you look when I fill you up with my cum."

Her toes curl, one hand moving to grip the side of the tub. "You're not playing fair," she groans.

"I told you, I'm playing to win. And I'll know I've won when I have you pinned underneath me, begging to come, those pretty pink nipples standing up for my teeth to sink into."

Her head bangs back against the edge, her hands moving faster. "More."

"I want you to present for me," I murmur. "Show me that perfect little cunt, empty and needy, holding yourself open. I'm going to sink my cock in, one inch at a time, until you're impaled on me, Bonded. Until I'm so deep inside you that you can't breathe for feeling me."

Her cry is fireworks in my veins, the pressure building up as I jerk, my cock threatening to explode.

"Up," I demand. "Lift yourself up, Bonded. I want to finish on you, so you can see exactly what your little show has done. Show me that pussy."

Her eyes almost drugged with pleasure, she pushes down with her legs until her body rises out of the water, her pussy puffy and swollen from her efforts.

My cum erupts from me in hot, thick pulses that land on her as she screams her own release. I vowed not to touch, but I can't fucking resist her, dropping to my knees and leaning in to rub myself into her skin, feeling her flutter under my fingers as she pants.

"Look what you do to me, Bonded."

Taking some of my release, I push it up inside her with two fingers, and her back arches. "*Tristan*."

It doesn't mean anything. She can't get pregnant unless she's in heat. But fuck, something primal inside me fucking *loves* the sight of my release pushing inside her, feeling her greedy pussy suck it from my fingers. I keep my fingers where they are, smoothing myself over her clit and into her skin until her hands reach for my wrist, weak and shaking. "No more," she begs. "It's too much."

I don't let her get out until I've cleaned her up, and then I lift her shaking body from the tub, drying her carefully with a towel and bundling her up in my robe. It swallows her, and I fold the sleeves up as she looks down, biting her lip.

I tug it free with my hand. "Don't be shy, Bonded," I whisper. "You were perfect."

She's perfect. So much so that the strength of feeling in my chest is almost a shock as I carry her into my room, lifting my covers and settling her into my bed.

She looks around. "What about—,"

"Stay here tonight. Please." I need her here, with me. Need to see her in my robe, in my sheets. Tonight was a lot, and I'm not letting her sleep alone.

Fuck, I always knew I'd be a possessive bastard, but this?

I can't let her go tonight, and I'm praying she doesn't ask me.

I pull on a pair of sweatpants before I climb under the covers. Sienna stiffens when I wrap my arm around her and draw her in, tucking her almost beneath me.

I swallow. "If you need to go, tell me now." I say quietly. "But I'd like to hold you tonight."

She softens around me until we're nestled together, my knee pushed between her legs and her head pillowed on my arm. "Just sleep?"

I push back some of the still-damp tendrils of hair from her forehead. "Just sleep. You still need to rest."

I breathe her in, long after her breathing deepens, her eyes closing.

I don't want to miss a single moment.

## 44

# SIENNA

It's the heat that wakes me, my eyes fluttering, still half full with sleep as I blink hazily.

It takes me a half-second of blinking at the unfamiliar ceiling before the memories slam into me. Tristan. The hallway. The *bath*.

Oh my god. I can feel the heat coming from my cheeks. I can't believe I did that.

Also, why the hell is it so *warm*?

I soon work it out when I glance down.

*I appear to have acquired a new blanket.*

Tristan is half draped across me, his leg pushed between mine and his hand cupping my breast, his arm half buried beneath his blue robe. I'm still buried in the thick material, and it's cozy and comfortable, but a bit much with the sun peeking through his drapes.

I give an experimental wriggle, and Tristan lets out a complaining noise. His hand squeezes me before he rolls over, taking me with him.

I land on top of him with an undignified squeak, and his eyes crack open.

"Good morning, Bonded."

"Ah – morning." I go to get up, but his arms lock around me.

"Don't leave," he whispers. "Stay with me."

The soft, sleepy words make me blink, my panic dissipating.

Why am I panicking? He's my Soul Bonded.

But I'm also really, really hot.

"Just a second!" I roll off before he can catch me, frantically untying the robe and tugging it off before I crawl back, gingerly curling up next to him. His arm wraps around me, and his body stills as he registers my lack of clothing.

"I was hot," I mumble into his side. He doesn't say anything, but his hand strokes down my bare back, long, sweeping strokes as he pets me.

I unashamedly stretch into his touch, hooking my leg around his as I wriggle to give him full access to my skin. It feels good.

There's a smile in his voice. "Little cat. You like being stroked."

The words bring back full, vivid memories of the night before, and I chew on my lip. Tristan pauses in his petting.

"Bonded. You're thinking very loudly."

Reaching out, I poke the center of his chest. A green eye cracks open. "Do you regret it?"

The words are soft, but I can feel the sudden tension in his body, the hitch in his breath.

I can't lie to him. "No. I don't regret it. Do… do you?"

He moves, and I find myself on my back, staring up into the face of a rumpled, sleepy Tristan. It's a dangerously addictive sight.

"I have plenty of regrets," he says, staring into my eyes. "but what we did last night isn't one of them."

I blow out a breath. "That's… that's good."

He leans down and rubs his nose against mine, drawing a reluctant smile. "I don't know how to do this," I admit.

I don't know how to do soft, sleepy mornings and gentle words. Maybe I would have, once. Maybe it would have been instinctive. But now my instincts keep telling me that this can't last.

"Nothing this good ever lasts," I murmur, and Tristan's eyes squeeze closed.

"Maybe it doesn't last," he whispers back, "because it gets better."

God, I hope so. I like this. Tristan dips his head, and my brief moment of morning breath-induced panic disappears as he presses a gentle kiss to my lips.

And my stomach makes a sound akin to the death rattle of a bear.

Maybe. But it's really loud, and Tristan's eyes widen. "We didn't feed you last night," he groans, and rolls off me, getting out of bed. "You need food, Bonded."

I shrug, stretching out in the warm sheets. "I'm quite satisfied with how my evening turned out."

Tristan grabs my hand, tugging me up. "And to have more nights like that, you need energy."

Come to think of it, I am pretty hungry.

I steal one of his shirts, sneakily inhaling the smoky scent he's left behind as we head downstairs. The rest of the pack are in the kitchen, Logan setting out plates.

His eyes grow wide as saucers as they move between me and Tristan.

"Morning!" he says brightly. Jax looks up from his coffee, a grin spreading across his face. Gray is frozen by the coffee, his eyes dropping down to my bare legs.

"Stop it," Tristan levels Jax with a glare, and he raises his hands with a smirk.

"I didn't say a thing. Shortcake, you look *ravishing* this morning."

Rolling my eyes, I move over to where Gray is standing. I remember this steel monstrosity. One of my many nemeses during the Trials.

Gray smiles when I scowl at it. "It looks worse than it is. I'll show you how to use it, but I'll make you a cup."

I give him a grateful smile. "Thank you."

His hand brushes my cheek as he moves around, taking a cup from the cupboard and pressing a whole load of buttons on the machine. I'm reserving judgment. It sure as hell doesn't look simple to me.

Sliding into a seat next to Jax, I jump when he leans in, pressing a kiss to my cheek. "Mornin', baby."

Wow. There's a whole lot of positivity floating around this morning. Logan beams at me as he sets down a plate. "You hungry? We have fruit, yogurt, cereal..."

In other words, everything that doesn't require cooking.

"What about... um. Pancakes?" I ask, tucking my hair behind my ear. "I could make them. If you want."

Jax groans. "Pancakes. Yes, please."

Everyone makes noises of agreement, and Gray slides a cup of coffee in front of me, the steam rising up. "Milk? Sugar?"

I shake my head, taking a sip of the hot liquid. "This is perfect."

Logan slips out of the room as I start to pull everything together, Gray and Jax helping me find the ingredients I need as I whisk up the batter. Gray adds some bacon to the grill, the scent permeating the kitchen as I split the mix in two and add some blueberries.

Tristan comes to stand next to me as I pour the hot mix onto the griddle, concentrating on getting perfect circles.

"Pancakes." He grins. "I haven't had pancakes for years. My mom used to make them for me when I was sick."

I vaguely remember his mom from the Bonding Ceremony. "She was a good mom?"

"The best," he says softly. "You'll like her, I think. I haven't spoken to her for a while."

I pick up the context. "She's not happy with you."

He shakes his head. "About as happy as I am with myself," he says quietly.

Flipping the pancakes, I almost dance when they come out a perfect golden brown, and Jax laughs. "You like this."

"I do." I shrug. "I'm not ashamed of being an omega. I love cooking for people. Housekeeping in general, really."

*Taking care of people.*

I'm dishing up when Logan comes back in, sliding into a seat as Jax takes the plates and passes them around. He slides his arms around my waist as I go to sit down, lifting and dropping down into a seat with me in his lap. "Sit with me, shortcake. I've missed you."

I protest half-heartedly. "Jax. I should sit down."

He gives me a charming smile. "You are sitting down."

Leaning over, he cuts up a piece of pancake and holds it up. Gray starts laughing, and I mock glare at him. "What is it with you guys and hand feeding me? Do I not have hands of my own?"

Jax tugs on my braid. "It's an alpha thing. Indulge us."

"It is?" I glance around, but they're all focused on me. Rolling my eyes, I lean forward and take the food off the fork, chewing it. "Are choo happy naw?"

Swallowing, I reach for my coffee. Jax continues to feed me in between eating his own food, and I take it grumpily until my plate is clean.

"There." I cross my arms. "Want me to show you my mouth, too?"

He groans in my ear. "Hell, yes."

God, he makes everything sound dirty. And tempting.

Before I can respond, Logan jumps up. "We have… some things for you," he says, clearing his throat. "For your nest."

My ears prick up. "You do? But I already have stuff."

Tristan tilts his head. "The store in Herrith didn't have much in the way of nesting materials, so I made do. But here, there are plenty of shops that cater for anything an omega might want."

My eyes round as Logan comes in, his arms full of pretty packages. Gray gets up to help him, clearing off the table so he can place them down in front of me.

So *pretty*. Even the wrapping is lovely, a mix of jeweled tones secured with different pieces of ribbon and string.

My hand hovers over one, and I look at them uncertainly. Logan gives me a nod. "Go on, Bonded. Open them."

They don't have to tell me twice. Carefully, I pick one out, a magenta-colored gift with dark blue ribbon. It slides away as I tug it with my fingers, and I lay it out on the counter to save it before I undo the pieces of tape.

Holding them up, I grin at Logan. "I love fluffy socks."

The socks are the same color as the tissue, knitted with a white cuff around the edges and little pom-poms hanging off.

I dive in, my excitement only growing as I show off each one. There's a large wire heart with an 'S' in the middle, decorated with pretty lights to hang on my wall, patchwork bunting with a mix of floral and stripes that I can already see hanging up, a variety of rocks and crystals for my shelves. My breath catches when I unwrap a thin, perfectly formed glass rose with a green stem and pale pink petals.

"I'm scared I'll break it," I say softly as I hold it carefully out. "These are beautiful, Logan."

Every single gift is something special.

Gray leans forward. "Here," he says. "Open this one next?"

I laugh in delight at the small, floppy fox teddy. "Oh, he's sweet. He'll go nicely with my *growing* collection of woodland animals." I wiggle my eyebrows at him for emphasis.

Gray holds out his hand, and I nearly bounce as he shows me the little raccoon in his palm. "For your collection."

I take it, holding the carving in my hand. "Thank you," I say softly, looking at them both. "For these. I love them."

"You deserve nice things, Sienna," Logan says softly. "This is only the start."

My ears grow warm, and I swallow. They're really trying. Maybe… maybe this could be permanent. Maybe this could be us. Jax's arms tighten around me, his chin settling into the crook of my neck. "Everything okay, shortcake?"

"Perfect," I whisper. Leaning back against him, I soak in his warmth.

For now, this is perfect.

Gray leans forward as I'm inspecting my things, my fingers tracing over the bunting. "There might be some more upstairs."

My feet are moving almost before he finishes his sentence, and Jax grumbles good-naturedly as I scramble off his lap. Grinning, I dart back and kiss his cheek, and his eyes widen. "Go on," he teases. "I'm gonna have to up my game, I think. Can't have the rest of them outshining me."

I take a moment to carefully collect my things, Logan carrying the glass as I dive for the stairs. I have a nest to build, and lovely things to put in it.

Today is a good day.

45

# LOGAN

Gray and I linger in the doorway of Sienna's room, watching her fuss with her new things, darting in and out of her nest. She pauses when she sees us standing there, her mouth twisting.

Holding out the glass rose, I smile. "This is yours, I believe."

She relieves me of the rose with a small frown creasing the middle of her forehead. "Thanks."

"What's wrong?" Gray asks her, clearly picking up the same vibe that I'm getting. "Is there something you don't like?"

"No, everything is lovely." She chews on her lip, her eyes flicking to us. "I'd invite you in, but…"

Ah. I get it now. An omega's space should be sacred, a complete comfort, with nothing disrupting it.

And we might have made progress, but she doesn't completely trust us yet.

"No need to apologize," I murmur. "We get it."

Sienna looks conflicted. "Tell us what you need," Gray urges.

She throws up her hands. "I want you to stay," she complains. "Just not… in here?"

I'll take it. Carefully, I settle down just outside the door, grabbing Gray's hand and pulling him down too. "Like this?"

She nods, a blush stealing over her cheeks. "Sorry."

"Don't apologize," I order quietly. "Not for this."

"You being uncomfortable with us in your space isn't your fault," Gray adds, stretching his legs in front of him. "It's ours. And we're happy to sit here for as long as you need us to."

Our Soul Bonded gives us one final, uncertain nod before she turns back to her nest preparations. We watch her carry things in and out, some of them thrown outside the doors of the nest with an irritated huff before a hand reaches out to drag them back in.

I grin. I can't help it. She's adorable. I glance at Gray, and he looks as enraptured as I feel, our eyes tracking our omega as she settles into her space.

She becomes more comfortable, her tentative movements becoming more confident as she works. She keeps looking out to see if we're still there. We're not going anywhere.

Finally, she emerges from her nest with a satisfied smile. "I think… I think I'm done. For now, I mean."

"I can't wait to see it," Gray says, then he backtracks, stumbling over his words. "I mean, not now, obviously. One day. At some point."

Sienna cocks her head. "One day," she agrees softly.

The sound of the doorbell rings through the house, and Sienna flinches.

"Hey," I soothe, getting up. "It's okay. It might be Jess. Or your family."

But when Jax appears, his face flushed from running up the stairs, it's not either of them.

"It's Ollena Hayward, shortcake," he says to Sienna. "She's asked to see you."

## 46

## SIENNA

Ollena and I sit awkwardly in the living room, opposite each other on the wide leather couches that frame the giant television on the wall. It's not a space I've spent a huge amount of time in, and I stare at the wide fireplace awkwardly as Gray carries in a tray.

"Coffee," he says to me softly, and I nod in thanks. His eyes move to Ollena. "Do you want me to stay, Bonded?"

I do, but I can tell by the purse of Ollena's mouth that she wants to talk alone. I shake my head, and Gray cups my cheek before he leaves. "Call if you need us."

When the door closes, Ollena releases a soft sigh. "Sienna. You look much better than the last time I saw you."

Maybe, but seeing Ollena is bringing back memories that I'd rather not dwell over, not when I'm trying to move on. Clearing my throat, I reach for the coffee, curling my hands around the warm cup for comfort. "How can I help you, Ollena?"

Ollena looks dismayed as she leans forward. "Sienna... I'm here for several reasons. First and foremost, to apologize. To you."

My head jerks back. "To me?"

Ollena nods, and for the first time, I see the bags under her eyes, the way her fingers quiver as she takes a cup. "For many things. But firstly, I am sorry that I wasn't able to overturn your Denied status. It… highlighted to me some of the injustices around our current system. Some things that need to change."

I take a deep breath. "This doesn't feel like it's going to be an easy conversation."

Ollena's mouth quirks. "I suppose that depends on how you look at it. You may have heard that the Trials have been disbanded."

"Isn't that only temporary?"

Ollena shakes her head. "It's clear that they cannot continue as they are," she says softly. "I won't stand by and watch another omega go through that. Not to mention that the omegas under my care would refuse to participate, as things currently stand."

My eyes grow wide. "They're refusing?"

Ollena nods. "Who can blame them? There has been much discussion over your Trial experiences, and what happened at your Bonding Ceremony. The omegas are scared, Sienna."

I sit back against the couch, needing a moment to think. The idea of everyone knowing about the Trials makes me feel ill. I don't want to be a topic of public gossip.

"What do you want from me?" I ask quietly. I'm not stupid. Ollena is kind, but she's the Omega leader for a reason. Her priority is the omega population, not one girl who had a bad time.

She sits forward, her eyes assessing me with renewed interest. "The Omega Gala is scheduled for next weekend. Everyone from Navarre will be there, and I believe there may be an opportunity to help reassure the omegas… if you were willing to attend with your pack."

I have to bite back the harsh rejection on my lips. "Unmated omegas don't attend the ball. I don't see how that would help."

Only the unmated alphas do, which has always struck me as incredibly unfair.

Ollena smiles ruefully. "Nevertheless, word will get around. The gala is the highlight of the social calendar, as you know."

Not really. I never paid much attention. Jess was always the one with the latest gossip.

"What do you really want, Ollena?" I ask. "What do you want to achieve from us attending?"

She raises a perfectly sculpted eyebrow. "I'm going to review the entirety of the Trials process, from start to finish. Maybe we'll find that it isn't needed. Maybe it is archaic, as some voices have been saying for years now. Maybe the alphas should be the ones proving themselves, and not the other way around."

My mouth drops open. Bonding Trials... for *alphas*. My fascination must show, because Ollena smiles. "It's difficult to argue that they don't need it after the last few weeks, no?"

"I can't imagine it," I admit. "But it doesn't sound like the worst idea."

"Whatever happens, my immediate priority is to help settle the omegas who are seriously concerned." She sits forward, scrutinizing me. "You, attending the gala, being seen with your pack in public, would help. I would also welcome your help in assessing the Trials, if that's something you would be interested in."

I blink. "I'll... think about it."

"Thank you." She settles back, smoothing down her dress. "I understand if it's too much. May I ask how you are?"

"I'm... okay. We're working things out."

Slowly, but we're getting there.

"That's good." Ollena watches me carefully. "I have been working closely with the Council to lobby for the removal of your Denied status. Depending on the appointment of the Beta representative, I don't believe it will be an issue."

The tension in my shoulders doesn't loosen. "I'm glad to hear it, but I've learned not to take anything for granted, Councilor."

Her lips tighten, but she nods. "I'll leave you in peace. Thank you for seeing me."

I follow her lead as she gets up. "No problem."

My head is spinning as I walk her to the door. Tristan is

leaning nonchalantly against the wall, not even trying to look like he's not lingering, and Ollena frowns at him. "It's unbecoming to listen at doorways, Mr. Cohen."

"Not listening, Councillor," he responds smoothly. "Just making sure my Bonded is well."

She eyes him suspiciously. "In order to ensure that, you need to look in a mirror, Tristan. I hope you're working to make amends."

Her voice is cutting, and I frown as Tristan looks down at the floor. "As I said, we're working through it. Thank you for your time, Councilor."

I open the front door, and Ollena assesses me. "I think you may be right, Sienna," she says softly as she sweeps past me. "I look forward to seeing you again."

I sink against the door when it closes behind her, and Tristan is there in a flash, his hands lifting to my cheeks. "Are you alright?"

"Did you hear?"

He shakes his head. "I really wasn't eavesdropping. I just wanted to be close in case you needed anything."

Nodding, I move his hands away and walk back to the living room, curling up on the couch. Tristan follows me, Jax, Gray and Logan slipping in behind him as I run through our discussion.

Gray's face twists in doubt. "The gala? Really?"

Logan nudges him. "What do you want to do, Sienna?"

I don't *know.*

"Can I use your phone?" I ask Tristan. "I need to make a call."

This is definitely a situation which calls for advice from my best friend.

47

# SIENNA

"**A**re you kidding?" Jess half-shrieks down the phone. "Hell *yes*, we are going to the gala."

I can't help but grin. "We?"

Her pout is nearly audible. "Like fuck are you going to the Omega Gala without me, Sienna Michaels. Besides, Emmett already had an invite."

I straighten with a frown. "He did?"

"Yep. Looks like David Cohen is seriously pitching him for the Beta representative job."

"How's he settling in?" I lie back on my bed, my hand over my eyes.

Jess quietens. "It's been an adjustment," she admits. "But he's doing okay. He could probably do with some male company. Monty's not been the most welcoming."

I bite my lip, remembering his caustic expression when he saw Emmett. "He's just protective over you, Jess."

"I know." She sighs. "But anyway. Back to the gala. I vote we go. And we go *hard*. Ballgowns, hair, the lot. We'll make the Cobutts regret every bad decision they've made when they see all the other packs fawning over you."

"Jess," I groan. "I don't want another pack. I have more than enough to manage with my actual *Soul Bonds*."

She snorts. "Maybe, but it wouldn't hurt to wind them up a little, Si. Make them sweat."

My stomach flips as I consider it, a tendril of interest snaking through my chest. "I'll need a dress."

Oh God. Another dress.

Jessalyn squeals in my ear. "I'm calling Helena. We'll need reinforcements. We're going to hit every dressmaker in town until we find you something perfect."

Oh, God. My *mother*.

I go to protest, but Jess has already hung up in her excitement. Rolling over, I bury my face in the pillow with a groan.

"Shortcake?" Jax knocks on my open door. "You okay?"

"No," I grumble into the cotton. "We're going to the gala. Jess and Emmett are going too."

He clicks his tongue. "If you don't wanna go, we won't go. I'll speak to the wildcat."

To his credit, his voice only wavers a *little*.

With a grimace, I wave my hand. "It's fine. We can go."

As much as I don't want to admit it, the idea of playing a little game with my Bonded is growing on me. They haven't exactly seen me at my best since our Mating Ceremony.

Maybe this is exactly what we all need.

## 4 8

# SIENNA

"There we go," my mother says. Her breath hitches as she carefully blots the ends of my hair with a soft towel. "All done."

I peer into the misted mirror opposite us, seeing the dark, telltale hue of pink hair. My lips tilt up.

"I'm glad to have it back," I admit truthfully. I didn't feel like *me* without it.

Mama doesn't let me linger, dragging me back into the large dressing room and the flurry of activity. Jess has gone *all* out on our gala preparations. She's lying back in a chair, her eyes closed as a beautician works on her eyebrows. One eye cracks open. "Champagne?"

"No, thank you." I grab an orange juice from the tray instead. "I need a clear head tonight."

Our dresses are hung carefully in the wardrobe, and my pack is downstairs, getting ready with Emmett. Jess's place is huge, and she's given them strict instructions on where they can go so they don't see us ahead of the big reveal.

It feels a little like how I did at my Mating Ceremony, *before* everything went to shit. A small frisson of excitement slips up my spine as I settle back in the chair, a blonde-haired stylist pursing her lips as she studies my hair.

"How do you want it?" she asks me. "Up or down?"

"Um. I was thinking – up? But kind of messy. Some tendrils coming down."

"Make sure you use the jewels," Jess instructs from her chair. "They'll look amazing in your hair, Si."

Leaning back, I take a deep breath as the stylist gets to work. Mama settles into her own chair next to me, holding out a hand for a beautician to do her nails.

"How are you feeling, sweetheart?" she asks me quietly. "About tonight?"

*Sick. I feel sick.*

Tonight we'll be on public display, the talk of the gala. There's no doubt about it, given the snippets my Mama has told me about all the questions.

Everyone wants to see the Denied omega with the pack who rejected her.

"Remember, you can leave at any time," she reminds me. "If it all gets too much, all you need to do is leave."

My spine tightens in resolve. I'm not going to let them run me off. Besides, I'm not doing this for them. I'm not even doing it for Ollena, despite her plea.

I'm doing it for me.

My eyes lock with Jess's across the room, and she raises her glass with a smirk. "To vengeance."

A grin tips my lips as I raise my glass back. "To alphas who need a little taste of their own medicine."

---

I step carefully into my gown, holding on to my mother as she keeps me steady. Madame Dumas lifts up the corset, fitting it to my waist, and I watch in the mirror as the stars on my bodice catch the light in a shimmer. Carefully, I draw on the thin gloves, tugging them up to just below my shoulders.

"Beautiful, Miss Sienna," Madame Dumas murmurs.

My eyes are wide. The stylists Jess brought in must be geniuses, because I barely recognize myself. My hair has been curled and swept up into a perfectly messy knot, tendrils snaking down to curl around my collarbone. My make-up is dark and glamorous, my eyes smoky and lined with sleek dark flicks.

And this dress. I wanted something *sexy*, something to make my pack sit up and pay attention - but something that still felt like *me*. And this is… it's perfect. My bodice hugs my breasts, dipping into a low v before flaring out in midnight blue tulle layers of stars, the long slit almost to my hips showing a glimpse of bare leg as I swish my skirt, topped off with a pair of elegant blush pink satin heels.

The stylist leans in, applying a light pink to my lips, and I blow a kiss to Jess. She looks radiant, her dress scarlet and sleek.

"They are going to fall to their knees when they see us," she crows, joining me in the mirror. "We look freaking phenomenal. Don't we, Helena?"

"You really do," my mother says softly, elegant in her own dark green gown. "I hope this evening is everything you might wish for, Sienna."

I meet her eyes in the mirror. "I hope so too, Mama."

Grabbing my matching satin pink clutch bag, the three of us make our way down the hall to the top of the staircase.

"Go on, Si," Jessalyn whispers. "This is your moment."

She nudges me not-so-gently, and my mother pats my arm as I move past her.

We're a little late, and I catch sight of my pack. Jax and Logan are talking quietly to each other, Gray leaning against a pillar with his arms crossed, and my breath catches in my throat as I take them in. Their hair is slicked back, each one of them devastating in black tuxedos.

*Mine.*

It's a heady thought, that these men might actually be mine.

Emmett is standing with the others but Tristan is pacing, his hands behind him as he stalks up and down the hall.

My hand is shaking as I set it carefully on the stair rail, and make my way down, lifting up my skirt and taking each step slowly.

Gray is first to see me. He straightens, his lips parting as his eyes drop, taking in every inch of me, from my heels to my dress. When he reaches my face, he smiles, and it transforms him. He doesn't speak, but he places his hand over his heart.

I'm too nervous to smile as Jax and Logan notice, breaking off mid conversation and moving to the foot of the stairs.

"Sienna." Logan's voice is low. "You look... I have no words."

Jax shakes his head, swallowing hard. "Beyond compare."

My eyes track Tristan as he pauses, his back to me. Holding my breath, I force my feet to keep moving as he turns around, his eyes moving straight to mine.

His expression... it's *everything* I ever wanted to see in my Soul Bonded. Everything I hoped for at our first meeting.

And maybe it's a little sweeter now, after everything.

I swallow back the emotion locking in my throat, giving him a wobbly smile as he moves to meet me at the bottom of the stairs. His eyes trace my face as he reaches for my gloved hand, turning it and pressing a kiss to my palm. His lips heat my skin, even through the thin fabric.

"Bonded," he says hoarsely. "You look like starlight."

My eyes move across them all. "Will I do, then?"

The affirmations ring out, and Jax steps forward.

"May I?" he asks, offering me his arm. Biting back a delighted smile at his charm, I wrap my hand carefully around his upper arm, and we walk out, escorted by the rest of my Bonded.

The car doors are open, waiting for us to slip inside. I glance around for my mother, and find her on the steps, watching us. She lifts her hand to wave. My dad is picking her up so they can travel to the gala together.

Jax holds my hand as I climb inside, Emmett handing Jess in after me so we can settle our skirts on the seats before they follow us inside, and the doors close. My pack is focused on me, so much so that I feel a little like prey. The hair on my arms stands on end as I glance around.

*Maybe this plan isn't the best idea.*

"So," Jess announces, clapping her hands. "Time for some ground rules, asswipes."

The tension in the car ratchets up a good few inches as my alphas peel their attention away from me. Tristan is the last to drag his eyes away, raising his eyebrow with a polite – slightly teeth-gritting – smile.

"By all means, enlighten us."

Jax groans audibly, and Jess crosses her arms. Across from her, Emmett frowns. It's clear that he hasn't been briefed in advance.

"We walk in together, and we sit together. But tonight is about networking. Working the room. So Sienna and I will be doing just that, and none of you are to interfere."

My pack freeze. I see the moment the penny drops for Tristan, the way his eyes move to mine, darkening dangerously. "*Bonded.*"

I shrug, flicking a piece of non-existent lint from my glove. "Jess is right. We need to network, Tristan. Maybe dance with a few people. It's nothing you shouldn't be familiar with."

My eyes flick up, meeting his with the edge of a dare. "Am I right?"

"You're treading a dangerous line, Sienna." His voice drops, intimate in the small space. "Are you sure this is a game you want to play?"

I smile widely. "Oh, yes. I think so."

Tristan folds his arms, but his jaw tics, betraying his frustration. "As you wish. Feel free to... network. But we'll be staying close."

I open my mouth to protest, and he gives me a look. "Erikkson is still out there," he says grimly. "A lot of people will be there tonight. So play your games, Bonded. We deserve every single one of them. But we will not be leaving your side."

He straightens his cuff. "And it's us you'll be leaving with at the end of the night."

The darkly possessive words wind around my throat, a whisper of the memory of his fingers gripping me. Pressing my lips together, I stare out of the window, trying desperately to dampen down the sudden surge of my scent.

He's playing dirty. But I'll play dirtier. I'm determined to give Tristan and the rest of my pack just a taste of some of what I've had to deal with.

49

# SIENNA

The car pulls to a stop outside the Council chambers where the gala is being held. We disembark in silence, Gray holding out his hand and winding my arm into his as he escorts me up the red carpet. The majestic building almost glitters in the night, thanks to the thousands of lights wound around each of the columns.

"You're going to give us a taste of our own medicine tonight, aren't you, Bonded?" Gray asks almost conversationally as we set a steady pace, the others following behind. I can hear Jess and Emmett hissing at each other, and my heart sinks. I don't want to cause any trouble for them.

"Maybe," I respond carefully. "Is that so bad?"

He looks down at me, a rueful twist on his lips. "It's a diabolical plan. We'll hate every single second. You know how many alphas attend the Omega Gala?"

I swallow. "No?"

"All of them." Music and laughter floats out of the doors ahead of us. "Have fun tonight, Sienna. We'll watch over you."

Tristan takes over from Gray as we join the queue for announcements. His face is closed off, but his hand squeezes mine. "Remember what I said," he murmurs as we step out to the top of the ballroom stairs. "Enjoy yourself. But afterwards, you're ours."

The promise in his words makes my mouth dry as our names are read out. Hundreds of faces turn to us amongst the thousands of glittering candelabras, each lit with at least a dozen candles, casting a warm glow. Tristan keeps a tight grip on me as I lift my skirts and we descend the stairs into the melee.

We're grabbed almost as soon as my foot touches the floor.

"Why, Sienna Michaels! What a surprise to *see* you here!"

I grit my teeth to greet an old classmate. I haven't seen her since we graduated from the Hub and it's very much for the lack of trying. "Clarissa."

Clarissa sidles up to us, not even trying to hide the fact that her eyes are greedily passing over my Bonded. She completely ignores her own pack, who are hanging back and muttering amongst themselves.

"Well, you hear these things," she whispers conspiratorially, except her voice carries like a damn foghorn. A few people look at us. "What an awful experience for you, darling. Sometimes these Trials can be so hard, especially when a pack is already taken."

Tristan turns to stone next to me as he looks down his nose at Sienna. "I beg your pardon?"

His tone is so hard that Clarissa takes a step back, her confident expression faltering. "Oh – well, I—,"

"You," Tristan says smoothly, "appear to have been misinformed. We are blissfully happy with our *Soul Bonded* mate."

Clarissa's eyes widen as they swing between us, and she manages a weak smile. "Oh. Ah – congratulations! If you'll excuse me, I think I see someone…"

As she almost runs away from us, I lean into Tristan. "I think you terrified her."

"Good," he responds crisply. "Some people need terrifying. Shall we?"

The further we move into the ballroom, the more I begin to doubt our plan. We take our seats around the table allocated for us, and Logan and Jax order drinks from one of the smartly dressed beta waiting staff. I catch Emmett watching them, his mouth set in a grim line. He and Jess aren't talking, and she keeps her eyes down on her champagne glass.

The first alpha appears moments after I've taken my first sip. "The elusive Sienna Michaels."

Jax sits back in his chair, crossing his arms with a drawl. "Perry. Always a pleasure to see you. How's mated life treating you?"

His eyes are hard. Perry laughs, although there's an edge to it as he brushes off Jax's question. He's handsome, with thick blonde hair and blue eyes, but there's a sharpness to his expression that smacks of cruelty.

He makes my skin crawl, more so when he looks down at me, his lip curling into a leer. "I've heard a lot about you. Would you care to dance?"

I lean back into the warmth of Gray's arm, slung casually across the back of my chair. "Not right now, thank you."

I'm not about to put myself in a potentially difficult situation just to wind my pack up. Gray's arm softens behind me, his fingers just brushing the nape of my neck.

"He's not a good man," he murmurs as Perry walks away without responding. "We'd only end up dragging him out by his neck when he tried to touch you."

Perry is only the first of a steady stream, none of whom make me feel comfortable enough to say yes to dancing. Jess catches my eye after turning down one of her own, a nice, slightly-awkward looking alpha who vanished fairly rapidly after seeing Emmett's scowl. She rolls her eyes, downing another drink.

"Dance with me," she says, grabbing Emmett's arm. "Since you insist on scaring off everyone else."

He looks like he's about to refuse, but then he looks at Jess's face. She looks close to tears, her lip trembling.

"Come on, then, Jessalyn," he says softly. Getting up, he holds out his arm. "Shall we?"

As they walk towards the dance floor, my view is obstructed by yet another alpha.

This one... doesn't set off any internal alarm bells. My pack straightens, and Gray's arm tenses again as the new alpha reaches us, offering us all a smile.

"Cohens. It's good to see you," he says, and he seems genuine. Enough that Tristan reaches over to shake his hand.

"Daniel. It's been a while."

"It has. Seems like you've been busy." There's a teasing lilt to his words, and he nods to me. "It's a pleasure to meet you. I'm Daniel. Pack lead of the Stevens pack."

I give him a small but genuine smile in return. "Hi. Are your pack here?"

He laughs. "They are. Undoubtedly causing mischief somewhere. But I was wondering if you're free for a dance?"

His bright green eyes don't move to my pack, staying steady on mine, and I respect him more for it.

"I am, actually." Tristan's head snaps to mine, and I give him a sweet smile as I place my hand into Daniel's. He bows, a ridiculously over-the-top gesture that pulls a laugh from my lips, before he leads me away. My back burns with the stares of my pack as Daniel pulls me into a waltz.

It's been a while since I last danced formally, but my feet remember the steps well enough, and it's easy to focus on him. His hands are light in mine as he keeps a respectable distance between us.

"So," he says, his lips quirking up. "You're a little bit famous, you know. Please forgive my curiosity."

He's direct, and I prefer it to the empty platitudes others have tried to offer. "You're forgiven."

He dips me before gently pulling me back upright. "Truthfully," he whispers. "I just wanted to wind Tristan up. We used to play quite a few tricks on each other in training, and the last time we met, he had one up on me."

Grinning, I wait as he spins me out, and we come back

together again. "Well, I'd say this is probably the way to do it. Does he look angry?"

"Furious," he says happily. "But I have to ask… why do you sound so delighted?"

I clear my throat. "You heard about my Mating Ceremony, I assume? It seems most of Navarre has."

He winces. "I did. I apologize if I've brought up bad memories."

"Not at all. It's about time he had a taste of his own medicine."

Daniel's eyebrows fly up, and he looks amused. "You're baiting him. Tread carefully, Sienna Michaels."

"I know what I'm doing." *I hope.*

"In that case…" I let out a shocked breath as Daniel pulls me closer. "Shall we give him a show?"

He waggles his eyebrows at me, and then he rotates, positioning us so I have the perfect view of my pack, all watching me with furious scowls.

Tristan's eyes burn into mine, the promise he made to me earlier engraved into my mind.

*Tonight, you're ours.*

When the dance finishes, Daniel bows, and I drop into a curtsey, tilting my head. "This was… surprisingly fun. You'll have to stay in touch with Tristan more often. He could do with some more fun in his life."

Daniel barks a laugh as he escorts me back to the table with his hand on my back, unfazed by the glares of my alphas. "It's been a delight, Sienna. I'll see you soon, I hope. Thank you for the dance."

He kisses the back of my hand, and Tristan growls. "*Stevens.*"

Daniel winks at me before turning to them. "You're a lucky pack."

As he melts into the crowd, I'm saved from whatever Tristan is about to say by the first course being served. There's no sign of Jess and Emmett as I glance around the room, seeking out familiar faces as I sip my soup.

My mother and father are seated a few tables away, and I raise my hand in a wave to them. The Council are seated together on the other side of the room, and I spot Tristan's mother next to David. Her eyes are focused on Tristan, but they wander across to me. I offer her a small smile, and she returns it.

Gray leans in as I finish, his words low and unhurried. "I hope that was worth it, because part of me wants to take you over my knee for that little show, sweetheart."

My hands clench on my napkin. "I'm not sure." Tapping my chin, I slide my eyes to him. "Do you feel suitably punished, Gray?"

He lifts his hand, playing with a strand of my hair. "It was a reminder," he says quietly. "Of what we could have lost through our own stupidity. Not having you in my life is unthinkable, Sienna."

I let his words soak into me, taking a needed sip of my drink as my parents come by to greet me. My father fixes the Cohens with a scowl. "How are you, sweetheart? They treating you well?"

"They are, dad," I murmur, allowing him to fold me into his arms. "I promise."

So much so that just the *teeniest* amount of guilt fills me when I say yes to another alpha asking me to dance. He's polite, but nowhere near as much fun as Daniel. Jax fixes me with a mournful look as I return to the table.

"Shortcake," he groans. "You're killing me."

"Really?" I raise my eyebrow, and he sighs. "And I deserve every second of it, plus more."

"Exactly."

Tristan gets up abruptly. "Excuse me."

The suddenness of his exit, the way he doesn't even look at me, makes my chest twist. Can he seriously not handle a few dances, after everything that happened?

Disappointed, I shake my head at the next alpha who walks up to me. "No, thank you."

Logan slips into Tristan's vacated seat, reaching out and

wrapping his hand around mine where it holds the stem of my glass, topping it up with champagne. "How are you feeling?"

*Frustrated.*

I'm about to unload on them when there's a squeal of microphone static.

"Good evening, everyone. If I could have your attention for a moment?"

My heart stops dead in my chest. I recognize that voice.

I spin in my seat so quickly that I nearly topple into Gray. His arms shoot out, steadying me as I take in Tristan. He's stood at a microphone, the orchestra paused with their instruments held up as they watch him.

Silence spreads across the room as my heart starts to beat faster, the champagne turning to dust in my mouth. Heads swivel to me, and I try to temper my panicked expression.

Logan leans in, his hand cupping my neck. "Breathe, sweetheart. This isn't a bad thing."

I can feel them all moving closer to me, Jax getting up from his seat and coming to stand behind me, and I try to take comfort in that as I watch my Bonded survey the room, his face the mask he prefers to wear in public.

He has everyone's attention.

"There have been a lot of rumors," he starts, "about our pack, and our relationship with our omega, Sienna Michaels."

The flurry of whispers silences as he holds up a hand.

"The details of our relationship belong to us, and us alone. However, given the level of interest in our pack, I wish to set something straight."

His chin tips up. "Sienna Michaels is our Soul Bonded. Our fated mate. And the *only* omega we want."

I can't breathe as I watch him, his figure swimming as tears blur my vision. Gasps and murmurs ring out.

"We will spend the rest of our lives atoning for the foolish, stupid decisions we made during the early days of our Bonding." His eyes find mine. "Never again. We claim you, Sienna

Michaels, publically, as our mate. You are the one we choose. Now, and always. Until the end of our days, and the end of all days."

*Never again.*

I wipe at my cheeks as Jax's hand settles on my shoulders.

"Our Bonding Ceremony didn't go as planned," Tristan says into the microphone. "We never had the opportunity to ask our Bonded to dance. So tonight seemed like a possibility to right at least one wrong."

My hands shake as he jumps off the tall stage, landing smoothly on his feet and stalking through the silent crowd towards me. Tristan holds out his hand, his eyes steady on mine.

"Dance with me, Bonded," he says softly.

The orchestra strikes up, and a male voice starts to sing as I reach up. His fingers close around mine as he leads me to the dancefloor, the faces around us a blur.

"Breathe," he coaxes, as he pulls me into his arms.

I finally let out a breath as we start to move, finding an easy rhythm.

He drops his head, his mouth brushing my ear. "Forgive me, Sienna. I will never stop atoning. But *forgive me*, so I can love you the way I want to. So I can keep making those memories with you, so I can wake up every morning to your face. *Please*."

I look up, into his eyes.

And I nod.

I don't want to tiptoe around, pretending I'm not aching for them, like the distance between us isn't painful.

I'll never forget. Neither will they. But I can forgive.

*It's time to move forward.*

He releases a breath, his eyes scanning mine. "Sienna."

We stop dancing in the middle of the floor as he cups my face and draws me into a kiss, his lips moving over mine as my hands reach up behind his neck.

When we pull apart, both of us are breathing heavily. But I'm smiling, and he's grinning, his face lit up.

"We should dance," he whispers. "I did promise you a dance, Bonded."

And then we *move*. I gasp as our feet fly across the floor, my feet easily finding the rhythm, and I send a silent thanks for all the hours of dancing tuition that led me to this moment, spinning across a dance floor, dressed in starlight in the arms of my Soul Bonded and feeling like a real, honest to god princess.

Tristan slows, smiling as his eyes move past me. And then Jax is there, spinning me into his arms with a sardonic lift of his eyebrow as I laugh in delight. He doesn't miss a beat as he picks up the rhythm.

"Shortcake," he murmurs. "Maybe I'll start calling you starlight instead."

"I like shortcake," I say as he dips me.

"Good." His voice is gruff. "I do, too."

As I come back up, his lips capture mine, leaving me gasping for air before he spins me away and Logan takes his place. His hands are warm against my bare skin as he whirls me away, his brown eyes completely focused on me.

"You deserve this," he says, holding me close as we move across the floor. "This moment, and every other one that follows, Sienna."

The words alone are dangerous enough, but their actions are knocking down my defenses one by one, breaking apart the last of my reservations like tissue paper. Logan has always been the most respectful of my boundaries. Even his hands are careful against my skin, like he's mindful of every touch.

So I wrap my hand around his neck, and his eyes widen as I tug him down to me. "Kiss me, Logan." I whisper. "Please."

He doesn't hesitate, stopping us mid-dance as his lips crash against mine like he's been holding back, waiting for me to ask. He tastes just like his scent, fresh and lemony, and I breathe him in as his hand grips the back of my neck and his tongue traces my lips.

There's a polite cough next to my elbow, and we break apart

with a gasp. There are a few chuckles from around us as I turn to Gray, and he holds his hand out.

"Room for one more?" he asks. His blue eyes are dark as Logan kisses me on the cheek, his lips lingering before he pulls back. He and Gray link their fingers as they pass each other, a heated look passing between them.

Gray waits patiently, his hand out, as I catch my breath. We watch each other, careless of the hundreds of eyes on us.

"I love you," he says, keeping his voice low. "I love you, Sienna Michaels. And I'm sorry it took me so long to realize it."

My fingers grip his, letting him pull me closer as I look up into his face. "Tell me again."

"I love you." We sweep smoothly into movement, Gray's hand holding mine as his other presses into the small of my back. He keeps it slow enough that I can rest my head against his chest, listening to his heartbeat pound, steady and sure.

He presses a kiss to the top of my head as we sway. "I'm not a fantastic dancer," he admits. "So this is probably the best I can do."

I smile into his shirt. "This is all I need."

When the music stops, there's a moment of silence before applause breaks out across the room. Blushing, I grip Gray's hand as we head back to our table, nodding to the people offering us well-wishes, the gossip of earlier this evening silenced for the time being at least, thanks to Tristan's declaration.

They're waiting for us, and my mouth waters as I take them in, all of them focused on me. Slightly disheveled, their shirts loosened at the top, their bow ties hanging down.

They all look freaking delicious.

I know what I want.

And I don't want to wait anymore.

I grin. "Take me home, Soul Bonds. I'm feeling…*tired*."

It's almost comical how quickly they all snap to attention, their eyes darkening. Jax swallows. "Are… are you sure, shortcake?"

"Oh, yes." I nod. "I'm definitely in need of an early night."

EVELYN FLOOD

I wiggle my eyebrows.

They burst into a flurry of activity, and I bite down on my smile as we hustle out of the ballroom. I catch my mother's eye, and she waves, a smile pulling at her mouth as she points to something on the other side of the room to my dad.

We bump into Jess and Emmett at the door, both of them disheveled but looking much more satisfied than the last time we saw them.

"We're heading back," I say to Jess. "Do you want to come with us?"

She shakes her head. "Emmett needs to go and speak to the Council."

"Um." I eye the way he's casually trying to flatten his hair. "He has a hickey on his neck," I whisper, leaning in.

"That's because he's mine," Jess says proudly. "They can deal. See you tomorrow, Si. Glad the plan worked."

With a wink, she's off, towing Emmett behind her.

I pause at the entrance. "Wait. I need... can you give me a minute?"

Tristan tilts his head. "Take all the time you need, Bonded. We'll be waiting."

With only a little blush, I scurry off, heading to the ladies restroom on the main floor. It's empty, and I grip the edges of the porcelain sink, staring at my flushed reflection in the mirror.

This is fine. I'm an *omega*.

Sex is practically our specialty.

Except now I'm wondering if offering myself up to all four of my alphas at the same time like some sort of tasty Sienna-flavored buffet might be a *little* more than I can handle for my first time.

I bite my lip. But I really, really want them all with me.

It's fine. We'll work it out.

After talking myself out of my mini-fritz, I take a moment to wash my hands, splashing a little water on my heated cheeks to cool them off. Reaching over, I grab a towel and press it carefully to my face, trying to avoid ruining what's left of my make-up.

And a damp, hot hand smashes over my mouth.

I'm yanked backwards as my hands reach up, scrabbling at the fingers gripping my face. A terrified noise slips out, but it's muted, and my eyes fly up in the mirror.

Erikkson sneers at me. His face is thinner than I remembered, his weeks on the run clearly having taken a toll. He smells like he hasn't showered since I last saw him, and I gag as his fingers shove into my mouth.

"You little bitch," he hisses. "You've caused me no end of trouble, but that ends tonight."

Still gripping my mouth, he starts tugging me backwards, and my heels scrabble on the tiles.

He pushes open the large window that leads out onto the grounds.

A terrified moan leaks out. *No.*

They won't know what's happened to me.

Erikkson clearly knows how to stay hidden, and I'll be shipped back over the wall within an hour.

I retch into his hand, and he grabs a section of my hair, pulling it back until I'm gasping, my head swimming as I try to take in air around his hand.

Think, Sienna. Fucking *think.*

My heel catches in the edges of the ornate tiling. Desperate, I lift it up and slam it as hard as I can into the top of his foot.

He screams like a little girl, his hand releasing my mouth, and I lurch forward, flying across the room towards safety. My hands wrap around the door handle before he catches back up to me, his hand winding into my hair and trying to drag me back.

But my hand is still attached to the handle, and it opens.

Pulling in the deepest breath I can, I scream out into the hallway.

"*TRISTAN!*"

"Fuck!" Erikkson shoves me forward, my head banging into the door before he scrambles back to the window. I shuffle back against the wall, gasping as the door splinters, and Tristan comes flying through.

His eyes move straight to the open window. "Jax," he snaps. "Gray. Go."

Logan's arms are around me, his voice speaking urgently into my ear, but it's all I can do to wrap my arms around him tightly.

*He came. They all came.*

"It's okay," he murmurs, over and over again as he holds me.

Tristan drops to his knees next to me, his hand going straight to my swollen mouth as he inspects it. His eyes turn to flint. "Tell me what happened. Are you hurt anywhere else?"

I shake my head. "I'm okay. It – it was Erikkson. He said I was causing him trouble."

Tristan looks grim. "Jax and Gray are going after him."

"What?" I struggle out of Logan's arms. "They can't. Tristan – those men have guns. If they're with Erikkson—,"

My panic is making it hard to breathe, and Tristan cups my face. "They are not helpless," he tells me firmly. "And there are security guards all over this place, Bonded. Erikkson slipped by them because he knows the layout, but he'll have a tough time getting back out."

As my breathing slows, there's shouting from outside the bathroom. Gray strides in, a long scratch across his cheek. His eyes move straight to mine.

"We got him," he says grimly. He kneels next to Tristan, his hand stroking my hair. "You hear that, sweetheart? It's done. We've got him. Plus two of the men who were looking for you in Herrith, I think."

I stare at him for a moment, before I throw myself forward, landing against him with an oomph. He rocks back, his arms locking around me. "Hey, now."

"You're an *idiot*." I thump him in the shoulder, and he yelps. "You could have died! You don't just run out into *danger*, Gray!"

Tears follow hot on the heels of my anger, and Logan gently pulls me back, lifting me up in his arms.

"Can we take her home?" he asks, and Tristan nods. "I'll get my father. He can deal with Erikkson's booking in. There's a cell waiting for him next to Alicia."

He touches my cheek. "I'll be right back."

"Come on, sweetheart." Logan carries me out of the bathroom, Gray hovering over us, and we move down the hall towards the group gathered.

Erikkson is spewing abuse at Jax, who's pinning his arms behind his back. A few Justice officers are gathered around them. Jax looks at me.

"I'll be done soon, Bonded," he promises. "I'm not trusting anyone else but us and David to handle this piece of shit."

Erikkson thrashes, but Jax holds him firm, and I wiggle in Logan's hold. "Put me down."

His arms tighten around me. "Sienna—,"

"*Now*, Logan."

With a reluctant grumble, he sets me carefully onto my feet. I wobble for a second before I launch into action. This man nearly stole my entire future, and I'm not about to let him waltz off into a cell without a little payback.

My heel catches Erikkson straight between the legs, and he folds over with a moan, dropping to his knees and nearly taking Jax with him.

"Asshole," I hiss. "You slimy, nasty piece of *shit*."

Jax grins savagely. "If I lift him," he asks, "can I *please* watch you do that again?"

I'm about to agree when the main doors spill open, more people heading towards us with raised voices. My lips tilt up. "No need," I say, grinning at Erikkson.

He blinks at me before a bushel of bronze hair swings in front of me, and I hear a thud.

I peer over Jess's shoulder. "You brought the knuckleduster?"

She hums, and Jax gapes as Emmett skids to a stop behind her, gaping down at where Erikkson is sprawled out on the floor. "Jess," he groans. "After the conversation we *just* had—,"

"Are you saying he didn't deserve it?" Jess demands, and Emmett rolls his eyes.

"It doesn't have to be one or the other," he grumbles. He lifts her around the waist. "Stay over here, and for the love of God, *please* put that thing away before that Justice guy sees it."

Everyone else arrives in a sudden rush of questions and worry, and Tristan appears next to me, his mouth tilting into a smile.

"Bonded," he murmurs. "Any idea why he was conscious when I left, but he's not now?"

"He put up a fight," Jax calls baldly. He eyes the Justice officers, daring them to disagree with him. "I had to subdue him."

Tristan's dad raises his eyebrow as he moves to look down at Erikkson's prone body. "Well, he's definitely out. Take him downstairs. Very considerate of him to come straight to our door."

He looks at me. "Are you alright?"

I nod, sinking back into Logan. My little moment of bravery wavers away, and I start to shake.

"We're taking you home," Tristan says. He nods at his dad. "I'll call tomorrow. Let me know if you need statements."

David sighs. "I'm sure Milo will insist on it. Make sure they all match up."

He glances at where Jessalyn is standing with Emmett, and she flushes, but straightens her shoulders. "Nice shot."

"I don't know what you're talking about," she says loftily, but she grins at me when he turns around. "Go home, Si. I'll call you tomorrow. *Late* tomorrow."

Emmett whispers in her ear, and she turns scarlet. "Maybe tomorrow evening!" she calls, her voice pitching higher as I bite back a laugh.

Tristan wraps his arm around me as we make our way to the car, fussing until I'm settled in with Jax on one side of me and Logan on the other. Gray slides into the seat opposite us as Tristan pulls out, heading for home.

I smooth down the material of my dress. This one actually

seems to have escaped relatively unscathed. Maybe my run of bad luck with dresses is finally over.

My nerves start to ratchet up as we get closer to home. Jax captures my hand in his, rubbing his thumb over my skin and stopping me from chewing on my nail.

"Nearly home," he soothes. "How's your head?"

I blink. "It's fine."

Gray leans forward, his hand rubbing my knee in what I'm pretty sure he thinks is comfort. "You need rest, Sienna."

This is not the pre-sexy times, sexy talk I was expecting, to be honest.

And like hell is Erikkson taking that from me, too.

As we pull through the gates, Tristan meets my eyes in the rearview mirror. "What are you planning, Bonded?"

It's slightly unnerving how much he picks up. As it is, I shrug casually. "Oh, you know. It's been a long night."

His eyes narrow. "Hmm."

Casually, I climb out of the car, accepting Logan's hand. Tristan slams his door and leans against it, his arms crossing as he watches me. Gray goes to open the door, holding it open as I move towards him. My heels click on the steps, and I pause in the doorway.

"Shortcake?" Jax asks from behind me. "What do you need?"

I wriggle pathetically. "My dress… it feels like I can't breathe, Jax. Can you undo it?"

His breath ghosts across my neck. "Baby, you know how much I love peeling you out of these things."

His fingers unhook the row of small buttons until my bodice gapes dangerously and I hold it up, smiling at him over my shoulder. "Thanks."

Gray sucks in a breath as I walk past him.

Then I drop the dress completely, letting it billow to the floor in a shimmer of blue fabric.

The choked sounds behind me are completely, utterly worth the time it took to find this underwear. For good measure, I shimmy, showing off the matching blue panties to go with my dress.

"You like them?" I ask casually. "I think they go well with the heels."

Stepping out of my dress, I leave it where it is for the moment, and head down the hall, wearing nothing but my heels and underwear. I hear shuffling footsteps and hissed whispers, and I swallow my grin as I place my heel on the stairs and turn around, raising my eyebrow.

"Consider this your *official* invite into my nest. The entry fee is orgasms. *Lots* of orgasms."

Jax swipes a hand over his face. "I want to carry you up," he says hoarsely. "But I want to watch you walk up those steps with that perfect ass more. Are you sure? Tonight—,"

"I'm sure." I interrupt. "He doesn't get to take anything else away from me, Jax."

His eyes flash. "Well then. Lead the way, shortcake."

Gray and Logan nod, but my eyes flick to Tristan. He's holding back, his face shadowed in the light from the hall lamps.

"And you?" I challenge him.

He takes a lazy, slow step forward. "I hope you can move fast in those heels, Bonded," he rumbles. "Because once we have our hands on you, we're not going to stop."

My eyes widen as he takes another step. Then I turn and dart up the stairs. Four pairs of footsteps pound behind me as I burst into my bedroom. With a breathless squeal, my feet are lifted from the floor and Jax seals his lips over mine. My legs part as he hooks them over his hips, his hands squeezing and moving over my ass as he walks us backwards towards my nest.

My hands dig into his hair, twisting and tugging the black strands between my fingers as he stops to kick off his shoes. "Hurry up," I urge, and he rubs his nose against mine, making me smile.

"We're not rushing tonight, shortcake," he murmurs. "We have forever."

My eyes move behind him. My alphas are tugging off their shoes, yanking off their ties and tux jackets. "And your shirts," I demand. The sight of them, all of them, here in my space with our scents mixing together… it's enough to make my head spin.

Jax strolls across the wooden floor, kneeling at the edge of the bed area and laying me down. I land with a slight bounce on my back, my legs still apart and my heels in the air. My breasts are on full display, my nipples pointed as I pant.

"Stay like that," Jax demands. "And hands above your head."

Slowly, I reach my hands above my head, and his eyes heat. "Good girl."

Squirming, I watch as Jax backs away, his hands moving to his shirt buttons, and Tristan takes his place. He climbs over me, his hand cupping my chin as he kisses me deeply, his tongue sweeping inside.

He leans until our bodies are pressed together, scraping my sensitive nipples with the golden smattering of hair across his chest, and I rub myself against him, my eyes closing. My hands start to come down, but he takes my wrist and pushes them back up.

"No touching," he murmurs, "not yet."

Gray and Logan appear on either side of me, their hands gently pinning me in place as Tristan's lips move down, tasting my neck and tracing down to my breasts. He presses soft kisses around my nipple, and I push against their hold.

"Patience, Bonded," Gray murmurs. He leans down, drawing me into a kiss, and I gasp into his mouth as Tristan's hot mouth seals across my nipple, and he takes a long, deep, suck, tugging it with his lips before he moves to the next one.

I can see the outline of Gray's cock straining against his trousers, and I look up at him as he breaks away. "Clothes off. Everyone needs to take their clothes off, right now."

Grinning, he keeps one hand curled around my wrist, the other moving to undo the button on his trousers. "Like this?"

I nod, my mouth dry as he unzips himself. I can hear the

others doing the same, Tristan still pressing kisses across my breasts, my belly, the sensitive dip of my abdomen. My arms tug uselessly against their grip as Gray pulls out his cock, his fingers gripping it as he pumps.

"Is this what you want, Bonded?" he asks. "Want to wrap those plump, pretty pink lips around my cock and take me in your mouth?"

I look between him and Logan, both of them so close to me, touching, stroking themselves. I'm pretty sure my eyes cross as I try to watch them both at once.

"Yes," I swallow, my mouth flooding with want. "I want your cock, Gray."

He leans in further, his swollen head brushing my lips as Tristan dips down, his tongue tracing the line of my slit through my underwear and making stars burst behind my eyes.

"Ah!" My body pushes up, my mouth opening, and Gray slips his head inside my mouth. "Suck, sweetheart," he murmurs, and I wrap my lips around him, taking in the slightly salty tang as he thrusts gently into my mouth.

"Look at you," Logan murmurs. "Taking it so well, baby." His hand strokes my hair and my eyes close again, overcome by the sensations dancing across my body. Hands slide in to play with my tight nipples, pulling, flicking, as Tristan continues his slow assault, moving to thick, laving licks through my soaking underwear.

His hands slip into the edges, and he peels them down, revealing me to them. I make a desperate noise around Gray's cock, my breathing harsh as his thrusts become a little deeper.

"Take it," he urges. "All the way, baby."

His hand cups the back of my head, pressing me forward until his knot bumps my lips. Stretching my lips as wide as I can, I seal my mouth around him completely, and his cock jumps inside my mouth.

"Fuuck," Gray curses, pushing my hair back. "Fucking perfect, Sienna."

His thrusts continue as warm air blows across my pussy, and my eyes roll back in my head. Gray pulls back, and I whine, reaching towards him.

He chuckles. "Later," he promises. I'm distracted by Tristan as he spreads his hands over my inner thighs, stretching me open. I can feel my slick, feel it gathering, and he dips his fingers to my pussy, brushing it and lifting them up.

"Look at all this mess you're making, Bonded," he says, his smile dark. I watch, my mouth open, as he sucks the juices off his fingers. "You taste delicious."

My breath catches as he lowers himself, burying his face into me, licking and biting until I'm convulsing, the waves growing to an inferno that has me sobbing out his name. "Tristan, *please*."

He sits up, his eyes burning into me and his face shining as he licks his lips. "More?"

I nod frantically. "More. Right now."

I push my hips up towards him as he takes his cock in his hand, rubbing it over my pussy, up and down.

"Tristan," I groan.

He notches the head of his cock to my entrance, a tantalizing promise of fullness as he pushes in, a single, torturous inch at a time until he's thick and full inside me, our hips pressed together and his arms holding me open, my hips off the bed.

He doesn't move. "Look how your body stretches for me, Bonded," he rasps. "Made to take me."

He thrusts, once, then again, pushing himself into me, his hands gripping my hips. His knot pushes against my entrance. Gray and Logan hold me steady, Jax's hands moving over my skin as Tristan *owns* me, his cock moving in and out of my body as he sets a pace that makes me jerk in their arms.

The wave starts to build again, my orgasm flashing like lightning down my back as my body bows in their arms. Tristan roars. My eyes close as his knot pulses, my body stretching impossibly wider as it pushes slowly inside, sealing us together as his heat empties inside me.

"Fuck, Sienna," Tristan croaks. His arms lower me gently to the bed, his body locked with mine as he leans over me. My hands are released, and I raise them shakily. He takes each hand, kissing my palms reverently. "Bonded. Are you alright?"

I nod hazily, adjusting to the feeling of his knot inside me. It's almost a burn, but it feels so fucking good that my eyes flutter. "Mmm. I think you broke me."

Tristan laughs breathlessly as he sets down my hands and leans in, his lips tracing over mine. My body still pulses, little aftershocks making me clench around the knot that's holding me in place.

Tristan sits up, his arms gathering underneath me, and I yelp as he lifts me, taking me with him so my breasts rest against his chest, my face pressed into his neck. His knot shifts inside me, and my whine rolls out into the nest.

I'm not done. But I'm not going anywhere, for the moment.

"More," I whisper into Tristan's neck. "Need more."

There's warmth at my back, the earthy, misty scent of Jax as he presses kisses along the damp skin at the back of my neck. I stretch back against him and his hands slide around to cup my breasts as Tristan watches us, our bodies still joined together.

"Do you want more, shortcake?" Jax rasps into my ear, his breath tickling the sensitive skin and making me shiver. "Because I can give you more. Shall we see if our Soul Bonded can take two knots?"

His words register, my eyes flying wide as his hand slides down my spine and between the cheeks of my ass. A finger presses against me.

"So wet," Jax murmurs. He drops his fingers lower, and I stare into Tristan's eyes as Jax rubs his fingers around where we're joined, taking the fluids and bringing it back up. I gasp as he uses my slick to push his finger in, just a little, moving it in and out.

"What do you think, Bonded?" Tristan leans forward to press a kiss against my lips. "Think you can take two of your alphas?"

I look around for Gray and Logan. They're lying on their sides, heads propped up as they watch me with Jax and Logan, their eyes full of heat.

"Yes," I whisper against his mouth. Tilting my head back, I look up into Jax's face. "Please."

Upside down, he leans down to kiss my lips, and I feel his finger push deep inside me. "Relax," Jax whispers into my mouth. "Remember, shortcake. You're made for us."

He pumps his finger in and out before he adds another, stretching me wider as I pant. My head rolls back against Jax's shoulder, and Tristan's hand comes up, circling my neck. "Eyes on me," he orders, and my gaze locks with his as I feel something much bigger than Jax's fingers pushing at me.

"Ah—,"

Jax presses a kiss to my shoulder. "Breathe, shortcake."

I focus on my breathing, Tristan breathing in time with me as Jax's cock sinks inside me, stretching me. Tristan's knot is still hard and hot inside me, and my lips part at the sensation.

"Just a little more," Jax coaxes, and my eyes close as he nudges through that final barrier, bottoming out inside me.

I've never felt so *full*.

He rocks inside me. "Everything I ever dreamed of, Sienna Michaels."

My moan is swallowed up by Tristan's kiss as his knot loosens inside me, his seed spilling down my legs as Jax wraps his arms around me and lifts me.

Tristan moves away, and I'm pressed down into the mattress, my cheek meeting the soft cotton of the sheets as Jax runs his hand down my back. "Arch that pretty spine and lift your ass up for me, mate."

My legs are shaking, but I do as he says, using my elbows to keep my balance. I'm rewarded with a hard thrust, my breath escaping in harsh gasps as Jax ups his pace, his hands sinking into my hips so tightly that I just know I'll see the evidence on my skin tomorrow.

The meeting of our skin echoes out into the room, and I groan into the mattress, my fingers gripping the material. Turning my head to the side, my eyes widen when I see Gray on his knees, Logan gripping his hair as he thrusts into his mouth.

The sight of them together, Logan switching between watching me and watching Gray, is enough to tip me over the edge. Jax follows me with a bellow, his teeth clamping down onto my shoulder and sending juddering spikes of lightning through me. His knot is even bigger than Tristan's, and a broken plea issues from my mouth as it pushes inside me.

I collapse into the bed, my face buried in the sheets as he follows me down, rolling us at the last second so I curl into him. I suck in deep breaths, our skin slicked in sweat as Jax presses gentle kisses to my hair, his hands stroking down my skin. Petting me.

I kind of love it.

I have the perfect view as Logan arches with a groan, the tendons in his throat standing out as Gray swallows down his release, his hands gripping his ass.

God, to be in the middle of that sandwich. It might have to wait until tomorrow, though. My limbs feel loose and lazy, and I'm not sure I can actually move right now.

I blink at Tristan sleepily when he appears, a damp towel in his hand. His hand dips down, and I suck in a breath as I feel the rasp of the cloth over my slit, cleaning me up even as I'm still locked onto Jax.

Tristan kisses my forehead. "Sleep, bonded."

I stir. "But Logan and Gray—,"

Strong fingers curl around mine. "We have forever, Sienna," Logan whispers. "Sleep now."

But I'm already out.

## 50

## TRISTAN

I'm overseeing the installation of our new security system the next morning, watching from the steps when a hand slips into mine, squeezing.

"Good morning. I brought coffee. And a muffin."

"You are an angel sent from heaven," I tease Sienna, and she blushes. We ate like kings this morning, thanks to our Soul Bonded waking up with an abundance of energy and turning into a whirlwind in the kitchen.

Sienna leans against me as I take a sip of my coffee, and I tuck her under my arm. "I've been thinking," she says carefully.

I take another sip before I answer. I'm starting to pick up on her tells, the hitches in her breath, the expressions on her face. And this particular tone tells me that I'm definitely not going to like whatever my Soul Bonded suggests.

"Tell me, Bonded."

She fidgets as I give her my full attention. "I want to go and see Alicia," she says in a rush.

It takes a second for the words to register. "Absolutely not."

"Tristan." Sienna chews her lip as she stands toe to toe with me, crossing her arms. "That's not a decision you can make for me. I can go around you if it comes to that. But I don't *want* to. I want you to come with me."

I frown. "But *why*? Why would you want to see her, after everything she did?"

Just the thought of Alicia within ten feet of my Soul Bonded makes my blood heat, anger pounding my chest.

Sienna sighs. "It's because of everything she did that I want to see her. I just… it feels unfinished. She tried to destroy my life, Tristan. And she nearly succeeded. I need to see her, need to close off that part of our lives so we can move on to the next one."

I cup her cheek. "I don't want you anywhere near her," I say honestly. "She's poison, Bonded. She'll try and get inside your head, try to turn you against us."

I trust Sienna to the ends of the earth. But we've come so far. Who knows what lies Alicia will throw at her?

"Give me some credit," she whispers. "I won't let her, Tristan. Will you come?"

I nod, brusquely. "If you need to go, then I'm taking you. I'll make the call and get one of the others to take over here."

"Thank you." She reaches up to stroke her thumb over my cheek, a teasing smile on her lips. "See? This is what adult, grown-up communication looks like."

I snap my teeth at her playfully, and she jumps back with a squeak.

"Before I make that call," I say smoothly, taking a step towards her. "I can think of something else that needs my urgent attention, Bonded."

"Oh?" She sucks in a breath, feeling for the edge of the doorway behind her. "What might that be?"

"I think you know." I lower my gaze, very deliberately. "It might take a while. Several hours, in fact."

She grins, waving her finger at me. "Oh, no. You're not getting out of it that way."

I pounce on her, taking in the breathy noise she makes when I hoist her over my shoulder. "Tristan!" She bats my back like a kitten. It's adorable.

I spread my hand over her ass, kneading it with my hand before I give it a light slap, and she groans, her fist curling into my shirt. "One hour," she gasps.

"Two," I counter with a squeeze. "And I'll throw in an extra orgasm."

She sighs dramatically. "Fine. Three hours, and *then* we'll go."

"Excellent negotiating skills, Bonded. I accept."

# 51

# SIENNA

It's late afternoon as Tristan and I walk up the steps of the Council chambers, retracing our steps from the night before.

His fingers hold mine tightly as he leads me across the huge marble antechamber and to a set of double doors.

"This is where they're keeping them?" I ask. Navarre isn't a huge place, but we have a larger prison building on the other side of town.

Tristan nods. His jaw is firm, the tic well and truly present, and I feel a small twinge of guilt for making him come here with me. Just for a moment, though.

We descend down into the bowels of the building, the air becoming cooler until we reach a locked door. Tristan reaches up and rings a bell.

"Are you ready?" he asks, wrapping his arm around me. I nod, soaking in his warmth. It's warm outside, but not down here, and the shirt I stole from Tristan to wear as a dress suddenly feels like it might not have been the best choice.

A grim-faced Justice officer opens the door, and he and Tristan exchange a few terse words as I lean around them both, taking in the surprisingly bright hall.

Maybe I imagined an actual dungeon, the odd rat scurrying

around. But the walls are a clean, faded shade of blue, electric strip lighting above us shadowing our steps as we follow the officer down to a door.

"She's in there." He motions to the barred door, a look of distaste on his face. "We've locked her down. We'll be outside if you need anything."

Tristan nods. "Thanks."

Taking my hand, he waits for me to give him the nod before he pushes the door open.

Alicia is slumped in a chair, chains locking her ankles and wrists to the metal. Her head is slumped, the lustrous shine of her hair dulled to a matted mess.

She raises dulled, bloodshot eyes to the door as we enter. Her eyes slide over me, dismissing me completely before they land on Tristan, and a spark of life appears.

"Tristan," she gasps. "You're here."

She strains against the chains, and they clank against the seat. "Look," she sobs. "Look what they've done to me. But you're here now."

Tristan's hand squeezes mine. "Alicia," he says quietly. "Sienna would like to speak to you."

"You're here." Alicia raises her face to the ceiling, a grin breaking out on her pale face. "I told them, I told all of them, and none of them believed me. I told you. I told you!"

Her voice rises to a scream as she pulls against the chair. Tristan puts his hand on my arm. "Sienna," he murmurs. "I don't think we should be in here."

I agree with him. But I hesitate as I turn to leave. "One second," I whisper, holding my hand out. "Just... just wait."

I approach Alicia carefully, stopping around a foot away as she mumbles.

"Alicia," I say steadily. "Do you know who I am?"

Her eyes slide to mine and then away. "Little omega bitch," she whispers. "You took him away from me."

"I didn't take him away from you." I step closer. "He was never yours, Alicia."

She hisses at me. "He was," she snarls. "He's still mine."

I feel Tristan shift behind me, ready to intervene, but I hold my hand out.

"This is the last time you will see him," I murmur. "We're going home now, Alicia. Back to our home, to a life that you will *never* be part of. After today, you will never be mentioned in our lives again. Do you understand me?"

Alicia snarls. "You're lying," she cries. "Tristan loves me."

She twists her wrists so hard inside her chains that I worry they might snap. I stare at her. She really, truly believes that Tristan is hers.

Turning away, I take Tristan's outstretched hand. "Goodbye, Alicia."

She screams Tristan's name, but he doesn't look back.

As we leave, I look at the guard. "She needs help. Proper, medical help, from a professional."

He nods. "Health Elio is overseeing her case."

"Good. That's... good."

Tristan holds my hand tightly until the door closes behind us, and he pulls me into his arms. I bury my face in his chest.

"I'm sorry," he says softly. He understands. He doesn't have to say it.

I don't know what I thought I'd get out of this. But it doesn't feel like a victory.

It just feels sad.

"Let's go home." It's time to move on, just as I told Alicia.

## 5 2

# GRAY

The beta working on installing our security turns to me as I walk up. "All done?"

He nods, pointing out the new cameras attached to the gate. "All remote controlled. They can link up to your phone, too."

I pull it out. "Show me."

I'm not taking any more chances with Sienna's safety, not after the events of the last few weeks.

As the security crew leave, my phone buzzes in my hand. My brows draw together as I take in the name of the person calling.

*Answer me, asswipe.*

I definitely didn't put that number in. But I'm also not going to let it go to voicemail. With a slight cringe, I put it to my ear. "Jessalyn. To what do I owe the pleasure?"

"Uh," a deep voice replied. "It's Emmett, actually."

I straighten, walking back into the house. "Oh. Hey. Everything okay?"

"All good. Listen – Jax told me you were involved with something to do with the beta housing? Outside the city?"

Frowning, I grab a bottle of water from the refrigerator. Logan walks in, his shirt spattered in red paint, and I hand him another bottle.

"Yeah," I say slowly. "I put some plans together a while back, but I was never able to get Erikkson to take them to the Council. Something about the budgets, but knowing what we do now, I'm pretty sure that was bullshit."

"I'd say so. Look, David Cohen is really pushing me on this position. I'm not sold, but I do want to get out there and take a look, get more of a feel for how things are working. You free to come? I can grab you in half an hour."

I check the time. "Sure. I can bring the plans with me."

"Great. Thanks, Gray."

Logan's hands slide around my waist as I hang up. "Who was that?"

As I explain, his eyes fly up. "Sounds like he is considering it, if he wants to go take a look at the beta housing."

A frisson of excitement runs through me. "Maybe. Guess we'll find out."

---

Emmett and I settle outside a small coffee shop, and I spread the plans out.

"Hell of a difference." Emmett shades his eyes as he looks around us. "From Navarre, I mean."

I know exactly what he means. The street around us is run-down as hell, litter overflowing the tiny bins, flowerbeds empty. Even the cars look beat-up, a reflection of the hierarchy. Betas don't typically have higher-paying jobs here, most reserved for alphas and even the odd omega. The Council position is the exception, not a rule, and it's always felt more like a box-ticking exercise than anything else.

I explain to Emmett, and he nods. "I thought so. Cohen seems keen to change that, though. Make it more equal across the three designations."

"If he said it, I'd believe him. Tristan is even more passionate about it, and he's taking over from David when he retires." I point at a spot on the plans. "You see this spot here? It's just a worn out piece of land. We could build temporary homes here, and move people around in batches, then move them back in when their homes are ready."

"How would we fund it?" Emmett asks. "And where would we get the contractors? You'd need specialists for some of this, and Navarre might not have the right skills."

We bat ideas back and forth for hours, getting our drinks topped off before we're ushered out at closing time by the friendly but firm older beta owner.

"So," I ask as we settle back into Emmett's truck. I slide the rolled-up plans under my seat as he reverses out of his parking space. "What do you think?"

He sighs. "I think it could work. It's a lot of work, though. At least a few years. And the Council would have to agree the funding, although it looks like they've been massively underfunding this area for years."

"I think Erikkson was probably skimming off the top." It makes sense, given what we know. "But definitely still underfunded, in any case. You should take the job, Emmett. It doesn't have to be a figurehead with no purpose. That's just what Erikkson made it."

He rolls his eyes. "You sound like Jessalyn."

But his fingers tap restlessly on the steering wheel, and he looks distracted when he drops me off. "Can I borrow those plans?" he asks. "I want to take another look, maybe make some notes."

"Keep them. I have copies."

I grin to myself as I walk back in, whistling. It felt good to get back to what really makes me tick, and to talk it over with someone else who feels as invested as I am. I've spent *years* trying to get people to pay attention to those plans, building a name for myself by designing more flashy, city-center pieces like the opera house.

I hope Emmett takes the job. We could use someone like him,

someone who understands what hard work looks like and can put it to use where it's needed.

"Lo?" I call, pushing open his studio door. He has his back to me, his shoulders hunched as he leans over an easel with his headphones over his ears.

I don't want to disturb him, so I grab a seat on the couch at the back of the room, tilting my head back and closing my eyes, breathing in the familiar scent of turps and oil.

My eyes open when the door squeaks quietly. Sienna pops her head around the door, her gaze moving to Logan. I wave at her, and she pads over to me, curling into my side.

I press a kiss to her hair, breathing her in. It still hits me, how lucky I am, we all are, that she's still here, safe and healthy.

"How was it?" I ask, my thumb rubbing her shoulder in circles.

She slumps, her tone dejected as she talks me through their visit.

"It makes sense," I muse. "That there might be another reason. Other than her being the world's biggest bitch, I mean."

Sienna shrugs. "I mean, I kind of wanted to shave her head. But I felt sorry for her, too. Not because she doesn't deserve what happens now. Just... her life is empty, Gray. All she has is her father, and he's in a cell next to her. And my life feels so full in comparison. I don't want to waste any more time on her."

My lips tighten. Pity is a stretch too far for me, not after what she did, especially during Sienna's heat. But my Soul Bonded is a far, far better person than I am.

Impulsively, I lift Sienna onto my lap, positioning her so she's facing me and pushing strands of pink hair away from her face. The white shirt she's wearing as a dress rides up, and she swallows as my hands land on her thighs, massaging into her skin.

"Gray," she whispers, darting a look towards Logan. He's oblivious as he hums, his back to us.

I grin. "I wonder how long it'll take him to notice us?"

Leaning forward, I grip the back of her neck and pull her into me, tracing her lips with my tongue. She sighs, her mouth opening under mine as I taste her, my other hand sliding up to cradle her cheeks.

"I will never get tired of that," I whisper in wonder. "Not in a million years."

Sienna's smile wavers as I trace my hands down, following the line of buttons on her shirt. Holding her gaze, I flick the first one open. The second.

Heat flares in her cheeks as I slide my hand inside to cup her breast, squeezing and rolling her nipple in my palm.

"You really don't like underwear, do you?" I ask, and she bites her cheek to hold in a laugh.

I spread my hands across her collarbones, She pushes against my chest. "I want this off."

Her hands slip under my tee, and I peel it over my head. Her eyes darken, and she licks her lips as she runs her hands over my skin.

Reaching up, I nudge the shirt back off her shoulders until it slips down her arms, the material pooling in the crook of her elbows.

"Beautiful," I rasp, tracing her curves. And *ours*.

Instead of answering, she leans in, pressing her lips to the crook of my neck. My hands move to her bare back, tracing the skin.

There's movement, and I look over at Logan. His eyes are bright as he watches us, and he holds up a hand. "Stay there," he says quietly. "Exactly where you are."

Sienna moves to sit up, but I press her head down gently. "Think the muse has kicked in," I murmur. "We're not allowed to move until he draws us."

Her breath hitches. "Oh."

I keep my hands where they are, only moving my fingers in gentle, soft strokes. Sienna melts into me, wriggling slightly, and I catch my breath at the feel of her pressing against my jeans.

"There," Logan rasps. "Keep your face just like that."

Time passes in a beautiful haze of torture. Sienna's scent deepens as Logan sketches us both, his tongue poking out in concentration. His eyes skate over my face, tracing the curves of my nose, my eyes, the touch of my hands on Sienna's back.

Our Soul Bonded lets out a tiny, breathless whine into my neck, and my hands clench. "Lo."

"One minute," he mutters, his hand flying across the page. "I'm nearly... done."

He tosses the page aside, and his hands join mine as they run over Sienna's back. I push the rest of the shirt from her shoulders, tasting the damp skin. "Bonded," I murmur.

She sits back, her hand rising to curl around Logan's neck as he presses into her, his mouth tracing down her neck. "Oh," she gasps, when his teeth just tease the edge of her skin.

I lean up, pressing my mouth to hers, before I tug Logan to me, my tongue tangling with his in familiar bliss.

Having Sienna with us is a new experience, and he raises his eyebrow at me as we explore each other, the three of us filling the air with harsh breaths and broken gasps.

"Logan," I say slowly. "Where do you want us?"

Sienna blinks, before her eyes fill with interest. Logan presses a last kiss to her shoulder. "I want you both," he says at last. His eyes heat as he gestures, and I twist, taking our Soul Bonded with me and laying her out on the wide couch. There's plenty of room for me to kneel between her legs, her knees up as she looks between us.

"What now?" she asks, biting her lip. In answer, I look at Lo.

"I think our Soul Bonded is wearing too many clothes," he says, a small smirk appearing on his face. "Take them off, Gray."

I slide my hands up her thighs and slowly peel her underwear away, revealing her soft, pink slit, already shining with slick. She squirms, and Logan strokes his hand over her hair from where he's stood. "I want to watch Gray fucking you, Bonded. Then, I'm going to fuck him, while he's inside you. How does that sound?"

Sienna moans, her pupils dilating. "*Yes.*"

My hands shake as I undo my jeans, my cock springing out, hard and ready as I press it into her dampness. I coat myself in her slick, working my cock up and down as she trembles beneath me. Logan moves behind me, his hands slipping down and cupping my bare ass as he pushes the rest of my jeans down.

"Look how wet you are, Bonded," he purrs, the vibration pulling a shiver from my chest as he nips my ear. "You're going to look so beautiful with Gray's cock buried inside you."

Sienna raises her hips, her eyes meeting mine in a plea. "Now, Gray."

I don't make her wait, pulling her hips up and sinking into her in one, smooth thrust that makes Sienna throw her head back, her groan rolling out across the room.

I start out gentle, gradually upping my pace as I pour all of the frustration and want I've been carrying around for weeks into my Bonded, our bodies slapping together, her moans coaxing me on as I give her everything I have.

Until a hand wraps around my throat. "Enough."

Sienna's eyes flutter open as I force myself to stop, panting as I run shaking hands over her skin. Logan shifts behind me, his hand cupping the area where Sienna and I are joined and gathering up fluids. His hand lands on my back as he pushes me forward, until my chest is pressed against Sienna's. Leaning down, I kiss her gently, feeling her gasp as Logan holds her legs, cupping behind her knees.

"Still with me, baby?" he asks her, and she nods. I drop my head into her neck as he pushes into me, working his way in, inch by tortuous inch until he bottoms out inside me.

"Fuck," I curse, and Sienna lifts her arms, wrapping them around my neck as Logan starts to move in shallow thrusts, getting us both used to the movement as he pushes my hips into Sienna's softness.

Both of us are entirely controlled by him, our eyes locked as our breathing speeds up and she throws her head back against the brown leather.

Logan rolls his hips into me, and I shudder as my release hits me in a rush. Sienna cries out as I jerk, coming in hot, thick pulses inside her, her pussy contracting around my cock as she twists her fingers into my hair. My knot slips in easily, locking into place inside her.

Logan growls, his pace slowing as his knot pushes at me, demanding entry. "Jesus," I groan, my eyes closing. Sienna arches her back underneath me, her legs opening wider as I settle amongst them, Logan filling me with his cum.

We lie there, sticky and breathless, my arms shaking as I settle carefully onto her, trying not to squash her with my weight. Logan balances his arm next to Sienna's head as he leans in. I feel the graze of his lips on my shoulder. "Was that – are you—,"

"Again," Sienna groans. She throws a hand over her eyes. "We need to do that again. The other way around, too."

Logan laughs as he rests against my back, the three of us settling in to wait for our knots to release us.

*I am absolutely not going to argue with my Soul Bonded.*

## 53

## JAX

"I'm ready."

Turning, I swallow down the lump of emotion in my chest. "Shortcake. You look *edible*."

She always does. But tonight, dressed in skin-tight black jeans that look like they've been spray-painted on, fuck-me black spiky boots, and a silky emerald green halterneck, she looks made for sin.

My mind scatters into the gutter as she looks me up and down, biting her lip. Fuck, but I love the way she looks at me, half innocent and half like she wants to pin me down and ride me until I'm gasping for mercy.

*Yes, please.*

It's been a week of experiences, of learning to love our Soul Bonded, of being together as a pack without the shadows of the Erikksons hanging over us.

And tonight, I get to perform for her. This time, I'll know exactly where she is in the crowd, and there'll be no sneaking off – unless it's with me. I can't fucking *wait*.

Logan walks in, his eyes moving straight to Sienna as he stops. "Fuck, we're lucky alphas," he says wonderingly. Sienna blushes.

I hustle them into the hall, itching to get going. Bouncing on my heels, I grin when I see Gray and Tristan already waiting for us. "Excellent. Time to go."

The trip to the club is a short one. This place is one of my favorites, and I keep one hand on my guitar, the other locked onto my Soul Bonded as I steer us towards the edge of the stage, my band heading past us to set up. Mal waves to Sienna as he strolls past, and she smiles back at him. "Hey, Mal."

He grins at her. "Sienna. Good to see you."

"Enough," I complain. "Stop eyeing up my Soul Bonded – although I agree she looks like a snack – and get out there. I'm coming."

With one last, lingering kiss, I head out, threading my guitar strap across my chest as the crowd swells into a baying mass.

"Good evening, Navarre," I purr. "Did you miss me?"

They scream for me, and I eat it up, launching into our set with a fury. My fingers fly over my guitar, buoyed on by the sight of Sienna dancing at the edge of the stage. She dances like she doesn't give a fuck, her hands up, her hair shaking, and it winds me up into a fucking frenzy as my hands smash against the strings.

I finally take what feels like a full breath at the mid-way point. Grabbing a bottle of water, I swig it down and grab the mic.

"You may have heard," I murmur into the mic, "that I am the luckiest damn alpha on the planet, and am Soul Bonded to the most perfect omega in the world."

The crowd screams, although I'm pretty sure there's a girl crying in the front row.

"I was an idiot," I say in a low voice. My body turns to Sienna. She's frozen, her eyes flicking between me and the stage as suspicion fills her face.

"I made some stupid decisions, and it nearly cost me everything I ever wanted. But thankfully, she's forgiven me for being an absolute dick."

Laughs ring out, the crowd slowly growing silent as they wait to see where I'm going with this.

"Just one more thing," I say slowly. In the corner of my eye, I catch Sienna shaking her head. "I'm told that my Bonded has music inside her, and even though she's ours – tonight, Navarre, I'm sharing a little bit of her with you, so you can see exactly how special she is."

The crowd erupts, cheering and whistling ringing out, as I jog over to where Sienna is standing.

"Jax," she hisses. She looks a bit pale as she looks out to the chanting crowd. "I can't play for them."

"You're not," I say, leaning in and kissing her. "You're playing for you. You have talent, shortcake. Just once, I want us to play together. Please?"

I can see her wavering. "I don't have an instrument—,"

Logan steps forward, holding up a battered case. Her dad's guitar.

"Come on, Sienna," I coax. "Share a little bit of that magic with us."

She purses her lips, but I can see her battling a smile. "You're incorrigible. You have not heard the last of this, Jax Cohen."

"God, I hope not," I say promptly. "Tell me it involves handcuffs and whips."

She laughs, grabbing the guitar from Logan. "I really do hate you a little bit for this, you know."

Maybe, but she's made for the stage. I can see it, clear as day. All she needs is a little nudge, to take that final step.

I keep her hand in mine as we walk out, the crowd growing louder as they spot us. Another mic has been set up next to mine, and Sienna lifts her strap over her shoulder, checking the strings.

"What song, baby?" I ask, pulling my guitar around. "I'll follow your lead."

She taps her lips. "How about… Embers?"

I whistle. "Appropriate."

She gives me a wry grin as she turns, adjusting the mic. Her eyes sweep over the crowd, and she takes a deep breath, her fingers dropping to the strings.

And then she plays.

It's everything I hoped it would be. The crowd silences as her voice rings out across the room. It's much deeper than I expected, a smoky cadence that curls around the words as she holds the crowd hostage.

*In the depths of pain*
*Where the shadows go*
*An ember flickers*
*Sinking low*
*This weight of hurt*
*It burns my soul*
*When is it time*
*To let it go?*

Carefully, my fingers dance softly across the strings.

*I'll forgive the past*
*Because nothing this good ever lasts*
*Embrace the journey*
*Make everything right*
*Drag those embers*
*Into the light*
*When will you see*
*The light in me*

Her voice trails off as she closes it off, and I follow her lead. The final note rings out, and there's silence. Pure, awed silence.

Sienna shifts uncertainly, and the spell breaks. Her mouth falls open as the cheers ring out from across the room. People are cheering, screaming for more, and her cheeks pink. "Jax…,"

"Listen to them, Sienna," I lean forward and whisper in her ear. "God, I knew you'd be perfect. They're screaming for you. Give the people what they want."

She rolls her eyes, but she's grinning. "One more, Jax. I mean it."

Something tells me I'll never get enough.

We tumble off stage, high on the buzz from the crowd, and

Sienna laughs as Gray grabs her, spinning her around. "That was incredible, Bonded."

She turns to me, her eyes sparkling.

"Am I forgiven?" I ask, a little meek and a whole lot of smug.

She tries to look stern, but her lips twitch. She wags her finger at me. "I'll decide when we get home."

"Excellent."

At the end of the night, we pile into the house, all of us giddy from the high of watching our Soul Bonded captivate an audience with her voice. The owner even pulled me aside to ask if she'd come back, do a gig of her own.

I grin to myself. I'll break the news to her tomorrow.

Sienna spins, full of endorphins and champagne as she laughs tipsily. Tristan darts to catch her. "Bonded. You need a glass of water."

"I need more champagne," she demands loftily. "But I'll take a glass of water too."

Laughing as Tristan sweeps her up, full of overprotective concern, I turn to Gray, but he's staring down at his phone with a frown.

"What is it?" I ask, peering over his shoulder as Logan follows Tristan and Sienna.

"The cameras," he mutters. "They're not working."

"What? We just had them put in."

He shakes his head. "I don't know, but I don't like this."

I open my mouth, ready to shout down to Tristan, when I catch the shadow in the corner of my eye. A shadow that shouldn't be there.

I crash into him as he lifts his arm, the shot going wide and hitting the wall, knocking off a chunk of plaster. There's shouting, Sienna crying out, and *goddamn* this piece of shit for ruining a fucking perfect evening.

I slam my hand down hard over his wrist, forcing him to drop the gun. Gray is there, kicking it away, and we both dive in, pinning the beta to the floor as he grunts.

"Get Sienna out of here," I shout to Tristan. There could be more of them. She tries to argue with him, but he throws her over his shoulder as he heads for the door. Logan appears next to me, grabbing an arm and helping to keep it pinned.

"Hey, asshole," I snap, banging his head into the floor. "Who the fuck are you?"

Sienna calls out. "Wait - *Tristan* - I know him!"

Tristan recoils. "What?"

She whacks him on the back, and he sets her down, his eyes scanning the hall. "It's the other beta," she gasps. "One of Erikkson's men. There were three of them, and we only got two at the gala. He's the third."

Doesn't mean he's the last, but it seems likely. "Get me a belt, or a rope."

Logan hands me the belt from his jeans, and I use it to secure the man's wrists. He groans, a nice-looking egg appearing on his forehead. Gray leans over, and I blink as he smacks his head down a second time.

*Goodnight, motherfucker.*

The Justice officers pull in a few minutes later and take ownership of our little parcel, and Tristan's dad isn't far behind them. He pulls Tristan into a hug, checking him over and turning to Sienna. "I'm so sorry this happened, Sienna."

She shakes her head, hugging her arms. "It's fine. I think he was the last."

David frowns. "I was actually already on my way with some news. Emmett Johnson has formally accepted the role of Beta representative on the Council. We took our first vote this evening, straight after his appointment."

Everyone pauses, our eyes moving to our Bonded. There's only one vote that we'd be interested in at this hour, and David knows us. "That was... quick," Sienna says. Her face is pale. "My Denied status?"

"Gone," David assures her. "It was a priority for both Ollena and I, and luckily, Emmett fully agreed with us. The Bonding

Trials as they currently stand have been dissolved. That includes Denial, and any omega currently under that status is free and able to stay in Navarre."

"Oh." Sienna wavers, and Tristan wraps his arm around her.

We all stare at each other. It's done. Over.

Sienna is ours, and we're staying.

David moves towards the door, following the Justice officers. "I'll leave you to it. But your mother wants you to come for dinner next week, Tristan."

Tristan swallows. "Tell her we'll be there."

The door swings closed behind him, and we're left alone, the four of us staring at each other.

## 54

## SIENNA

I can stay.

The last, horrible sword hanging over my head is gone.

Alicia and Erikkson are locked up, and their goons with them.

I'm no longer a Denied omega.

And my pack... my breath hitches.

We're free. All of us.

The grin spreads over my face. Tristan, Jax, Gray and Logan gather around me.

"Bonded?" Tristan asks, looking down at me. His arm is warm and secure around my shoulders, his scent soaking into me.

Jax grins. "It's done, shortcake. No going anywhere."

Logan reaches out, stroking his hand across my cheek. "Coffee, I think," he says quietly. "A moment to let everything sink in."

I nod gratefully.

Coffee with my pack sounds like exactly what I need.

And after that... who knows?

## 4 YEARS LATER

"Fuck," I moan. My hair is pulled back, Logan's hand slipping around to grip my throat as he pounds into me, my hips pinned in place by the counter in our kitchen.

"They're going to walk in," he pants, "and see you writhing around my cock, baby. No rest for you tonight. Gonna fill you up, get you nice and ready for your heat."

My response is a groan, my fingers gripping the edges of the worktops Gray and I chose. It's taken us three years from start to finish, but today, we *finally* moved into our new home.

The home Logan and I are currently christening.

"I like this kitchen," he says thoughtfully, and adds a slap to my ass that makes me see stars. He's far too restrained for my liking, and I clench my muscles around him.

"No," he scolds. "No knotting. I haven't seen the upstairs yet."

"Logan." I convulse around him, gasping out my release as footsteps sound outside.

Logan whips out of me, tugging my dress down, and we're both leaning against the counter by the time Gray walks in. He scans us, his eyes narrowing.

"Already?" he asks. "We just took the wrap off that counter."

I can't control my laugh, and it bubbles out of me as he comes over, his lips brushing mine. "I'm feeling a little left out, Bonded."

*Well, we can't have that.*

I'm about to suggest that we relocate to the nest upstairs - the beautiful nest that looks uncannily like my nest in our last home, because I couldn't bear to leave it behind. But we're interrupted by gentle scolding.

"You can't put your head through the railings," Jax says with exasperation. "You'll get stuck. We'll have to take your ears off to get you out."

There's a horrified gasp, and my lips stretch into a smile as he walks in. Jessie is nestled in his arms, a bundle of vibrant and far too adventurous two year-old.

She holds her arms out to me. Mixed blue and green eyes, a mirror image of Tristan. They make me catch my breath every time.

"Daddy cut my ears off," she mumbles, and I laugh.

"Naughty daddy," I say, and Jax gives me an outraged look. I whisper in her ear. "Find Daddy Tristan. He'll tell Jax off."

Grinning in a way that reminds me strongly of her namesake, she nods, and I carefully set her down. Logan chases her out, making her squeal as she pelts down the hallway.

"Where is Tristan?" I ask, as Jax folds me into his arms.

"On the phone." Gray rolls his eyes. "He'll be here in a minute."

"Big day tomorrow," I remind him. "I think we can cut him some slack."

I take Jax's hand, and we follow Logan and Jessie down the hall, taking in the high ceilings and the picture walls. Our memories are everywhere, a little touch from Tristan. There's a framed note in the middle.

*To making new memories with you.*

Tristan walks in through the door. "Sorry," he says with a sigh. "I promise this will all be sorted by tonight."

"No, it won't." I lean into him as he comes to stand next to me.

"The wall is coming down tomorrow, Tristan. It's a big day. Don't worry about us."

He kisses my hair. "You will always be my priority."

Jessie runs back in, laughing, and hides behind his leg. He grabs her, swinging her onto his hip. "Little miss. What are you doing?"

She grins. "Cutting my ears off."

After reassuring a slightly panicked Tristan that our beloved child is not, in fact, going to cut her own ears off, I take Jessie as they all head out to the truck to grab the first of many, many boxes.

I'd offer to help, but they'd only say no. Besides, Jessie is normally snuggled up to one of them, and I'm taking the chance to breathe her in before everyone arrives. Jess, Emmett, my parents, Elise, my alpha's parents, even Ollena. Everyone is coming over to celebrate our new home, and the removal of the wall.

I look over. From our front door, I can just see the edge of it, glimmering in the light.

It's the end of an era.

And the start of a new one.

"You can be whatever you want to be," I whisper to Jessie. "You know that?"

She kicks her legs. "Okay. I want to be cake."

I laugh, catching Tristan's eye. He grins at me, blowing hair out of his face as he carries a heaped box towards our home.

Home. It took a long time, but I finally found it.

Home is wherever they are.

# DEVOTED PLAYLIST (IN ORDER)

Find it on Spotify

Impossible - Shontelle
Left Outside Alone – Anastacia
Train Wreck – James Arthur
Running Up That Hill – Kate Bush
Falling – Harry Styles
Missed – Ella Henderson
Nobody's Perfect – Jessie J
Let Me Down Slowly – Alec Benjamin
War Of Hearts - Ruelle
Blank Page – Christina Aguilera
I'll Keep You Safe – Sleeping At Last
Some Kind of Heaven – Sleeping at Last
Love Is Gone – SLANDER, Dylan Matthew
Never Seen Anything Quite Like You – The Script
Can I Be Him – James Arthur
Fire On Fire – Sam Smith
All I Need – Within Temptation
I'll Stand By You - Pretenders
Until I Found You – Stephen Sanchez

DEVOTED PLAYLIST (IN ORDER)

## A note from Evelyn

Writing the Bonding Trials has been... well. I don't really have any words, actually. (I know. And I call myself a writer). I could probably go on at length, but I will just say that it has been a privilege to share these stories with you, and to see the reaction that these books have had.

I think the Cohen pack earned their redemption. I hope you think so too. And they're still there, in my head, making new memories with Sienna and earning her forgiveness every single day.

This duet is complete, but I do feel that maybe Jess and Emmett deserve their own moment in the spotlight. That won't be just yet, but if anyone has earned a spot as a main character - even if it's a short story or novella - it's Jessalyn freakin' Rogers.

If you'd like to keep up with the latest news and updates on my releases, join the #IHateAlicia or the #IHeartJessalyn club, or just shout at me for emotional damage caused by my books, come and hang out in my Facebook group, The Evelyn Flood Collective.

If you enjoyed this book, please consider leaving a review on Goodreads or Amazon! Reviews are so, so important for indie authors to help us keep doing what we love.

Thank you!

Evie x

# OTHER BOOKS BY EVELYN FLOOD

## THE OMEGA WAR

Omega Found

Omega Lost

Omega Fallen

Knot Forever

# STALK ME!

Newsletter: https://mailchi.mp/449ab054db99/evelynflood
Goodreads: https://www.goodreads.com/evelynflood
Bookbub: https://www.bookbub.com/profile/evelyn-flood
TikTok: https://www.tiktok.com/@evelynfloodauthor
Instagram: https://www.instagram.com/evelynfloodauthor/
Facebook: https://www.facebook.com/groups/evelynflood/

Printed in Great Britain
by Amazon

24556034R00158